Marion Halligan was born in Newcastle on the east coast of Australia and grew up by the sea. She now lives in Canberra, with her husband and, occasionally, two children. Her books have been nominated for most of the major literary prizes and have won several, including the Steele Rudd Award (for best collection of short stories in its year), the Braille Book of the Year for *The Living Hothouse*, and the Geraldine Pascal Prize for critical writing. Her last novel, *Lovers' Knots*, won the *Age* Book of the Year Award, the ACT Book of the Year Award, the 3M Talking Book of the Year Award and the inaugural Nita B. Kibble Literary Award.

Her other books are the novels *Self-Possession* and *Spider Cup*, two more collections of short stories, *The Hanged Man in the Garden* and *The Worry Box*, and *Eat My Words*, a collection of essays about food and other things.

She has published over sixty short stories in journals and magazines, and has been widely anthologised.

She is currently Chairperson of the Literature Board of the Australia Council.

Also by Marion Halligan

Published 1995 by Minerva
a part of Reed Books Australia
22 Salmon Street, Port Melbourne, Victoria 3207
a division of Reed International Books Australia Pty Limited

First published by William Heinemann Australia 1994

Typeset in New Baskerville by Abbtype
Printed and bound in Australia by Australian Print Group

National Library of Australia
cataloguing-in-publication data:

Halligan, Marion, 1940– .
Wishbone.

ISBN 1 86330 450 9.

I. Title

A823.3

Wishbone

Marion Halligan

MINERVA

To Cosmo, with all my love

Contents

acknowledgement

I wish to thank the Literature Board
of the Australia Council for the grant which gave me
time to write this novel and the encouragement to do so.

My thanks to Judy Pearce and Neil Porter
who persuaded my computer to release its secrets.

merrythought (1607): The Furcula or forked bone between the neck and breast of a bird, also called the wishbone. The name has reference to the custom of two persons pulling the furcula of a fowl till it breaks, the notion being that the one who gets the longer piece will either be married first, or will get any wish he may form at the moment.

Shorter Oxford Dictionary (1959)

Once upon a time ... Let me tell you the story of the poor peasant couple who are offered three wishes. They are filled with excitement, and some anxiety. They are cold, they are hungry, they live in a hovel, they have no livelihood. They must choose carefully. Suddenly the husband says, I'm so hungry. I wish I had a black pudding to eat. And there it is before him sizzling on a plate. You fool, shrieks his wife, you've wasted a whole wish. Oh, oh, I wish that black pudding was stuck on the end of your nose! And there he is, with a black pudding on the end of his nose. What can they do with their third wish but wish it off again?

Note: some stories reckon it was a sausage, not a black pudding. It's hardly important.

The Glade

The difficulty of a love affair between a young woman and a married man may be its logistics. Where can they go? He lives with his wife. She lives with her parents. They can't afford hotels, and besides they may not be appropriate if the town is not large. Clumsy encounters in cars are not stylish. Work places may be monuments to indiscretion. The affair develops layers of loss and longing out of having nowhere to go. It feels like the doomed lovers of history. Me Tristram. You Isolde. A young woman may read Keats with burning heart, wishing she could be so lucky as to have a storm to flee away into.

Brian knew of a good place. It was just over the edge of a cliff. This cliff seemed to be a simple right angle, the land flat at the top, rimmed with bushes, then falling sheer to the sea. But in one place it dropped in steps and hollows. You climbed down a hidden path and there was a wide ledge, wide enough for trees and bushes and some rocks and a big enough space amongst all these for a blanket. It was sheltered on every one of its sides, even from above. The sea was below, but to the people lying on the blanket only the sky showed. Their only observers were lazy birds catching thermals. It was a perfectly secret place. Of course it needed fine weather.

The glade, Brian called it. When he had it in mind he would whistle the tune of Handel's *Where e'er you walk*. Hearing this tune always gladdened his wife's heart because she knew her husband was feeling cheerful. He would move around the house getting ready to go to work and small things would not irritate him. He would not get into a bad temper because he could not remember where he had put certain books, or had mislaid a necessary pen. She knew the tune quite well, and could also sing the words to it. She liked it because of the grammar. *Where e'er you walk Cool gales shall fan the glade.* They were not words of blessing, or hope, they were words of command. *Trees where you sit shall crowd into a shade.* She liked the idea of being able to command even the natural world to give pleasure to the beloved. When Brian had gone out she would sing it through several times, taking particular pleasure in the *shalls.*

If only Brian could be often this cheerful. His blitheness was a weight removed from her chest. She could stand straighter and more gracefully, she could breathe air into her lungs and release it in song. *Where e'er you walk*, she carolled. *Trees where you sit.*

The song told her about the walking and sitting but what she didn't know about was the lying.

Emmanuelle always thought of the glade as their place. Shall we meet in our place? she'd say to Brian. They went in the bus, at different times and to different stops, each meeting a different secretive plot. Brian usually let her go to the terminus, a gravel roundabout beyond the thinned-out suburbs, while he got off a stop or two earlier. Even from the terminus there was a considerable walk, through the hot bush and the noise of cicadas. Once Emmanuelle met a friend of her mother's while she was waiting at the bus stop in town. You look like a picnic, the woman said, because Emmanuelle was wearing a shady hat and a sundress. Her hair in a long thick plait tied with a ribbon. Well, I have to walk through the sun to uni, she said, and wondered what she'd do if her bus came before Mrs Faulkner's. She'd have to miss it, she couldn't let the woman see that she was travelling in a different direction. What happened was the university bus coming first. She looked at it in horror. Isn't that your bus, said Mrs Faulkner. Oh yes, said Emmanuelle. A number of people were getting on, she couldn't do anything but follow. She got out at the next stop which meant the fare wasted but the plot not ruined. All the way out to their place in the slow hot bus trundling and stopping, trundling and stopping, she felt the sharp edge of nervousness, of fear, made sharper and harder to bear by desire and the pain of the separation which these stolen meetings could never dissipate. As she walked along the track the noise of the cicadas was the whirr of passion winding her up so tight she might burst with it. Her plait slid over her bare shoulder, her arm, silky and prickling. Brian would pull the ribbon undone and the straight fair hair would unfurl itself slowly from the crinkling braid. Mermaid hair, he would say. You have mermaid hair.

Down the cliff face; the glade, the blanket, Brian waiting. Reading Chekhov. The lovemaking. Then they were lying together and he was sliding his fingers over the skin inside her thighs. She knew how it would feel because she liked doing it herself. She was about to ask him what words he would use for this smoothness; words like silk or satin didn't apply because those things were dead and her flesh was alive. She liked it when he described her in little broken passionate immediate words, or later in poems. Like the one where her hair was like the sun shining on the green sea and men dive in and never escape from its tangles.

Do you ever think you're perfectly happy, he asked. I do. At this moment I am perfectly happy.

Are you? I'm not. Not perfectly. I remember that you're married.

Each of these meetings was a disappointment, because each time she expected him to say, At last, my marriage is over, we can be together always, or some such thing; there were dozens of ways of expressing it. She tried them all out. In the bus she said to herself,

Today he will say it, and wondered what the exact words would be. Every time he greeted her with kisses and began taking her clothes off, and while she gave herself up to this she was also overwhelmed with pain that he did not first of all offer the longed-for words. Every time, and not till afterwards, when they lay soothingly together, every time it was a matter of waiting a bit longer, not too long, a bit longer, the right moment, it would come, soon, and in the meantime ...

Married, said Brian. That's future. And past. I'm talking about this moment, now, and now I am perfectly happy. I wish it would last forever.

If wishes were horses beggars would ride, she said.

If turnips were watches I'd wear one by my side, he finished.

She cannot bear to be parted from this man who has the same words in his head as she does. She breathes a sigh. The tightness of passion and fear and desire and the pain of loss is not much relieved by lovemaking. The cicadas still whirr on the cliff path. She sighs in order to believe: something so wanted, so needed, so necessary will happen; next time he will say, Today I am no longer married, today you and I are together for ever, or some such thing.

She wraps herself in his arms. The summer may be passing, on the ledge above the sea.

I wish we could stay like this forever, she says.

We will. We will.

She learned that believing you can't bear something doesn't mean anything. She stood on the platform of the underground railway and heard the boom of the train in the tunnel, felt the concussion of air it pushed out. Three steps forward at the right moment ... Every afternoon this release offered itself. Every afternoon she rehearsed it, the three steps forward at the right moment, not too soon, not too late, the timing not overly precise, a little leeway either way. In her head she did this, but her feet never moved. Nor did she say, tomorrow I'll really do it, she simply stood, each afternoon in her head taking the three steps, her feet not moving, and once when a man running down the stairs stumbled and fell against her she felt the anger of fear: he could have pushed her under a train. After a while she stopped thinking I cannot bear it; she realised she had borne it. The impossible loss, and yet there she was, not stepping, never stepping, under the saving train. Or off a bridge, or swallowing pills, except they had never been an intention, the train was always her solution.

She still thought of Brian with pain but not all that often. The winter had come. Too cold for cliff faces. He'd gone to a job in Perth, a senior lectureship. His wife had gone with him. She compared other men who took her out with Brian and they never measured up, but then she met Lance Latimer. He didn't measure up either at first but after a while she stopped making comparisons. Lance's real name was Lancelot, which he kept a secret, along with two other given names and the first part of a hyphenated surname, but he trusted all of them to Emmanuelle and shortly afterwards they got engaged, and then married, in the grey stone church that his family always called ours, just like a church in an English village said her parents. There were photographs in the newspapers, and in the *Women's Weekly*. Lance worked in his father's firm and she went on with her job at a publisher's until Maud was born. They moved from their terrace in Paddington to a larger place in Pymble with a garden that gave on to the bush and space to bring up children. Emmanuelle had several miscarriages before William was born, and suffered from toxaemia during that pregnancy, so when she brought him home from the hospital they hired a nanny to help with the children.

Sometimes the family went on picnics to places where the rocks and the bushes and the thin sapling gums looked and smelt the same as those in the glade above the sea but they didn't remind her of Brian. Not in this context of husband and children and being responsible for them having a good time. Occasionally she thought about him; it was like trying to remember a novel that she'd once read, maybe back in her publishing days when going through the slush pile was her job, just in case a good book had come unsolicited. The plot and the events were a bit vague; what had it really been about? What were the characters really like? So that she wished she had a copy of the book, could turn the pages and read it again and try to understand the story. But it was a manuscript that had been lost, not just mislaid, thrown on the fire maybe, somehow destroyed, she'd never be able to go back to it and read again the hero's words when he breathed undying love and wished that they might never be parted. It seemed a common enough tale of an affair between a teacher and a student, you might even say banal, typical slush pile stuff, and yet there had been something of grace and beauty in its telling, hadn't there? A truth that had saved it?

Sometimes she would see the name Perth, and think of Brian in that city, giving perhaps the same lectures she had listened to, leaning forward in tutorials with the same intense eyes: Tell me, Miss Parry, what do you make of Tolstoy's ... Sometimes she thought of herself going to Perth with him, beloved wife of the brilliant new lecturer in the English department, but it was like writing a new ending to a novel, like having Anna Karenina not step under her train but go on to live happily in a cottage in the country; it didn't work. And she was living a quite different plot, with hardly the time or the desire to consider alternatives.

Smashing Meissen

Maud was dressed ready for kindergarten in a pink tee-shirt and dungarees when she decided she hated these prickly trousers and wanted to wear a dress.

I wish you'd make up your mind, said Emmanuelle. They'd already spent a long time deciding on the dungarees. Now she was dressing William. She'd got rid of the bossy nanny for an *au pair* girl from New Zealand who was doing classes in hotel management, several days a week. When she went into Maud's bedroom the child was strewing clothes around, looking for a dress. Emmanuelle had got a firm which specialised in creating wardrobes for individual tastes to design one for Maud, which meant she could reach all her clothes and pull them out and leave them on the floor, when it was supposed to have the opposite effect, of enabling her to hang them up and be neat.

Maud, Maud, look at the mess. I wish you could be a tidy girl and put things back in your wardrobe, said Emmanuelle. Maud didn't care about such remarks because she knew there wasn't anything her mother could do to make her behave well. She found a navy dress with a red sash and they put that on and then they had to rush because they were late.

7

When Emmanuelle got back from taking her to kindergarten the cleaning lady was thumping the vacuum cleaner through the kitchen so she went down into her back garden and picked violets, dozens, hundreds, nipping off their long stalks with her thumb nail, making a round posy, surrounding it with leaves. She squatted down, sitting on her heels, close to the damp shady dew-strewn leaves whose scent wafted up as she disturbed them. Her hair was shorter now, no longer possible to plait, inclined to fall across her face so she would slide her fingers through it and lift it behind her ear like a curtain behind a hook, not thinking about it, concentrating as here on the odour of flowers rising from the mulchy ground. William played in the sand pit. She put the flowers in a small Meissen bowl in the middle of the kitchen table. Magda had finished the ground floor and gone upstairs; faint booming noises marked her progress. Magda was a Croatian who spoke almost no English; she puts all her frustrations into housework, said Emmanuelle, it makes for a very clean house. Her friend Susie Prothero who had a child about William's age called in and she made coffee.

Susie picked up the vase of violets. It was a three-footed cream pot with babyish gilded lion's paws, painted in a mild purple colour with the sacrifice of Abraham, fierce man and child. There was an angel with a sword in the sky and in the distance a riverbank with two men fishing and further off houses and a mountain. All on a bowl small enough for violets.

Frankie had some nice Meissen in the Mosman gallery, Susie said. Wish I'd bought some. It's all gone now, must have been a good price.

Hard to believe, of anything of Frankie's.

Maybe somebody told him about loss leaders.

Emmanuelle laughed. They both bought things from Frankie, and complained about his high prices. As though in buying the things they also bought the pleasure of complaining.

Susie took deep breaths of the violets. Essence of violets in my oxygen, she said. I can feel them doing me good. Turning me into a nicer person.

Better than hay fever.

But really, don't you think that smelling something so perfect as this must really have a good effect on you?

I've never thought of it. Maybe I should spend a few days smelling violets, and you can tell me if I'm a nicer person.

Emmanuelle took the frail pot in both her hands and drew in a deep breath of the odour, then held it up like a grail.

Do you ever feel tempted to drop something like this?

Good god, no.

Like on a cliff, wanting to jump off. Not being able to resist.

She held the Meissen over the tiled floor. Both women saw the shards of expensive porcelain shattered on its hardness. Needing to be picked up with care so their sharp edges didn't cut.

Shit, Emmanuelle, here I am coveting it and you're talking about breaking the thing. Give it to me if you don't want it.

Oh no. It's the breaking that counts. Smash. The violence. Emmanuelle looked at Susie over the violets. Do you want it all that much? I mean, would you ask for Meissen if you got offered a wish?

What do you mean?

Suppose the good fairy drops in and offers you a wish. What would you ask for? Not china, I reckon.

Susie looked sly. For all my wishes to come true, of course.

I don't think you can do that. There must have to be some kind of etiquette. Emmanuelle put the vase down on the table. Being greedy wouldn't work. Remember the woman and the flounder.

Should I?

Don't you know the story of the poor fisherman who caught a flounder? It told him it was an enchanted prince so he let it go, then when he gets home his wife says why didn't you get it to give you a wish? Why should we live in this miserable hovel. Go back and ask it for a little cottage. So he does, and the wife's happy enough for a while, but then she wants something better, so she sends him back for a stone castle, and that's okay for a bit, and then she wants to be king, then emperor, then pope. Poor old fisherman has to go and call up the flounder and ask for all these things, he hates it, but she makes him do it. And the flounder obliges. Ilsebil, she's called, isn't that a greedy name.

Pretty sharp woman, you'd have to say. King, emperor, pope. Nice male ambitions. No female modesty for her. She knew where the power was.

Mmm. But she went too far. She wanted to be the good lord. I suddenly realised when I was reading it to William the other day what that meant. She wanted to be God. That's what did for her.

What happened?

Lost the lot. Ended up back in the hovel.

Interesting. Looks like she could have had all the earthly power she wanted, if she'd stopped there. It was the heavenly kind that wrecked it.

Yes, but fairy stories always have to go to their end. You can't say, stop there and it'll be all right. There's a fate working out.

I like the idea of a woman being pope, said Susie.

Is that what you'd ask the good fairy for?

Oh, I don't think it's my style.

Of course, mostly you get offered three wishes. That's the magic number.

Number one, the sausage. Number two, the sausage on the nose. Number three, the sausage off the nose, said Susie.

My book said black pudding. Yes, well, you've got to watch careless words when there's wishes around. That's why it's a good idea to have a little practice. So, seriously; what would you wish for? Emmanuelle leaned forward, watching Susie.

One wish? I dunno. I'm torn between perfect eyesight and being able to eat as much as I like and never get fat.

You're not fat. And you look great in glasses.

Susie jabbed her bold black frames back up her nose.

They're heavy. They hurt. They steam up. They get grotty. They get lost. They never work properly. Imagine waking up in the morning and being able to see the spiders on the ceiling. Or the man in your life. Well, you can, you do. I just wish I could. I loathe glasses. Nearly as much as I loathe going without them.

What about being rich, said Emmanuelle. Beautiful. Successful. Loved.

Why would you wish for any of those things? You are already. Susie lit a cigarette. Give up smoking, she muttered.

Emmanuelle frowned. No I'm not.

Yes you are. Of course you are. That's how the world sees you. Maybe you don't. Maybe you're like the flounder woman. Don't know when you're well off. Not grateful.

When I was a kid, you know what I wanted? I wanted black curly hair. Just like yours.

Poor you. Stuck with being a natural blonde. That's what I wanted to be. Hair like corn silk, don't they say? Peaches and cream complexion.

Why peaches, I've always wondered. Aren't peaches yellow?

William and Nathan came jostling inside. Nathan was bawling because William had thrown a truck at him. Both children were wet and covered in sand that began to shed on the floor and make gritty noises underfoot. The women realised it was raining.

Blast, said Emmanuelle. I've got to go to town. I hate rain and trains and shopping.

She got towels and they rubbed at the children, who leaned against their mothers in a proprietary way, each staking out his territory.

What are you going shopping for?

A dress. There's a cocktail party next week. Some people Lance wants to impress. I'm supposed to look glamorous. A business dress,

I suppose you could call it. Will it come off the tax, we ask ourselves.

Susie rubbed away at Nathan's wet hair until he squirmed out of her grasp. You know what you need? You need a chauffeur.

Oh yes. Drop one at the door of DJ's. Come back at four, Jeemes. Hold the umbrella. Carry the parcels. Open the door.

That too, said Susie, laughing like a trumpet. I was thinking of some spunky guy, with muscles. Doing wonders for my sex life.

A chauffeur?

Why not? Why else have one?

I was thinking of being driven around, said Emmanuelle.

That's taken for granted. I'm thinking about the extracurricular activities.

Emmanuelle looked at her curiously. William and Nathan had gone off to the playroom. Susie was leaning with her elbows on the table, smoking with the dreamy intensity of a thirties film star. That could be a wish, she said. A handsome chauffeur, who's besotted with me. Who thinks I'm as sexy as he is. Long afternoons of passion.

What's wrong with a husband, ditto, asked Emmanuelle. If it's a matter of wishing. And anyway, what about AIDS? You're not supposed to do that sort of thing any more.

A wish wouldn't have AIDS, said Susie.

The Man in the Train

Mel the *au pair* girl from New Zealand is twenty years old. Some of the best things about Mel are the bad things she doesn't do, like not bullying the children, not making arbitrary demands, not setting her standards of behaviour or tidiness too high. She is easy-going, lazy at times, distrustful of dictums and formulae. A change from the nanny who constructed their days on a strict grid of rules and was anxious to let no act, no moment, slip through any space between them. Rules being good for the character, their meaning or usefulness not counting. Whereas Mel treats the children as though they are human beings and together the three of them will work out useful ways to conduct their lives; mostly they respect her for it and behave as if they are. Human beings. Not always well, but not gratuitously badly. Sometimes with irresistible anger or irritation or mischief. Then Mel looks at them and even William will soon calm down and be civilised again. Emmanuelle thinks of her as a kind of treasure: not perfect; flawed? A flawed treasure. Not immortal gold, but silver tarnishing. Did she mean her spirit or her heart or simply her way? Mel had narrow eyes and her hair and skin were rather dingy. Emmanuelle wished that somebody would take her and scrub her pink and glowing. Susie said, A treasure is a treasure. What's dingy skin got to do with good child care?

Nothing at all, of course, said Emmanuelle. But it's to do with Mel.

I reckon it's not anything she can do anything about or she would. Mel's okay.

But she could be better.

Why?

Aren't you interested in things being the way they should? Getting them right?

No.

It would be nice for Mel to be prettier.

Not for you. No. You think it would be nice to have a prettier Mel about but it wouldn't. For one thing she'd probably not be so good at minding kids. Beautiful people have better things to do. Beautiful people are smug.

Why do you say that?

Because they are. Look at you. Susie jabbed her spectacles up her nose and blinked at Emmanuelle through them. Maybe I should try contact lenses again, she moaned. Make it, what, six times, is it? She took off her glasses and rubbed the red marks they'd left on her cheeks. Her eyes looked naked, suddenly rudely unclothed. Like the undeveloped breasts of a child prostitute Emmanuelle had seen in Bangkok. I like you in glasses, she said. They suit you.

Shit, said Susie. Never say that. Smug, she repeated. And for a second thing a slightly scungy child carer is less likely though of course there are no guarantees to seduce your husband.

I'd wish her luck in that department. I suppose he could schedule it for the occasional breakfast meeting. Early breakfast meeting. Provided it didn't take too long.

Morning glory, giggled Susie. You'd be surprised what a busy man can find time for.

Do you really think I'm smug, asked Emmanuelle.

Mel doesn't actually go to hotel school, she doesn't go to any classes at all. She only says she does in order to make sure she has time off.

And perhaps to seem like a serious person with a career in mind. She would like to be this but can't think what the career would be. She doesn't have the education for anything requiring study. She tried out for the Dorchester Hospitality Course but didn't get in. The Regency wouldn't have her either and neither would the Palatial. Too many immaculate highly mannered young ladies with good accents and dumb but charming young men from public schools. She goes to town and looks in shops and feels dissatisfied since she has neither money nor figure for the clothes in them, and envies her employer, who has both. She wonders how riches can be acquired and then perhaps the figure to go with them willed, or bought. At the moment she wears black Doc Martens with white socks, very short flowered skirts, rusty black tee-shirts and her hair in spiky bunches with battered hats on top. Emmanuelle finds this peculiar even though she knows it is fashionable among the young.

Going to town to buy her dress Emmanuelle wore a trench coat and a beret and high-heeled shoes because of needing the right line for trying on a cocktail dress. She looked like a woman in a Humphrey Bogart movie, the blonde who comes to him for help but does not tell him everything. She carried a large yellow umbrella with a polished wooden duck's head handle. She parked her car as close as she could to the station but even so with the rain blowing slantwise and the asphalt deeply puddled she got wet. Her shoes were soaked and so was the hem of her coat. A chauffeur would have been useful simply for chauffering. Nevertheless she sat in her seat on the train without giving much thought to these things. The carriage swayed along its track with a rhythmic rackety motion and she swayed with it. She sat in a trance, not reading her book, not thinking, simply being the dreamy erratic motion imparted by the train. There was a man sitting opposite her. Each knew the other was there, but took no notice. As they swayed their eyepaths crossed but didn't touch.

After Chatswood the train filled up and people had to stand.

Their umbrellas dripped and there was a smell like wet dog. Behind her a woman said loudly, I wish this bloody rain would stop. The gardens need it, and the farmers, said her companion; I just wish it'd do its raining in the night. The man opposite Emmanuelle caught her with his glance and said, What would you wish? Emmanuelle replied, without thinking, I would wish for the gift of making dangerous choices.

The man pursed his lips and put his head on one side. His cheeks sucked in a little, as though the wish were a mouthful of wine he was tasting, then he nods his head, that is satisfactory, the waiter pours it into glasses and everybody drinks. The man smiled with pleasure, and at the next stop got off the train.

Emmanuelle went to David Jones Sixth Floor. She tried on a number of dresses but none of them would do. Too dowdy, she said, too matronly, I want an exciting dress, too elderly, too dull, too careful, too modest, though they were the sort of thing she usually bought, until the assistant brings her a dark silk dress in an ancient purple that is the colour and has the shine of an aubergine. It is a piece of elegant engineering, very tight round the waist and ribs, then opening out into an organised crumple of silk taffeta forming a kind of shelf, cantilevered, on which her breasts sit and are pushed up in two little globes like round quivering fruits in a nest of crumpled silk. It's an eighteenth century dress, in the top half anyway, the skirt is quite short. Her legs stretch a long way down to her wet shoes. That is a dress for a decadent society, a man at the party will say. And he doesn't even know what it's cost. Nobody does, Emmanuelle would not dare say except of course Lance will find out when he pays the bill but then he did order it. Though on the evening it is designed to grace he does not appear to notice it, being worried about being late. Mel whistles like a brickie on a building site, envious of the waist and the cash, she can tell it cost a lot though she wouldn't imagine how much, but is good natured enough to admire. Maud smooths her palms across the silk of the skirt and wants a dress just like it, William is mainly interested in burying his head in her breasts when she bends over to say good night.

I do think we ought to hurry, said Lance. It won't look good if one of the hosts is late. He had the Mercedes in front of the door, engine running, so they could just jump in and take off.

It was too early for even William to go to bed, so Mel was going to read a story. There was a batch of new books that Emmanuelle had bought on her shopping trip. Maud chose one called *Borobub's Space Adventure*. After several pages, in which Borobub had built a space ship and taken off in it, there was a pause, and a series of questions. Where does Borobub land? Is it on a planet threatened by giant green bees? Does he come down in a lake and find a mysterious underwater city inhabited by merpeople? Does his space ship crash into an asteroid and break up? Each of these possibilities had a page number, to which you turned, and when you'd read on through a bit more adventure you were presented with another set of choices, and so on all through the book. William got first choice and since he was into disaster chose the crashing on the asteroid.

Of course it isn't too bad. Borobub isn't killed or even hurt, but the space ship is damaged. He is worried that it won't ever fly again. When it comes to Maud's turn to choose from several forms of rescue, one by giant green bees, or to leave him marooned on the asteroid, she refuses. She doesn't want to choose, she shouldn't have to choose, it's a story, it is, it exists, she doesn't want to have anything to do with making it up, just hear it read. William however is keen to get to the end, he wants to know what happens. Yes, says Maud, if it's a proper story. So Mel reads on, making the choices herself, so that it appears to be a seamless narrative, and both the children are happy.

Merger

Emmanuelle and Lance were not at all late for the reception, in fact
they were extremely early, there was no one else there at all until
after about ten minutes one of the partners, called Donald Slatkin,
arrived, looking rather put out because he'd expected to be first.
He worried that Lance didn't work him hard enough. Lance still
didn't remark on the aubergine dress. Even if he hadn't noticed
how glamorous it was, or how it suited her, Emmanuelle had
expected him to find it too low in the neck, but even that hadn't
registered. He strode around examining the refreshments and con-
ferring with the waiters which was all rather pointless since the hotel
would manage everything, all had been planned in meticulous
advance and nothing could be changed now. The guests arrived and
she received them, standing in a line with Lance and the partners.
The party was to celebrate a merger, in which their company had
merged rather more successfully than the other. So the old family
firm as it still thought of itself though it was now multinational and
conducted much of its business off-shore, the firm of Hugues
Latimer Hallett (Hugues-Latimer was the hyphenated name Lance
had confided to Emmanuelle before he asked her to marry him,
and tried not to use, along with his middle name which was

Delattre) had merged with Bunbury Knight to call itself Latimer Hallett Knight, since the Hugues part was a grandfather who wasn't around to fuss. Bunbury didn't get a choice in the matter. The reception would introduce all the right people to the right people and confirm how right they were with Moet et Chandon and nibbles of a rare and fishy nature.

Emmanuelle in her marvellous dress the taut and shining colour of the skins of ripe aubergines, a dress apparently invisible to her husband's eye, Emmanuelle is talking to one of the Knights. She bites into a canape that crumbles and doesn't manage to catch all of it with her tongue; a morsel, a crumb, falls on to her breast. His hand darts out and finger and thumb scoop it up with a small nip like a bee nearly stinging. He puts the crumb in his own mouth and kisses his fingers at the same time. Emmanuelle dabs her breast with the tiny square of linen napkin and with her finger presses on its roundness (that quivering fruit in a nest of carefully crumpled silk) so that the nipple pops up over the edge of the neckline. She looks at him and then down at the nipple round and brown poking over the edge of her dress. His eyes are round and brown too but shining; brown eyes regard brown nipples; over the rim of the saucer-shaped glass her blue eyes watch him. She goes to the lavatory and takes off her knickers. The party is being very successful if noise is anything to go by, and people are quaffing the Moet as if it were local bubbly of the cheapest kind. Lance tells the head waiter to keep it coming. This is his first grand occasion since his father retired; he doesn't want it to be mean.

Later, at the restaurant where a favoured dozen are being given dinner Emmanuelle contrives to sit next to the Knight. The table has a starched white cloth that flares across their laps. She feels his hand slide up the slippery black nylon of her stocking, pause at her skin, silkier than silk, more satiny than satin, and fondle there, then on to her knickerless wet flesh.

You're not eating, she says. He picks up his fork in his right hand and stabs meat.

I prefer sea shells, he says, tracing her whorls with his finger. It becomes necessary to push his hand away. He rubs his fingers thoughtfully across his nose and turns to his neighbour. Dinner table conversation is like a dance. There is a moment for changing partners.

She wads herself with a tissue. The dress is lined, but that won't stop the damp seeping through. She wriggles her skirt out from underneath her and feels the pattern of the cane chair pressing into her bare flesh. She imagines her white buttocks patterned with crosses and circles from the cane seating of the chair. The man on her left is keen to discuss the beauties of the merger. I can see that you are more than just a pretty face, he tells her.

I'll give you a bell, says the Knight, bending over her hand in quite a French way as they take their leave of one another. She smiles the enigma smile of the woman in the aubergine dress. There is something about this dress that doesn't need conversation. It is curious, because usually she is full of chatter. She hasn't even learned his first name.

In the car going home Lance was very pleased that she'd got on so well with Knight. Some people might not think it important, he said, but I do, I think it essential for business colleagues to get on well. Essential. Especially at delicate times. He's a good man, Knight.

Emmanuelle wondered if Lance was a bit drunk. She'd suggested driving but he'd refused. Now he was threading his way through the traffic, swearing at the half-wits who had taken all the fun out of driving in Sydney. What you need is a chauffeur, she said. Then you could sit in the back and relax.

Not a bad idea. Let him have the worry of the morons. Get a lot of work done that way.

Emmanuelle's picture had been of them sitting comfortably in the back together, perhaps holding hands, certainly having time for the conversation of husbands and wives. Paying attention to one another. Their eyes sometimes meeting, and their heads bent to listen to the words their mouths spoke. She sighed. Lance said, I expect you're tired. Pretty gruelling, this sort of evening.

No, not tired, she said. She felt full of sap and energy, she wanted something to happen, she wanted Lance to make love to her. She put her hand on his knee, only for a moment, he didn't like to be touched when he was driving.

Made in Heaven

Marriages are made in heaven, Emmanuelle's mother-in-law has a habit of saying. Real marriages, she sometimes adds, when she needs to take account of all the divorces happening around her.

How do you know beforehand that it's going to be a real one, Emmanuelle asked.

Well, it's not easy, she said. Nothing in life is. But with the right spirit you can do it.

When Lou said spirit it sounded as though it meant energy. She herself was spirited, in the way a horse is; she cantered through life enjoying the fresh air and the scenery, and not baulking at difficult jumps. When Lance brought Emmanuelle home to meet his parents Lou said, not in public, her manners were nice, but to Lance: She looks good; is she? and Lance who'd developed an automatic answering habit when talking to his mother said Of course, ma. Lou who knew what the answer was worth decided it was probably true. She'd be good for Lance, anyway. Lou was worried about Lance still being single, at his age. He was handsome, and kind, and clever, but there was a coolness about him, a cold charm that could take people or leave them. As though his eligibility chilled him. Lou wanted for him the heat of passion, or at least the warmth of love.

Emmanuelle seemed a person to manage both. Lou had also determined to like her daughter-in-law, whoever she was. Emmanuelle made it quite easy. Though Lou herself was harder going. Emmanuelle, she murmured. An unusual name. Where does it come from? And when Emmanuelle replied that it came out of a novel her mother was reading before she was born, Lou said: I'm not sure young women ought to be allowed to read novels when they're pregnant.

Maybe they should read history, said Emmanuelle, then they could call their kids Napoleon or Hannibal. Or what about the legends of King Arthur?

There was a moment of balance, when the two men watched to see if friendliness would humpty dumpty tumble down and break into pieces that would need a lifetime's mending, but then Lou and Emmanuelle laughed and all four suddenly felt safe. I had a choice, said Lou. Lancelot or Percival; a change seemed a good idea.

When Maud was born Lou remarked, Been reading Tennyson, I see. They already trusted one another to see the jokes they made.

Emmanuelle's only unsatisfactoriness was not going to church. Lou went every Sunday. She walked through the lychgate and up the stone paved path and every Sunday she thought I was glad when they said unto me, let us go into the House of the Lord. And that was it, she was glad. That was why she went to church, because of the gladness. She wished Emmanuelle would go with her. After Maud's christening, when she said You'll be sending her to Sunday School, I hope, Emmanuelle replied without any doubt, Oh yes, I want her to go to Sunday School. She needs to learn about religion so she can choose.

Did you choose, asked Lou.

No, not really. I had nothing to go on. It's a regret.

Maybe one day you'll be chosen.

Ah, said Emmanuelle. It made her sound as though she had an open mind.

Failing church, Lou liked Emmanuelle to go shopping with her. Come and give me your advice, lovey, she said. She never took it. Emmanuelle was somebody to talk to while she made up her own mind. They always had lunch, always at a different restaurant that she was keen to try. At first Emmanuelle had imagined her being a person who would want to go each time to the same place, with staff who knew her and paid attention, but she quickly learned that the things she imagined about her mother-in-law were often wrong, not always, so it wasn't dependable, which made it interesting.

We'll cross this one off our list, Lou says, eating mushy pasta at a placed called Oodle's. Jane told me it was good. She's getting married on Saturday, you know. To her Jason. Stars in her eyes. For the pasta too, I reckon. Never trust lovers when it comes to restaurants.

Another marriage made in heaven, asks Emmanuelle.

So far one would think so.

What could you do if you thought yours wasn't?

Work on it, says Lou. What else?

You mean it's a matter of will? I thought being made in heaven was exactly the opposite, that your will didn't come into it. That it was a gift.

All marriages need work, says Lou. Let's have some dessert. We must be able to garner something from this ... experience. She calls the waiter to clear the uneaten food and bring the menu, and when all this is done she leans her elbows on the table and says, Did I ever tell you about me and Lance's father? No of course I never did.

She settles back and waits for a moment, the storyteller testing her audience.

I was engaged to be married at the time. To a man named Sunny Bell. A desirable man. His family had properties near Scone, one of them was his. He was tall and had long legs with that slight bow as though they are expecting a horse between them. And one of those big-brimmed hats, not at all the sort of hat a city man wears. His skin was brown and his eyes were blue ... oh, it was a grand thing to be engaged to a man like Sunny Bell. I knew it. My friends knew it. My parents were delighted; all their ambitions coming true. Stars in the eyes? And bubbles in the blood. Life was one long glass of champagne, with a hollow stem so the fizz keeps coming.

For a wedding present his parents were giving us a flat in town. A nice little compliment to me the city girl, and of course a good investment. They were very generous, we had a say in choosing it. A young man from a firm of estate agents showed us a number of properties in the Eastern Suburbs. A pleasant young man, in an unglamorous way, not very tall, my height in fact. You wouldn't look at him beside Sunny. Three days we spent viewing desirable apartments. None of them pleased Sunny, they were all too pokey, and I laughed and said that his trouble was thinking of Whiteacres and he couldn't possibly expect such grandeur in town. Why not, he said, and I looked at him, and at the young man from the estate agents, and I thought marriage is for all your life and I don't want to spend it with Sunny Bell, this man here is the person to live with, in flats pokey or grand, or houses or caravans if need be, at least there's likely to be quite a choice in his line of business, and that night I gave Sunny back his ring, it was a square cut emerald with sixteen diamonds, pretty snazzy, he was astounded, and so were all my friends, and my parents too, they were enraged as well, they thought I must have gone off my head. Especially when they saw who I was choosing instead.

Lou took a mouthful of dessert and put down her spoon. She didn't push the plate away, but it was evident she would eat no more. I rang up Percy first thing next morning, oh yes of course he was the young man, and arranged to look at yet another flat, a pretty one as I remember, with leadlight windows and a view over Rushcutters' Bay, and there I told him that I was no longer engaged to Sunny Bell. Percy knew what that meant. He knew what to do. Lou smiled.

An estate agent. I can still hear my father's voice. The scorn. An estate agent. Of course Percy wasn't really that. Though I didn't know it at the time. It was the university holidays, he was working in that branch of the firm, for the experience, Lance did the same thing. But it took papa quite a long time to cotton on. He thought I was making the most appalling *mésalliance*. I remember when I told him Percy's name, all the bits, he said, he roared, my papa roared, Jumped up, of all the jumped-up little ... My mother cried. Sunny Bell married the chief bridesmaid-to-be. My old school chum Jill. Dear old Jill. Things aren't too good on the land these days. Last I heard Whiteacres was in receivership.

So you see, my marriage made in heaven. But I had to make it happen. In the face of all that anger and amazement. And that was just the beginning.

Wow, said Emmanuelle. That's a marvellous story. She looked at her mother-in-law with admiration; romance, and riches too, her reward for recognising the right man.

The thing is, though, how did you tell?

Lou leaned forward. Her shoulders gave a little ripple. The sex is how you tell. And when you get it right it lasts forever. At least, as far as I can see. Fifty years on.

Emmanuelle flinched. Did Lou notice? Of course, of course, sharp Lou missed nothing. But she appeared not to be looking and that was a help. Emmanuelle took a gulp of the coffee, hot bitter coffee, and pulled her mouth into shape. So Lance doesn't take after his father then, she thought of saying, but instead she murmured Sex, and smiled, as though there were unspoken volumes in the word, volumes well-thumbed if not tatty and dog-eared, thoroughly well-read by Emmanuelle Latimer.

Of course, she added, Percy is still a very handsome man.

Oh, do you think so? It never occurred to me he was handsome. Sunny Bell, now, he was a good-looking man. He turned the heads and the hearts.

There was a thoughtful silence. Both women sipped at the coffee. Lou put hers down half finished, with a sharp clink in the saucer.

Shall we go, she said. You can tell me what to buy Jane for a wedding present.

Emmanuelle followed her out of the restaurant. Over seventy, and Lou still walked like a graceful horse.

She knew what she wanted to give Jane and found it and bought it without any help from Emmanuelle. It was a silver epergne sort of thing, an intricate pierced shape atop a slender fluted stem. An object of beauty and almost no use, said Lou. Not essential use, anyway. Just what you need at the start of a marriage. Useful things are always with us, but objects of *virtu* not always. Now, how about a cocktail?

I better not, said Emmanuelle. I'd better be getting home.

You are looking a bit peaky, said Lou. On the other hand, maybe a cocktail ... No? Well, off you go.

Emmanuelle sat in the train and thought about her own marriage. She'd never considered it made in heaven, that wouldn't have been relevant. Consenting adults, they were. They fell into conversation straight away. They went to plays and films and restaurants and to bed, and got pleasure from all these things. Her spirit lifted when she saw him come into the restaurant where she was waiting, found his car parked outside her flat, heard his voice on the telephone. He was a man who took care, paid attention, his hand, his arm, his eyes always available. Whose company was always available; no pain of absence, no misery of loss. She knew the moment when he touched her heart, it was when she saw his eyelashes, thick, stubby, very black, beautiful childish unexpected eyelashes that belied his rather correct face, eyelashes that she noticed every day of her life, though she hadn't known this would happen. But what if she'd been engaged to a Sunny Bell; would she have considered his world well lost for a Lance of whom she had no acquaintance, no knowledge? A Lance idly met out of context, just himself, no roles, no trappings? Or was it perhaps that Lance, handsome, oh yes he was handsome, handsome Lance with his good life evident about him, wasn't he her Sunny Bell, and the other, the true love of her heart, had gone unperceived by her?

She didn't like that idea at all. Not only because she didn't like being wrong, especially on such a grand scale. Because it was unfair to Lance, and unfair to her. She loved him. Passionately? Yes, passionately. When she got the chance. Lou for all her sharpness was a sentimental old woman, and who was to say that she possessed the truth.

The unexamined life is not worth living, said a soft voice. Opposite her a man with a speckled beard was talking to a young woman, who scowled and wriggled her shoulders. When he saw that he had Emmanuelle's attention he nodded his head and repeated his words. That's Socrates you know. The unexamined life is not worth living.

The train was pulling into her stop. Marriages are made in heaven, she offered in return, and got off.

The Good Wife

The good wife knows her husband doesn't like being touched while driving and only briefly puts her hand upon his thigh. She wishes him to be happy. She shapes a little fantasy of the passion that will bind them when they step through the door of their bedroom. She's left a rosy light burning, she'll step out of her shoes, he will bend and kiss her breasts with delicate butterfly lips, all so slow and the excitement rising until their bodies cannot contain it ...

Lance said, I wish I could spend more time with you and the kids. I feel they're growing up. The moments passing, precious moments that will never come again. His voice slow with sadness.

Yes, that's true. Time is passing very fast. But there are choices to be made.

Oh, choices. A or B. It's not so simple, Emmanuelle. This merger ... you've no idea ...

Well, maybe, now it's done.

Maybe, I'll try. It's what I want, to see a bit more of my family. But we can't always have our wants.

Emmanuelle wonders. She thinks she may be in the presence of the most common human delusion, that we are not making choices, that our lives are not in our hands, that we could not have done otherwise. She considers saying this to her husband, of adding, What about Donald Slatkin, all the Donald Slatkins, you don't have to do all the work yourself, but he is driving grimly, quite fast. If she wants him to play his role in her scenario of lust she had better not get into an argument.

Ah, she says, in a seductive voice. Ah. Wants. But sometimes what we want is what we've got. If we're lucky. She wriggles luxuriously into the seat. The silk dress whispers. Lance turns the radio on. Perhaps the wish is father to the thought, or is it the act, she murmurs, as the radio bursts into song.

If you were a camera you could pull back out of the comfortable back seat of the Mercedes, where the scented leather is soft and properly supportive of a sprawling body, pull out and look down on it speeding home through the late night traffic. Pause for a moment and admire this silver capsule, shaped to slip through the buffeting air with no let, so that the wind its passage makes slides past like a caress and none of it finds its way through the cunningly sealed doors and windows to trouble the ideal environment it creates inside itself, chilly in the sweaty summer days or as now warm on a sharp spring night. Pause to rejoice with the cosseted couple who are the masters of all this comfort, contained, transported and now entertained; Kiri Te Kanawa sings just for them Songs of the Auvergne, such passion, such longing, such melancholy that you feel weak with the pleasure of it.

The car swings through the traffic of the highway, then turns off into the narrow crossword-puzzle streets of the leafy suburb where its owners live. Leafy: this is how the press describes such suburbs when disasters happen in them, as in Children Abducted from Leafy Sydney Suburb, or Triple Murder Suicide in Leafy Northern Suburb, as though leafiness makes damage more shocking. Though of course leafy is a good word to distinguish these from the mean and sun-baked man-botched slums-in-waiting of certain outer districts, or the severe angles of brick and iron lace in the fashionable inner city, where the Latimers lived until the next generation gave the previous one an excuse to move out of the family house, they would never say mansion though an outsider might, and into a harbourside apartment, harbourside being a word like leafy, a label of instant communication.

The Latimer property deserves its leafy adjective as well as any could, from the grove of silver birches at the front to the great oak under which tea may be taken at a green iron table on the back lawn, past the bougainvillea and jasmine that thread through the lattice of the cloistered swimming pool, and here it could be remembered that leaves are simply a nuisance where swimming pools are concerned, and have to be scooped out with a long net, down to the eucalypts at the bottom of the property which merges with the native reserve that cuts a wide swathe through this suburb, stretching along a gully and across the small rise beyond, so that owing to the skill of the architect who designed this house with its important rooms and gardens at the back, the necessary amenities like garages and chauffeur's flat and nursery forming wings to shelter and enfold them, you can look out upon the prospect of a large park that seems entirely to belong to you. And the architect who some would say was the most brilliant and loving of his day, had in his head Mediterranean villas and ochre colours and the tense new geometry of art deco, and built a house which was or had none of these things exactly, but was a perfectly Sydney house on the edge of the warm eucalypt scented bush.

And now the camera having whipped ahead to give us this view of the house (*Vogue Living* devoted six pages to it in the winter issue, if you want to know about its cool marble rooms and warm Tuscan patios) moves back to where the car is still negotiating its puzzle streets towards home. These have been pictures without sound, except for the yearning of the Auvergne songs, which like a lot of art make us long for something they do not quite give us. The pain of desire is not quite assuaged by the pleasure of possession and so we must keep coming back to it in the hope of satisfaction, this time. Whereas with material things the pleasure of possession is surely completed; the Mercedes, the graceful dwelling, they are, they fully occupy their present, they leave no room for desire. So Emmanuelle and Lance in this car turning into the driveway of this house, should be perfectly content, except for that small lost edge of longing in Kiri Te Kanawa's singing.

But the words of the couple belie this. I wish, they say, I want, I would like, were I, if only, would that it were so. Their dialogue with themselves and with others is subjunctive. Is contingent, is hypothetical. It is constructed in the wishing tense, its syntax is desire. Its message is discontent. Subjunctive, disjunctive. Contentment doesn't seem to lie in possession. So, what's new. People have always known this. Some people. That's why the flounder sent the old woman back to the hovel, in the end.

Lance stops the car at the front door. There's a circular drive, and just here a roof with pillars. He gets out too. I'll leave it here tonight, he says, something he never does. Always the car must be put away; he lets Emmanuelle out at the front door and then drives round to the garage. But tonight: It'll be okay here, he says. Something that Emmanuelle always thinks but has given up saying. Tonight there's a tautness about him that she responds to by putting her arm round his waist as they go up the steps.

Inside he deadlocks the door and then turns to her. Em, he says, in a thick growling voice, Em. The voice is urgent. He grabs at her. His passion cannot wait even as far as the bedroom. Em, he says again. He has no other words. He has her, his arms around her, is leaning hard against her, is sagging, falling against her, her flimsily-heeled feet lose their grip on the marble of the floor and they both sprawl in a heap. Steady, she murmurs, steady, with a little throaty laugh, thinking are we here at last and not wanting to add but does it need to be so violent? And afraid that he is more drunk than she thought and it is booze not passion that has brought them together.

Come on, she murmured, pushing at his weight heavy against her on the marble floor, and it struck her that he was too heavy, that his weight lying upon her was nothing to do with her, that his body twitched and bent and had no thought of her. She pulled herself away and knelt beside him, his limbs fell away loosely so he lay half on his front, breathing in loud snorts. His face was dark red as if full of old angry blood. She thought, he's passed out. How can he be so drunk. She stood up in fury, to go and get a blanket and leave him there foolishly snoring in the front hall until he should have slept it off. To an evil hangover and stiff from the cold stone floor. Then she knelt again; Lance had never fallen down dead drunk before. Very drunk she's seen him, morose, or madly merry, or grumpy, but never falling down. She felt his pulse, it bounded under her finger with a dreadful power, and yet his arm was heavy. She remembered that thick growling voice. Em ... Em ... Lance always calls her Emmanuelle ... Never Em.

She went to the phone and dialled three noughts. Her legs trembled so much her voice came out in gasps. Then she rang Mel's extension, and sent her for blankets and a pillow. The blankets she tucked over him, but didn't want to heave him on to the pillow. The ambulance men were deft, turned him over, gave him oxygen. Stertorous breathing, said one. They manoeuvred him on to the stretcher. The Mercedes was in the way, they had to back and fill, the stretcher on its high legs and small wheels teetered. Emmanuelle saw it tipping over and spilling its load on to the cobblestones, but they righted it.

She sat in the front beside the driver, the other ambulance man was in the back with Lance. They drove steadily through the night streets, long ways round but easy. In the hospital they took Lance away through wide flapping doors. There was a plastic seat for her to sit on. The smell was the same as when Maud was born, when she was in labour for thirty hours and Lance put his face close to hers so she could feel his will flowing into her and it saved her from despair. It was cold; her breasts in their nest of crumpled silk were grey with

34

gooseflesh. She was in some sort of corridor, echoing and brightly lit, full of bits of equipment waiting to be used. There was a high bench bed parked in a corner with a cellular blanket folded at its foot and she wrapped that around her. The well-washed cotton, pale green like a mint lolly, was comforting. The aubergine dress felt a very foolish garment in that place.

Talk to Him

Lance knew he was lying somewhere quite hard and rather hot; the sheets had a breathless feel about them that meant plastic underneath. People were talking around him, their voices boomed faintly in his head, confident voices in the habit of speaking these things, except that they were wrong, he could hear he could understand he wasn't in a coma. He opened his mouth to put them right but it didn't obey him nor did the hand his mind lifted to catch their attention. I can hear, I can understand his brain said but the words didn't get through. A terrible squeezing of all his body parts tried to come out of his brain and was trapped there, buzzing. I know, I understand, I'm not in a coma, his brain yelled but his body lay there like a dummy. The self-possessed voices receded and were replaced by a soft whispering one he recognised as Emmanuelle's. A voice gentle and low, an excellent thing in a woman, Percy would say whenever he heard a strident female voice, apparently that was King Lear talking about his daughter Cordelia. Percy had no daughters, no more sons either, only Lance, and Lou's voice though low was hoarse rather than gentle.

Now Emmanuelle's voice was murmuring, close by his ear, she was talking to him as though he were William, not even William, she'd always talked to the children as though they were sensible human beings, made a policy of it, got it out of some bringing up your baby to be intelligent book she'd read at one time. Now her phrases were broken, fragments of endearment and hope and news strung together into repetitive beads of desire, like a rosary. Lance heard her talking to him, like a rosary, muttered, repetitive, noted the booming doctor voice, Talk to him, Mrs Latimer, he may hear you, wanted to scream Of course I hear you, fools, couldn't you say something interesting, but his body was a cold clay coffin and no one could hear the words he couldn't utter. He ground his teeth in despair, and the noise in his skull was silent as a tomb.

Time passed unpunctuated by bodily functions. Drips and catheters stole the passing needs. Voices came and went. Emmanuelle would be there, wittering on as to a gormless child. Black eyelashes. She held his hand that gave no heed to his anger, lay limp and smarmy in her grasp. She held it against her chest whose fluttering he could have matched had the idiot hand not disobeyed him.

Oh Lance my dear my love I can say my love though in life you would not have liked it. Wrinkle brow in life you frowned. In life, of course you are in life though no sign shows you lie like a man of wax in the way they say is perfectly formed, you were always perfectly formed and is this wax so different, haven't you been wax to me and should I be honest I to you wax indeed for a long day. She sighed and squeezed his hand. Oh wax my love for a long day.

Waxing and wailing, Lance thought to say. Waxing and wailing, and lightly punch her arm. Lightly and quite hard. But his hand hung soft in the hollow of her cheek and damp too and when she was no longer there his waxiness seemed a fact. She came again and her voice mumbling on made his brain near burst with the distance of her closeness, or did he mean the closeness of her distance, the hand that would not put out and stop her, the shoulder that would not shrug, the deep sigh not fetched up from where the intestines coiled with no orders from him. The booming voices with their strangely rotund words and mysterious syntax were easier to bear. Though afterwards there could be terror left behind. But the words came in clusters like curious fruits that asked to be bitten and chewed and rolled around the tongue, and if they were poisonous well that was their nature. Cerebrovascular incident indeed. The certainty that cerebral eschemia. Subdural hematomes which can present as. Subsequent embolic events. Artheroma. The narrowing of the lumen.

That gave him luminous. He wished to live in a world that could be called luminous, which welled with light, shining but not bright like the harsh crack in the furry dark that lay over his eyeballs. If he were to pray he would ask: Give me a luminous world. May my world be luminous.

And not frequented by weeping women. Here was Lou, saying in a whispery voice, I will never forgive myself San Francisco. He remembered now. Percy and Lou feeling like a little trip, San Francisco a nice distance. Never been there. Unaccountable, said Percy. Lou like a girl in a 60s movie never been kissed in a cable car. And here she was weeping. How was the cable car he asked. I met my love on the cable car he sang but she stood snuffling and then sat by him and said things the likes of which and the manner had never passed her lips before, not in his hearing, he felt like a voyeur. Stop, stop, I should not be seeing these things! but on she went. His flesh quivered with embarrassment under its wax its cerements, perhaps he was dead after all and in a winding sheet, a shroud, wax cloth against wax skin.

Lou held his hand in hers and babbled was the only word. My child, my son, my only one, allowed only one and now you're taken going from me. Two stillborn and three miscarried, only one allowed and still too much. Hysteria whispered in her voice. Shush ma he would have said but the panic was rising in him too like the intestines coiling and then there was Percy's voice an old old man saying Cheer him up, love, cheer him up that's what's to do. Tell him about the waiter in that restaurant on the wharf who juggled the fish. A great spot San Francisco my boy. You should consider it when next you're thinking of a holiday.

And Lou hardly audible. Oh yes, yes, Percy's right, you'd like it, you and Em, oh yes.

Again the booming voices. Damage to smooth endothelial lining. Heparinisation. Apoplexy. Lance could have laughed at apoplexy. Gone the way of antimacassars and aspidistras. Not forgotten, just a joke. People don't have them any more. Like choleric butlers, not any more.

Supportive medical care followed by rehabilitation therapy. That was Emmanuelle's voice. An excellent thing in a woman, hey Dad? Then Percy's asking How long? but there didn't seem to be an answer. Until a strange female voice said, He's tired now. Come back tomorrow. He likes it, you know, he loves being talked to. Come back and talk to him tomorrow.

The Chauffeur

Emmanuelle and Susie stood at an upstairs window watching Stuart swimming laps of the pool. Every third turn he changed his stroke. I like the butterfly best, said Susie, regarding his flailing arms lift his brown body out of the water and shoot it forward. They were in Maud's room because that was where the best view was to be had. At ground level the latticed fence threaded with vines kept out curiosity as well as drownable children.

So there you have him, said Susie.

What?

Your sexy chauffeur.

It was you that wanted a sexy chauffeur.

For the sex. But you were quite keen on being driven around, as I recall.

Emmanuelle stared at her. Susie! You did it on purpose. You meant ... that to happen.

Meant what to happen?

You know perfectly well what I mean.

Em, you can't possibly think that. I'm not that clever, for one thing.

Emmanuelle leaned her forehead against the window pane. She

felt tired in her bones, these days, though she didn't need to go into the hospital so often, could have a morning off, like now, with Susie calling in and Nathan and William playing. At first she'd driven in twice a day, sometimes three times, spending all day and half the night there. The doctor saying, keep talking to him, you never know what gets through. The real weariness of these visits came from there being no news, not good or bad, just waiting and seeing. Watching for a change, a flicker of mind, to cross his waxen face. There were a lot of tests; she waiting in his glittering room while he was wheeled away. The bed cost more than a new car, the porter said, very neat to drive. Then, suddenly, Lance did come back; a flutter of his eyelids and she could feel him seeing her. On Friday afternoon the doctor said, yes, we could hope that Lance would be all right, a matter of rehabilitation and eventually the chance of a more or less complete recovery. Quite a good prognosis for stroke patients, really, generally, once they'd got through the initial ... er ...

She called in to see Susie on her way home, suddenly needing the comfort of her yellow sunflower family room and Susie's cheerful cynical kindness. Her trumpeting laugh driving the cloying hospital silence out of her head. She sank into one of her deep chairs, and relief released her into the exhaustion she had until now not admitted.

You look terrible, said Susie, once the news of Lance's prospects had been discussed.

Thank you. You're a good friend.

More than you realise. I know just what you need. Susie went into the kitchen. There was the whizzing noise of a blender and she came back with two huge brandy balloons filled with a pastel-coloured frothy substance and a whole strawberry stuck over the edge of the glass. Drink this, she said.

What on earth is it?

A magic potion. What else?

Yeah?

Yeah. Designed to turn you into !Superwoman! Susie pronounced this with the whooping emphasis of is-it-a-bird-is-it-a-plane-no-its-Superman on the television.

Good. Just what I need. Will it be instant? She tasted. The creamy pale pink drink was comforting, faintly sweet, mysterious, like being a child having a treat. She drank it gratefully, in small spaced sips.

Seriously, though.

My new thing, said Susie. Like a milkshake. Milk, obviously, a whack of cream, a lot of strawberries, pureed. As you see.

You mean, no grog.

Oh, a bit, not a lot. Susie watched Emmanuelle enjoying it. I bet you didn't have any lunch, she said.

Lunch. What's that?

Okay. There's something nourishing. Just what you need to keep you going.

Mmm. And I had better be. Going. Emmanuelle stayed sunk in the chair, a picture of weak flesh overcoming a spirit willing. I must go, she said. Poor old Mel needs some time off.

Susie went out to the kitchen again and came back with the blender jug. Have a bit more. I put more strawberries in. It'll have a good energising effect. You've got to avoid getting run down and worn out, you know. Everybody depending on you.

Em liked being taken charge of. She drank the second milkshake. So much less effort than chewing food. Smooth and soft in her wizened stomach. Her blood seemed to flow more energetically. I can feel it doing me good, she said.

I'm trying out different combinations. I may give up eating and just live on cream cocktails.

Cocktails?

Well, that's basically what they are. I had a couple the other night at the Regency, it gave me a taste for them. This one's called a Paradise Lost, with extra strawberries. They have great names.

There's the Gone Troppo, that's rather yummy. And the Orange Orgasm, haven't tried that yet.

That was how Emmanuelle came to lose her licence to drive. Round the corner from Susie's were flashing blue lights and policemen in fluorescent orange waistcoats and baton torches who pulled the Mercedes over with she thought a certain glee, certainly when she spoke into the machine, they made her count and her voice wobbled so the words hardly uttered, louder, they said, you have to speak louder, and came out over the limit. Not a lot, but as the young policeman said with a laugh, it's the over that counts, not the how much. Especially when added to all the points she already had for speeding.

Afterwards she rang up Susie. What was in that drink, she demanded.

I told you. Strawberries, milk, cream ...

And the rest? The alcohol, Susie.

Well ... A bit of Kahlua, some Grand Marnier ... and a drop of Amaretto just to take the sweetness off. Oh, and some Fraise as well, for the strawberries ...

Shit, said Emmanuelle. No wonder.

Susie thought it was funny, in a way. Em who never took more than a glass of wine, done for drink driving. She was contrite too. I never would've thought, she kept saying. I don't know whyever not, said Emmanuelle, you could get pissed just reciting the ingredients.

I thought a morsel of alcohol would put a bit of life into you. Like St Bernards in the snow. It never occurred to me that it'd put you over the limit. Not for a second. You must be extremely susceptible.

Lou was amused too, now that the news about Lance had brought her sense of humour back. All those shopping lunches when she'd order a bottle of wine and Em never would drink her half. It was Percy who came to the rescue and offered Stuart, who was a driver for the firm, and could help with Lance when he came home from hospital.

The cocktails stayed a sore point. Like slipping somebody a Mickey Finn, Emmanuelle said. You knew they had alcohol in them, said Susie. Not so much, said Emmanuelle. Now she was accusing Susie of doing it on purpose so she'd have to hire a chauffeur. Of course, she didn't really believe that. But she didn't like being a person who had lost her licence for drunken driving. It changed her view of herself. She didn't like the loss of control it implied. There was a trap she'd never thought could catch her, and she'd fallen in. Susie knew she wasn't keen on drinking liqueurs, that's why she hadn't mentioned them. She'd exploited her weariness, and her gratitude. Out of kindness. Susie had made choices for her which she knowing about would have rejected. But Susie was her friend, wishing her well, Emmanuelle accepted that; seeing her tired, wanting to make her feel better. She wouldn't have thought for a second of breathalysers lurking in the two or three deeply suburban streets separating their houses. The main thing was bad luck.

And yet—she would never let on to Susie—there was a kind of exhilaration in it. It got her into a more dangerous world. Nice well brought up always doing the right thing Emmanuelle: if accident could so easily put you in the wrong was there much point in good intentions? It was as though there was a pale she'd been put beyond; beyond smugness, beyond safety, and maybe it was a good place to be. Behind her the white picket fence of neatness, ahead a soaring landscape, with wide prospects and hidden grottoes, and playing through her hair a little sinister breeze that might become a gale.

Paradise Lost, the drink was called. She remembered Brian, who came into her thoughts from time to time, these days, spending a whole term on *Paradise Lost.* Milton's. The Fortunate Fall. How humanity needed it. An unchosen Paradise not being worth having. Whereas now we know good and evil and can choose and that's what makes good valuable. She'd been passionate about Milton, the way Brian offered him. The Fortunate Fall. Except that Susie had chosen it for her. Adam could have said no to the apple, but then probably he was as ignorant of its implications as Emmanuelle of the cocktail's.

And now they are in Maud's room so Susie can look out the window and see Stuart. That's what she's come for. So she can check out the spunky chauffeur.

Why don't you put on a bikini and go and join him? says Emmanuelle. The cruelty of this remark is intentional. She still has a desire to punish Susie. Put on a bikini and go and join him, she says, knowing bikinis are not for Susie, nor she for them. She is a person of abundant flesh, opulent, voluptuous: words that fill the mouth as palpably as her body the spaces it moves through. It's handsome, this abundant flesh, left to itself, naked, but when you draw the sharp lines of a bikini across it, apply the garment's mean shapes to its plenitude, you mock it. I am too fat for a bikini, says Susie to herself; Susie is too fat to wear a bikini, thinks Emmanuelle; it occurs to neither of them that it is the bikini which is not suitable for Susie, that the garment, not the woman, it is that fails. Imagine any of Rubens' Venuses in bikinis; they'd look as silly as moustaches round their pouting rosy lips.

I just might at that, says Susie. She won't let Em see her words hurting. Anyway, it's a small revenge for the lost licence.

The hum and thump of Magda vacuuming sounds in the passage outside. They go downstairs. Emmanuelle offers coffee. She's not at the hospital because Lance is having another CAT scan. X-rays, swimming, physiotherapy, electro-encephalograms, they set her free for periods of each day. And soon Lance will come home.

Bonking

You know what's wrong with me, says Susie. I'm suffering from lust. Unalloyed. Unslaked. Unrequited. She uses these ambitious words to give a faintly comic air to her situation, at the same time as she means them.

She and Emmanuelle are drinking coffee in the kitchen of Em's house, the enormous 1920s room that was meant to be an enlightened working place for numbers of servants. It's got wooden cupboards with glass doors offering glimpses of flowered china (there's a copper sink in the scullery next door for washing it, copper not so likely as stone or enamel to break frail china or scratch its gilt) and plates and bowls and pots and pans; the heart's desire of any cook could find requital here. The floor is covered with pinkish ochre tiles worn into hollows, there's an Aga where the fuel stove used to be. Victorian mansions had such offices, but this is no basement. It could be a kitchen on a farm, where people live. Emmanuelle is the third generation of women to take pleasure in it. Renovation has been discreet; french windows to the garden, a dishwasher, a covert microwave. Lou would never have moved out if she'd thought her daughter-in-law was the kind of person to call in a creative kitchens firm.

I don't know how you can stand it, Susie once said. It's all so old and gloomy. She has a creative kitchen.

Gloomy? Rubbish. Mellow, maybe. Look how beautiful the light is.

I suppose so. What there is of it. Must be a killer to keep clean.

Emmanuelle shrugged. No more than any other.

It's a whim. A rich person's whim.

Whim became Susie's word of the moment. She pronounced it with a kind of whipping hum. It's a whim, she said. It's your whim. It made Emmanuelle feel she lived in a fantastical world at the wrong end of Susie's telescope.

Now they are sitting in this kitchen at a large long table, old yellowed pine with turned legs painted blue, a milky turquoise colour that Susie reckons is Tuscan. Why, asked Emmanuelle; Susie said it just was. If you had an eye for such things.

Lust.

Yes, said Susie. It's like being a teenager again, when you didn't know what it was all about. Except now you do, so it's worse.

Susie's husband is called Gavin and he has a computer business, doing nicely, but he's never home, there's no time, no conversation, no sex, no life together. Susie spends the long nights alone, drinking cream cocktails, and maybe believing them innocent as milkshakes, watching videos with Nathan in bed and the house around her, the house that she has cosseted and adorned, clicking softly and rustling as though it had a life of its own and cared nothing for her, was maybe not even friendly. I feel it's watching me, she said, waiting for its moment. I'm glad Nathan's there, and I have to be ready to look after him.

Isn't Gavin ever at home, asked Emmanuelle, thinking of Lance and no time, no conversation, no making love.

Well, sometimes, and we go out, usually businessy things. But you know, I don't feel I get any attention from him.

And there are Lou and Percy and fifty years. What's gone wrong with our generation, Emmanuelle said. Here we are, not even pushing forty, and all we can talk of is the absence of love. That's what you really mean, Susie, not sex.

Susie pushed in and out the little drawer in the side of the table where the egg-beaters were kept. It was worn and stuck slightly. What does a stroke do for your sex life, she asked, but seeing Emmanuelle's face went on, yeah, well, I don't know. It all started out all right. Remember at uni ...

Uni! I didn't know you went to uni.

Only lasted a year, said Susie, but boy, it was good while it lasted. There was this guy in the English department. We used to bonk on his study floor. People said he had a Lilo that he used to get out of the cupboard and blow up but he didn't. We used the cushions off the chairs. You rolled off them and on to the floor. Lino tiles. Gritty. Gritty sex. Oh yeah.

In his study. Didn't people know?

I suppose they did. Who can tell. It didn't seem to matter. Of course you had to be quiet; that was the hard part, but fun too, wanting to shriek out and holding in till you thought you'd burst.

What happened in the end?

There wasn't an end. It just stopped. I failed. Every single unit. Didn't go back. He had a wife of course. I suppose he bonked some keen kid from the next year's intake. There were lots of other guys. Though I have to admit Evan was fairly special. He'd talk to you. Poetical things. Ah Susie, he'd say, ah Susie, thy beauty is to me ... I turned into Susie that year. I'd been Susan up till then. Remember little friend Susan in *Milly Molly Mandy*? God what a wimp. How could my mother wish that on me. Well, I know, she was giving me a nice English name for a nice English life. Susan. Susie was going to be a fun person. Anyway, Evan used to look in your eyes and say poetical things, of course you knew he got them out of books but still you had the feeling he was making love to you, not just bonking. I suppose all his girls did.

I wonder if any female gets through university without sleeping with one of them? The lecturers.

You too? Susie laughed her trumpet laugh. Who'd've thought it. I imagined you much too well behaved. The cold beauty.

And there I was, bonking with the best of them.

Lecturers–lecherers, hooted Susie. So what happened?

The usual. Nothing.

Just bonking. The word thumped in Emmanuelle's head. Bonking put in a box. Nailed down, got rid of, out of the way. Even if it still rattled sometimes. A child bangs its head against the wall, against the bars of a cot, jig a jingle, the rhythm's the same, only slower, and the brain sloshes in the skull's fluid.

She said, I've got to go now, pick up Maud. There's Stuart bringing the car round. William, she called, Time to go. Nathan!

Can I have a lift home?

I thought you wanted to walk. The exercise.

Exercise, trumpeted Susie. There's exercise and exercise. I haven't met Stuart yet, remember? Only perved on him.

The car was waiting outside the front door. Magda was vacuuming the hall. She bent over to turn the machine off and there was a faint tinkle across the floor. Emmanuelle picked up a little gold wheel with cogs. Magda snatched it out of her hand. Is pray, she said. Bus. Pray bus. Magda's conversation was the triumphant discovery of words but syntax forever escaped her. She held the little wheel with its axis between her thumb and middle finger and turned it with the pad of her index finger, like a treadmill.

For praying, said Emmanuelle. Is it a kind of rosary?

Pray, nodded Magda. Not hoover. She made a loud vrooming noise and kicked the vacuum cleaner, putting her hands over her ears. Bus. Pray little boy. She patted William on the head. Pray boy. Good.

I have a daughter too, said Emmanuelle, though she had no faith in praying.

Daughter okay, said Magda. Not need. Boy. She took a comb out of her pocket and began to comb his hair.

I think you should pray for all of us, Magda, said Susie. Sit on the bus and turn your little wheel and pray for all of us. Heaven knows we need it.

Pray, nodded Magda. Pray son. She licked her fingers and would have sleeked William's hair, but Emmanuelle hustled him into the car. The comb had made tracks in his hair, but he and Nathan played gibbering games with one another that required a lot of head shaking, and they quickly disappeared.

Luck

When old Percy Latimer offered him the job of chauffeur for his son, Stuart took it because it seemed like a change might be a good idea. What he was doing was a bit boring, sitting round in the security men's office waiting to drive someone somewhere, at least this'd be in a house, and a pretty ritzy one at that. The woman who'd be his boss was extremely attractive. Nice, too, polite, the kind of politeness you'd like to have belonging to you, and you could do things with it. Not rough things. Being strong didn't mean rough, he wasn't rough with women. Nor men neither, though that might be tougher. The aggression there, under the skin. Good fun. He wondered what her skin would feel like under his fingers. It'd be good to get his hands on her. When he oiled his own body, rubbing in black pepper oil to warm his muscles, he thought what if it was hers he was stroking with some nice scented oil. What perfume for her? What was the one Yvette used to wish she could afford, the most beautiful of all she said, it smelt of orange flowers, sweet and bitter at the same time. Neroli, that was it, she'd named the baby that. Not his baby, so she said. He believed her, well, pretty much, they'd used precautions except that one time he got a bit carried away, and she left after that. It might have been quite nice if it had been his, but anyway. Neroli. Sweet and bitter would suit this lady. Her husband was sick in the hospital, maybe she was the kind that'd need a bit of comfort, sooner or later. Calling him in and he'd know she needed a bit of a cuddle, the smart clothes she wore peeling off her, sliding down to the floor, his foot kicking them away in slithery heaps.

The flat that came with the job had a bathroom all mirrors, he could see his back as well as the front, he really was fabulously cut, he hadn't been able to get that angle on himself before, but he'd noticed her looking at him with that little open-mouthed smile she had, you could see she liked his body. Sometimes he'd lie on his bed and imagine her there beside him, not in this bed, in the house, in a large room with marble floors like the entrance hall, he hadn't got past the marble floors and her slippery clothes in a heap on their smooth surface. And yellow, that was in his head too, the yellowness of the lady's bedroom, though he had no reason for it.

Not that he spent a lot of time lying on his bed. Though the job wasn't too heavy, not yet, anyway, while the husband was in hospital, and she was good about telling him the times when she needed him. What's your name, she'd asked him, in a gentle way, as though he might be a friend, and when he told her William Stuart she said Do you mind if I call you Stuart which of course was a polite way of saying she was going to, because of her little boy being called William, that way there'd be no confusion. He didn't mind, though people didn't call him William, mostly he was Bill, but being Stuart in this lady's soft voice felt like being a different person, maybe a smart person who'd go places, though being Bill had been okay, Bill got along all right. But not with rich people, like this lady. Stuart maybe would be a person to sleep with a rich and beautiful lady. He'd be driving her round, anyway, and that was quite erotic.

Stuart, said Mrs Latimer each evening, about tomorrow. First of all we'll take Maud to school, and then you can drop me at the hospital, you needn't wait, come back and pick me up at three, then ... So she made a scheme of each day, and so far there were plenty of holes that belonged to him. He brought the car round and stood beside it, dressed in the pale grey suit that was his uniform. Please don't wear your cap, she said on the first day, so he kept it on the seat beside him. The suit sat uneasily on him, its thin fabric pulling across his muscles. He'd brought his gym with him, and set it up in the cloister by the pool house; when he'd done his jobs he worked out, or else swam laps in the pool. Sometimes Mel who looked after the kids came and joined him. She was a funny looking girl but okay company. As well as good at keeping quiet. She understood that when you're working out that's what you're doing, not yapping away at women's gabble. Sometimes she'd have time to sit and have a beer afterwards, and then it was all right if she talked.

It's not a bad life here, she said one day. Is it. She was lying on a reclining chair, in her swimsuit with a sarong wrapped round it, he'd noticed she wasn't comfortable in just a swimsuit. She waved at the green salt pool, with its cloisters and statues, the trellises of bougainvillea, the pale ochre house beyond.

Yeah, said Stuart.

The only thing is, it'd be nice to live in it, really live, instead of just working in it.

You can say that again, said Stuart.

I'll say it as often as you like, said Mel.

What d' you reckon it'd be worth, he asked. One million? Two?

That much? Mel sucked her breath in. It's the old family house, you know. The grandfather built it. Lance grew up here. Then his parents moved out when Lance and Emmanuelle started having kids, give them space. The parents make do with a giant apartment at Elizabeth Bay. Only as big as two ordinary houses.

Money, said Stuart. It goes round and round in its own rinky dink and more and more sticks to it. Like a magnet. But hardly ever any comes off.

I know. The thing is, why are some people rich and some not?

You a socialist?

Hell, no. I want to be one of the rich ones.

Don't we all.

I mean, really want. Don't you think, if you really want it enough, you should be able to do it? It's just a matter of working out how.

I do lotto every week.

I hate that, said Mel. It's admitting defeat. It's saying that only sheer blind one in a billion chance will ever save you. Lotteries. They're to give the poor suffering masses hope. They're admitting that everything's despair, except this one hopeless hope.

Still, I wouldn't mind winning. Somebody has to. Why not me. Stuart stood up and stretched, his muscles moved in their well-oiled pleasurable patterns. He knew he looked as good as he felt.

That's it, said Mel. You're accepting despair. She plucked the sarong away from her body. She didn't want it to stick to her wet swimmers and show her shape. What if she had a body she could offer as Stuart did his? Serene in its knowledge that it was desire's ideal. She couldn't imagine what it would be like not to want to hide yourself, not to search out at all moments the disguise that would protect you from scornful eyes. She looked at this body preening before her, its brown and gleaming surfaces. No hair. She'd heard that serious body builders waxed off all their hair. Wouldn't the skin prickle? What would it be like, flesh against flesh?

Stuart looked at the pool. He stood on its edge, rocking up and down on the balls of his feet. I dunno, he said. Okay. So this doesn't belong to us. But we enjoy it. Now, this minute, it's ours. Do you see them doing that? Enjoying? Madame off at the hospital all the time? And as for him, what fun's he having?

But it's not ours. Not mine.

Yes it is. This pool, right now, it's mine.

He kicked himself off and dived in a high sleek curve into the salty green water. And yes, his body did own the spaces it moved through.

But there's no security, she yelled. I'm thinking of more than passing moments. Oh shit, she said. What's the time? Oh god, I'll be late picking up William.

There was a fine if you were late. Forty dollars. To discourage you. Mel had already had to pay it once, and Emmanuelle hadn't been pleased.

What's he like, Susie had asked when Emmanuelle had first told her about Stuart.

Oh, he seems nice. Quiet. Seems to be a good driver.

What's he *look* like?

Lots of muscles. He's got his own gym. Portable, more or less. He works out a lot.

Susie gave a big bosomy sigh that came quivering down the telephone. Maybe I should join him. Get myself a lustworthy body. I'll come over and check out his equipment, she said.

No you won't. You jolly well won't. I wish you'd stop going on like this. He's not a gigolo, or a toyboy. He's a chauffeur. He knows his place. So should we.

Yes. I do like the servants to know their place, said Susie.

Shit, said Emmanuelle. You know what I mean. His role. His job. But okay. Come over and have a look at him. But politely. From a distance. Hire your own if you want to screw him.

Emmanuelle had thought quite a lot about Stuart. Not in lustful Susie's way. Late one evening, putting out the garbage, she'd seen the pool lamps lit and heard the creak of his machines. There he was, cultivating his body until late at night; she wondered what was going on in his head. Did you think while you pulled and pushed, pumped and pedalled? No, of course you didn't, that was partly the point, you were your body, its effort, its straining, the mind was of no more account than a little finger and would get no more attention. Emmanuelle liked that idea. A smooth bulge of muscle, a smooth bulge of brain. No crinkles or worries. Whereas her brain was a portable gym where her thoughts went through the same distressing motions over and over and were neither exercised nor soothed by the process; never any results, none of that marvellous healthy tiredness that good exercise brings.

She knew what love was now, it was fear and impotence, looking at a person helpless in a bed and feeling your chest filling with a love that was afraid of its simple powerlessness. Every night when she came home from the hospital Mel handed her a list of telephone messages. One day there was a note that Knight had called, and she thought, Knight, who is that? supposing some dutiful well-wisher, not remembering his fingers under the table in a restaurant, the cane pattern of a chair against her bare bottom. Lust was another country and the memory of desire was dead.

Stroke

Emmanuelle hadn't told her children much about what was happening to Lance. She didn't need to, since they weren't troubled by his absence. They were used to him wordless rushing off in the morning, and getting home after they were asleep. Even at weekends there wasn't much contact. My children are growing up and I'm missing it, he said to Emmanuelle over late dinners, when all he'd seen of them was sleeping heads, tiptoeing in the dark so as not to wake them, dropping kisses, staring down though there was little to see, smelling new-bathed children and listening to their solemn breaths in beds full of inanimate fabric creatures. I need to spend more time with them he said. Saturdays sometimes he took them to breakfast in the village, where they drank mugs of hot chocolate and ate croissants while Lance read the papers, but this wasn't a regular occurrence so they didn't question the absence of the treat. Emmanuelle wondered that the disappearance of their father from their lives could cause so little anguish. Though they did notice daddy not sleeping at home, and she told them that he wasn't feeling very well, and had gone to hospital which was where they made people feel better. She wondered what she'd do if this turned out to be a lie, but if it did then so much would be terrible that one small exploding lie would be the least part of the damage.

Gorn to the horspital, said William, in his gruff voice. Where did he learn his vowels. Is Daddy still gorn to the horspital? When will he be got better?

At first he asked this question often, but then it lost its charm. Emmanuelle wouldn't take them to visit Lance, they couldn't see him like that, in that sleep of the dead, though she did wonder if their small voices, William's gruff and classy vowels, Maud's piping singsong, might pierce his closed-off brain. Perhaps she should take them along, put them through it, take the risk of upsetting them to do some good to Lance. But would they talk? That waxy father lying so heavy in the high bed, his lids not quite closed over a jelly slit of eye, the tubes and wires and machines that ticked and clicked and drew their jagged lines: would children speak to that? Shh, daddy's sleeping, she'd say on rare Sunday mornings when Lance stayed in bed. Shh, said Maud, said William, tiptoeing, whispering, really being quiet. This machine-bound father wouldn't be a person to chatter to. The innocent lisping of his babes wasn't something you could engineer.

And when he came out of the coma she even more didn't want to take them. But then the doctor said his rehabilitation could proceed better at home.

Daddy's coming home from the hospital, she told her children.

Is he all better, asked Maud.

Well, not quite all better ...

Think of a computer, Mrs Latimer, said the doctor. It offers quite a good image of the human brain, and the ways in which it functions. At the moment a certain amount of interruption in the circuits, a certain breaking of connections, has occurred. You could say, the messages aren't getting through. What is necessary is for the terminals of the body computer to hitch up to some new wires so that messages can travel back and forth again. Time is of the essence here, of course, time and patience. Now, with the strokee — Emmanuelle winced at that, but the doctor didn't notice, he was not talking to her but at her, thinking about his words and not her hearing of them, hooding his eyes to look down at the sheet of paper on which he was drawing, upside down so it would be right way up to her sitting opposite — with the strokee, the brain is still there, just like the computer on that desk beside you. Mmm. Stroke is as it were like destroying the disk, so you can't gain information from the computer, the information stored on the disk has been lost. We must create a new disk, a new program, and of course if it is to be useful the disk must be compatible with the computer. In other words, the old skills aren't lost, it's just necessary to relearn how to tap into them.

I'm afraid I don't actually know very much about computers, said Emmanuelle.

Well of course I'm mentioning them as an illustration. In layman's terms. As I was saying, to make a brand new program takes time, just like recovery from stroke. Give yourselves time. Stroke is quite a challenge.

No definite article, Emmanuelle noticed. The effects of stroke. Living with stroke. Confronted with stroke the family. The absence of *a* or *the* gave the word immense weight. The heaviness of the hand of God. Dropping bolts of lightning to fell at random. Striking down. For nobody seemed quite sure why this had happened to Lance. He was rather young. Statistics favoured the elderly. But did not of course preclude the young. There was stress of course. And who knew what heredity. If you wanted to lay blame which of course was not necessarily profitable then heredity was the place to look. This doctor despite the eye-hooding was optimistic. The coma had probably not lasted too long. Health and he imagined will were on the patient's side. You know Walt Whitman, he said. The poet? He had a stroke at thirty-nine and recovered completely. Handel had one and four years later wrote the *Messiah*. So there's no need to be pessimistic.

You're aware that your husband's was a right hemisphere stroke. Less disabling, indeed. Though seat perhaps of the personality ... his voice faded away. Certainly it's in the right hemisphere that an understanding of space lies. Your husband wasn't by any chance left-handed? Or his parents?

His mother is, said Emmanuelle.

Good. Neuropsychological recovery tends to be more rapid, and complete, where there is a family history of left-handedness. The sinister can be useful, he said, with a little chuckle.

Emmanuelle wondered if anybody had written a study of the syntax of doctors. The constructions with which they made little parcels of the truth that you had to take away and unwrap and puzzle over. The jokes and euphemisms and sudden cold truths like knives carelessly hidden in tissue paper. The multiple qualifications that defeated reassurance. She thought, all I do lately is wonder, there's a huge hunger of wondering inside me like a tapeworm gnawing and not anywhere a crumb of certainty to feed it.

So Lance came home. Isn't it lovely, Emmanuelle told her children, we'll have daddy home all the time now. She set him up in the guest flat which was on the ground floor of one of those enfolding wings of the house, since the stairs made their bedroom impossible. It had french windows opening directly on to the garden. Stuart took him to a day-care centre and entered into the spirit of his rehabilitation. He looked on it as another aspect of body building. He put Lance through the day-care exercises at home, and took him swimming in the pool, and got him working out on the portable gym. Emmanuelle increased his wages, now that he was so much more than a chauffeur. And less; she found herself taking taxis and trains most of the time.

Mel

The part of New Zealand Mel grew up in was the Kapiti coast, in a town called Paraparaumu, a name which in Maori should have each of its vowels separately and lovingly pronounced. The locals say Parapa as though they were intending to offer you parapet, then suddenly put ram on the end. They ram it on. There are right circles for both these versions, and it's embarrassing to get them wrong. Kapiti with no emphases after the first syllable is a lovely long island off the coast, a beneficent presence saving it from the Tasman Sea's westward onslaught. Some people say this coastline has the healthiest climate in the world. There are long sands strewn with pumice stones, gifts from a volcanic past, and in the river mouths there are whitebait to be fished. Birds snatch shellfish as they burrow into the sand, fly high up into the air and drop them so that the shells break, then swoop down and swallow the creature inside. The limpid shores are littered with the debris from these meals.

It's a benign coast, the sun sinking in mists behind the island, the waves gentle, the sands a silver mirror for the evening light, a coast to make you believe nature intends kindness to humans.

One of Mel's grandmothers was a Maori woman from the

Paremata area but the family first of all suppressed this and then forgot, so Mel is not aware of this now desirable heritage. Her father was a linesman for the electricity authority; when she was six he disappeared, leaving her mother with two smaller children as well. Paraparam, they said in that house; the announcers on the radio dwelt upon the syllables of Paraparaumu as though it were a foreign language; the kids laughed. Pa-ra-pa-ra-u-mu they hooted; you had to get jokes where you could. Forget the taste of the bitterness in that small wooden house by the highway, the narrow busy road north that was always killing their cats, bitterness like metal in the mouth even through the white bread and sweet red jam which was what mostly filled their hungry tummies. Except when the whitebait were running, and they made fritters of the tiny fish and ate them with lemon from the raggedy tree in the garden. This is a feast, said Mel, the year she was eleven, and her mother laughed. A feast, she said, fancy that, a feast. The next year her smallest brother Dan was drowned where the river met the sea, nobody knew how since he swam like a small fish himself, and the whitebait tasted bitter too. The benign coastline was no help to a teenage girl. Mel looked to the west and thought maybe without that stupid island you could see Australia, where life would be. At fifteen she left Paraparam for Wellington, though there was one teacher who tried to persuade her to stay on at school, he said You've got a brain worth using you silly girl, why waste it? Mel thought the waste was staying on in an eventless coastal town. Two years later she made it to Australia, where she got a good reputation as an *au pair* girl, or mother's help she mostly called herself, not being at home with the foreign phrase. She was good with children, all that practice with two little brothers while her mother sat in the window and smoked and stared at the cars on the highway and hated the husband who'd gone she didn't even know in which direction.

Stick with other people's kids, her mother said when Mel left New Zealand. Doesn't matter what a man says to you, don't believe him. Mel was happy to take this advice, had already done so with the

Paraparam schoolteacher, and does so still while she minds Maud and William and waits for the real future to start happening.

With the warming of the season she began to swim in the Latimers' pool, often at the same time as Stuart. Because that was when they were free. Her skin turned brown in the sun. When she swam she had a sleek solid body like an otter, burrowing through the water with its own grace, and when she climbed out of the pool and shook the sliding water drops from her skin that grace remained with it, the grace of a stocky sturdy body that has its own function in its own element, even the useful layer of subcutaneous fat and the high heavy waist, especially those; in the water her body was happy and stepping out of it some of that happiness remained, though Mel herself had no faith in it and swiftly wrapped it in her sarong. This swimming body was what Stuart saw. Not muscles but the sleek shining of fat, the cleaving of flesh through water. He didn't like women with muscles.

Knowledgeable eyes might have seen the lineaments of certain young Maori women in the brown solid body with straight thin legs and crumpled black hair, but there were none of those around. Not even Mel's in the mirror. Instead there were Stuart's lustful ones. He watched her swimming the length of the pool and thought, she's comma-shaped like a sperm. Every time he thought of this he grinned, but would never tell her why. He made it clear that he liked her. Mel was used to this with men, the fathers of the children she minded usually tried something, kissing, or feeling, sometimes screwing, and talking to her because she was new ears for their problems, not their wives who'd heard it all before. The good thing about Stuart was no wife, and no same dreary problems. She found out what his hairless waxed body felt like. He wanted her to swim with nothing on, but she wouldn't go without her black covering swimsuit, what the magazines called this flattering one-piece. What if somebody were to come and catch us, she said, it's not private here.

That wouldn't worry you, said Stuart, would it? I bet you're not a girl who cares what people think.

She was silent, because she did care, and she didn't want Stuart judging her, so she just kept on shaking her head, not seeing him admiring her. Even when he made love to her she didn't think that, and wanted the bedroom dim, and a sheet handy. Though after a bit, at night, if she was sure the people in the house were in bed, she would give in when he urged, let's do it in the pool, but only after the lights were turned off. It was good, in the warm dark water and the stars like salt in the sky. Mel was swimming a lot and screwing a lot and getting fit, but not changing her shape which was what she really wanted.

If some of her grandmother's people had seen her, if she'd been standing naked on the edge of water, with her heavy breasts free and her hair flowing across her shoulders, they would have recognised her as their kin and one who might walk with innocent reclaiming feet across her own country. But these were ifs Mel knew nothing of, having a quite different set in mind. Resenting the magazine looks of the thin blonde woman, for whom they came so easily, not able to see herself with the candid eyes of a Stuart who cared nothing for the images of fashion. But didn't think either to tell her so.

Lunch in the Garden

The house where Emmanuelle and Lance lived was called Peppertrees. His grandfather who built it had named it, and it was evident that he had wanted it to be known by its name, to be identified by it, instead of by number or even street, so there was a dream of letters addressed to Percival D. Hugues-Latimer Esquire, Peppertrees, Sydney, but that never happened. The name was carved into the tall pillars by the gate, but wasn't much used. Your place, people said, our place, home, hardly ever Peppertrees.

Emmanuelle, when she first went there, when Percy and Lou were still living there, observed its various trees: the grove of silver birches, the oak, a liquidambar by the garage, the grape arbour, the apple tree, the lemon, the walnut, but no pepper trees. Why that name, she asked.

There were pepper trees, said Lou. Right here where the house stands. So of course they had to be chopped down when it was built. Percy's father liked the smell of them. He was sorry to see them go, so he named his house after them.

Couldn't he have left some somewhere, asked Emmanuelle. All this land, and all of it cleared. No natives. You'd think he could have left one.

They're not natives, said Lance. Not here. They come from South Africa. *Schinus molle*'s their name. Like the wine.

I suppose he didn't like them as much as he wanted an English garden, said Lou. An English garden, with Italian bits.

That's one story, said Percy. There's another. My father came here by way of the West Indies. When he set up in business the first thing he imported was pepper. He used to say the pepper tree made his fortune. He loved eating the stuff too. Used to grind it over his food long before the habit took on. It would ruin the lining of his stomach, my mother said. All those little chips of peppercorn scratching away.

You never told me that, said Lou.

Didn't I? I suppose I thought I should have some secrets.

There you are, said Lou to Lance. You can choose. Your father's version or mine.

Maybe I should make up my own, said Lance.

The garden was still English with Italian bits. The bougainvillea by the pool hardly altered that. Emmanuelle liked its calm spaces. She went to live there first in winter, and on certain afternoons the low sun shone yellow through its green grasses, casting the trunks of the trees into long shadows, and it was as though another place and another time were there in a moment's gift before the twilight came. The kind of moment that makes you yearn for those others, and if you are lucky, to realise that just for a moment you had them.

When Lou and Percy moved to their harbourside apartment Emmanuelle saw no reason to change the garden. She looked at it from her bedroom window and sat in it sometimes and set meals there. And sometimes caught that luminous melancholy moment when the late sun lay yellow over the grass, and wondered what her yearning was for.

One autumn Sunday after Lance's return she served lunch outside. It was a way of saying I believe we are now beginning to lead a normal life. She didn't go so far as inviting any outsiders, she was still turned in on herself and the need to contain the grief of Lance's illness, but the lunch was a small festivity, the garden not quite the wide world but also not the sick chamber she felt they'd all been confined to. She put out interesting food and tall glasses for wine and napkins embroidered with daisies. Mel and Stuart were included too; they all sat at a round green table under the pergola covered with grape vines. The air was warm and still, threatened by the coolness of morning and evening but resplendent sunny midday still, the sun more golden for the yellowing of the leaves. Mel had been swimming so she came in her swimsuit with the sarong wrapped round. Lance said Great tits you've got there girlie. Show us your tits Mel. Come on, show us your tits. He grabbed at the strap of her swimmers and she recoiled, which set him off balance and he would have tipped out of his chair if Stuart hadn't reached and righted him. Lance slapped his hand down on the front of Stuart's shorts. You're pretty well hung yourself, aren't you boy? How about showing us your dick, Stuart? Two tits worth a dick, eh?

Emmanuelle had a book about strokes which said that talk like this was quite common. The healthy partner may find it difficult to cope with inappropriate sexual remarks, the book said. The strokee may become lascivious, bawdy, coarse. But the strokee was Lance, discreet, polite. Urbane was the word Emmanuelle would choose for her lost Lance. Replaced by this man leering and grabbing. She couldn't help thinking that these crude responses had been there all the time, that what the stroke had done was remove inhibitions and reveal Lance's true nature, but the book warned against that. You must forget the old person, it said. The familiar face and voice may remain (though she wasn't sure about that, either) but the person you know and love has gone. New patterns and ways of dealing with the strokee must be developed, if disappointment and frustration are to be avoided. It may be difficult not to mourn the lost one.

Another thing the book talked about was sex drives. Diminished libido, fear of not being able to perform leading to impotence, was quite usual, or else heightened arousal. This seemed to be Lance's state. Come to bed, woman, he said in the middle of lunch. Now, he shouted, throwing a grilled sardine at her. He ate greedily, and swallowed wine in gulps. She hid the wine bottle and filled his glass with mineral water. Yuppy designer piss, he sneered. He banged the glass on the table so that the water flew up in a fountain and told her she was a rotten housekeeper letting the wine dry up and the guests go thirsty. Feeding them crap, too; he pointed at the salad bowl. Rabbit food, yah. Lance had never been fond of salad. Pretty lucky rabbit, said Mel, helping herself to a pile of elegant leaves. I suppose it does keep them fucking, said Lance, and was back to calling Emmanuelle to bed. Emmanuelle pretended to be a calm and gracious hostess so that the children wouldn't notice anything amiss. Eddie's got a rabbit in a cage, said William. Does he feed it lettuce, asked Mel. William nodded. It's got a black ear, he said. My dad keeps rabbits, said Stuart. White angoras.

Not you. Lance shouted suddenly. Not you. Keep your filthy self to yourself. He reached out to a tall majolica bowl that Emmanuelle had piled with green and purple grapes, and the oriental scissors for cutting the stems, pretty scissors with short pointed blades and big looping handles, the kind sold in Chinese shops for snipping herbs and vegetables. He picked them up back to front so his fingers through the handles held them in a dagger position, and glared at Stuart. She's my wife you know, he said in a sinister sneering voice. You shan't have her. Oh we know all about you chauffeurs. Filthy beasts. He raised the scissors and lowered them in a stabbing motion, raised and stabbed them down over the Brie soft on its plate, but not touching it, sitting otherwise still and bright-eyed contemplating the violence of the action. His words paused, his hand still stabbed. The people round the table watched, breaths held. He had the children's full attention. Raise, stab. The elegant kitchen tool transformed into an ancient weapon. Look to your eyes my friend. Look to your dick. But do not look at my wife. Oh, do not think I haven't seen you. Do not think I do not know.

Then he went on to chant a sneering clumsy song:

> How about a wish
> Wish for a dick
> Stick it on his nose
> Dick on his nose
> Dick sausage nose

He made it fit to the first two lines of Three Blind Mice, repeated, and sung rather flat. Emmanuelle began to laugh in a kind of hooting throaty way. Stuart held Lance's arm and gently removed the scissors from his gasp. He cut off a bunch of grapes and put it on Lance's plate. Here, have some grapes, he said. They're very good. Not off this vine here, but.

The tension round the table loosened a bit, then tightened again. They'd all sat with such attention, muscles clenched tight in their watching of Lance's stabbing hand above the Brie, they had hardly imagined the next step, the stabbing hand reaching out to flesh, to eyes, to the discreetly nestled penis inside the denim shorts, the scissors plunging. Could it have come to that, they wondered now. Lance had drawn the line at actually stabbing the Brie, Emmanuelle said to herself.

Lance said Grapes, and stuffed the bunch into his mouth. Mmm. Very good, he said, smacking his lips. He'd become cheerful again, and was enjoying himself like a farcical connoisseur. He put his head on one side and palpated the grapes with his tongue, pursing his lips in a long tunnel and sucking in air with little whistles. Not of course as good as the finished product, but we don't seem to be allowed any more of that, do we. As we are not allowed to take our wife to bed on this fine sunny day in the autumn of — what year is it?

Emmanuelle offered to make coffee but Mel said she'd do it.

Four large butterflies, black with white and red patterns, flew over the table in a complicated vertical dance that charmed the silence; the remaining lunchers could watch them, and not worry about what to do next, for the moment. Can they see us, whispered William. But when Mel came back with coffee and a plate of honey cakes Lance began to talk again about bedding his woman and after a while Emmanuelle couldn't bear the ever more explicit invitations and went with him, slowly across the lawn and along the terrace to the guest room. It was like a parody of a marriage feast. Mel and Stuart and the children sitting over the half-eaten lunch and watching with large grave eyes their painful progress, the new couple off to a consummation while the faithful retainers watch and witness and imagine what's going on in the bride bed. The children a peculiarly modern touch.

This new Lance liked Emmanuelle to perform for him. Take her clothes off, let him look at her. Do you think I'm a nincompoop, he growled. I'm no nincompoop. He spat the word like phlegm out of his mouth. Don't think you've got a nincompoop for a husband. Dance. Come on. Kick your legs. You've got skinny haven't you. Far too skinny. Time to fatten yourself up old girl. A bit more meat in the right places.

Out of love for him, and pity, and maybe in mourning, Emmanuelle did what he asked. He was still not visualising his left side properly, so he lay on his back and she sat over him. His eyes glittered and his mouth was wet. You're a gorgeous woman, Em, he said. Emma, lily lily Emma. His hands were tremulous on her body, scarcely believing, anxious to hold what love never can get, and his voice was urgent with strange endearments. And the brief name he's never used before except that one night and then it seems because he tried for the whole and couldn't complete it.

It was exciting, in a dark and fearful way, love-making and this was love, but she didn't like it much. And afterwards she remembered the reproach of too skinny and this made her feel like a sex-aid doll not suiting a man's whim, needing to be blown up and made more pneumatic. She lay beside him, on his good side, and held him in her arms. They slept, she out of simple weariness. He woke up first, and when she opened her eyes she found him staring at the window curtain, where a chink of sunlight glared. He took no notice of her when she got out of the bed and went into the bathroom and came back and began putting on her clothes. She talked to him in an idle polite way but he went on staring silently at the curtain. Apathy said one of the books was another common response. Though it should pass.

Lance made no move to get dressed. Come on, she coaxed. You can put your clothes on. Why don't you come to the kitchen with me and I'll make a cup of tea? This is thirsty work, she said in a rather flirtatious way. Lance humped his right shoulder at her. Suddenly he began pulling at his left arm. Get it away, he said in a low panicky voice. Get it away. It's not mine. It's only pinned on. Nothing to do with me.

Yes it is. It's yours. Look at me, two arms. And so have you. Come on, love, look in the mirror, you'll see.

But Lance lay on the bed, occasionally pulling at his left arm. It wasn't paralysed, he could feel things in it, it flinched at pin-pricks, he could move it, but he believed it didn't belong to him. Mostly he ignored it, sometimes like now he tried to get rid of it. He wasn't good at walking through doors, he behaved as though his left side wasn't there and often banged into the lintel. He didn't dress it. There was a video that showed how to do so. Emmanuelle played it to him from time to time and Lance said Yes of course I see, but he still couldn't manage. This too was supposed to pass. Hemineglect was the name for it.

Emmanuelle kissed his forehead. Have a nap, she said. She stepped tentatively out into the garden, but the witnesses were gone. The debris of lunch lay in the sun, quite altered. The butter was greasy and rancid. The Brie had oozed to the edge of its dish so that it was flat as a plate, and the bread was dry and scratchy. Two sardines lay stiff as fossils. The honey cakes crawled with ants. She got a garbage bag and scraped the whole lot in. For a moment she thought of putting the plates and glasses in too but why punish them for the corruptions of flesh. She loaded them on to a tray and carried them inside to the dishwasher. All the time she did this she remembered Lance's voice murmuring I am not a nincompoop. Don't think you've got a nincompoop for a husband. What had put this word into his head?

There was a right way to pack the dishwasher. A place for tall glasses, short, small plates, large ones. Not the hand-painted Italian faience, they had to be washed by hand, she only used them when she was prepared to do this. Though sometimes she regretted it. The cutlery basket fitted in various places, depending on which bowls and saucepans needed to be accommodated. Emmanuelle had done it so often she could work automatically, and yet take pleasure in the orderliness of it, the knowable precision of these small acts. You could get it right, and it would work. The glasses would sparkle, the cutlery gleam. Her minor skill part of a transformation from dirt to cleanliness. An extravagant cleanliness, crowing its victory.

Cleo the cat jumped up on the bench. Wicked Cleo, you know you're not allowed, said Emmanuelle kindly, and putting her arm around her hindquarters half pushed half lifted the cat off the bench so that she curved through the air in a small arc and landed gracefully on the floor where she sat and began to wash. William came in and began to handle her with his usual violent affection.

William love, don't pummel Cleo. Stroke her. Stroke her gently, the way I showed you.

William suddenly went rigid. He threw himself backwards, and since he was kneeling on the floor this bent his knees at an alarming angle, they went white with gristle. No, he shouted. No. No. No. He began to sob in a hiccupy chest-wrenching way. Emmanuelle rushed over to hold him but his stiff and thrashing little body resisted her. She had to use all her strength to get a grip on him, and all the while her voice murmured sweet words to him, until finally he stilled and clung to her, and she kept murmuring her soft-voiced words while she rocked him tight in her arms. As his sobs turned into distant shuddering sniffs he buried his head in her neck and muttered. Don't want to. Don't want *you* to.

Sweetheart, don't want to what?

Don't want to, he said, in a passion again, shouting. Don't want to stroke Cleo. Don't want her gorn to horspital and made better. It might die her.

So Emmanuelle realised what had terrified him and tried to explain that stroking the cat and having a stroke didn't mean the same thing and William looked at her in disbelief and then gradually with a willingness to listen as she stroked his leg and hers and Mel, who'd come running and Maud too, Mel said they're quite different words they just sound the same and swore there'd be no hospital for the cat. Look, Mel said, she loves stroking, listen she'll purr, but Cleo looking affronted walked away.

The book says that children of a stroke person often show a fear of death, and feel that they may be to blame for the parent's illness. Show them that you still love them, says the book, written by a team of neurologists, psychologists and occupational therapists. Reassure them that they are still important in your life.

Emmanuelle sat on the floor with her arms around her small child. His body still shuddered occasionally. Daddy really will be better soon, she said. He'll be our dear daddy, just like he was. Soon, she said, soon, for the soothing sound of the word more than for its meaning. Maud gazed critically at them. William's silly, she said. Everybody knows that stroking a cat hasn't got anything to do with hospitals. Cats don't go to hospitals.

Yes they do. Rabbits do. Eddie's other rabbit did. And cats can too, can't they Mummy?

Sometimes, said Emmanuelle, uncrouching her stiff legs on the floor. She reached one arm out and Maud came and sat beside her. All three sat on the floor in her tight embrace. If they're sick and the doctor makes them better, she murmured. But it's not stroking that hurts them.

It was a dog bit Eddie's rabbit. His other rabbit, said William.

Maud leaned her head round. Was there blood, she asked.

A huge lot, said William.

Emmanuelle stayed sitting with her arms around her children while William told the story of the rabbit, as Eddie had told it to him at kindergarten. As she listened to this delicate finding and offering of words, and Maud's considering responses, and heard the shapely tale they were constructing between them, she marvelled at the minds inside their soft-boned childish skulls, so fine, so complicated, so frail. Minds a little in her care, but not entirely, minds their own spaces, but not inviolable. She was afraid of what might happen to them. You couldn't keep them safe in a dangerous world. Even when you tried, and what about when people didn't try. Hurt their children, shook them till their brains came loose, beat them to death. She held hers so tight that Maud said in a small voice, Mummy, you're hurting me.

Moonlight

Show us your tits, sniggers Stuart. He's lying on his back in his dark bedroom. Come on Mel, show us your tits. Two tits are worth a dick. He slaps his stomach, kicks up his legs and laughs aloud. Mel beside him under the sheet doesn't comply, she knows he's only quoting. She giggles a bit, but fearfully. She remembers the old Lance, the polite employer, the pleasant man of manners who often put a little extra in her pay packet, just to show our appreciation.

He never used to be like that, she says.

Well, he still isn't all the time. But Jeesus. Did he let rip. And did you see her face. He slaps his stomach again and guffaws.

Yeah. Mel sighs. She still looks as though she's just stepped out of *Vogue*, but.

What's that got to do with it?

Just that she always looks so glamorous, that's all.

Wonder what she'd be like in the sack, says Stuart, running his fingers over his chest, enjoying the feel of the smooth pads of muscle. He still thinks of clothes slithering to a marble floor, a little silky pile stepped out of, left behind.

Why don't you ask him? He'd probably tell you, the way he is, says Mel, sliding out of bed, the sheet still around her, picking up her underwear with her toes. I've got to go, she says. Maud's been having nightmares.

You mean you have to get up in the night too?

Well, not usually. But Emmanuelle's rather far away to hear.

Mel walked back through the garden. She felt a bit nervous, all that bush at the bottom there, but Stuart wasn't far away. The moon was full, the garden was drenched with its mysterious colour-stealing light. She remembered being a small girl on the beach when the moon shone like this, the sand and the sea whitened and coldly blazing. Kapiti humped like a whale. The same moon, she thought, and rarely for her wondered how her mother was. Here the shadows were black as India ink. She avoided the wisteria walk, skirting around it with a shiver, anybody could be in there. She slipped under the arch where it met the house and across the lawn to the kitchen side, where there were back stairs leading to the children's end of the house. Emmanuelle standing at her window gazing at the moonlit garden and thinking how changed were all its values of shape and colour saw Mel step out from the darkness where the french windows of the guest room gave on to the wisteria walk and scoot silently across the lawn and into the house. The guest bedroom which was now where Lance slept.

Right Hand

Emmanuelle had kept her promise to send the children to Sunday School but it had got neglected during Lance's illness. After the first chaotic days when nobody knew what was happening, and fear left space for coping with nothing but itself, Lou paid attention to the children. Several times she took Maud to church, and waited while she went to Sunday School. But then Lance was on the mend, danger was over, tedium set in, and Lou and Percy went to Alaska. Travel was what they did, now Percy was retired. Emmanuelle was glad that they weren't there to see Lance in his lascivious phase. Or rather, that she didn't have to be there, seeing them see. Maybe he'd be out of it by the time they got back. Phase was the word the books used; it had a comforting quality. Phases aren't permanent.

People had phases of going to church. Emmanuelle had one when she was a child. She collected the small coloured texts they handed out to children who went to the service. You didn't have to stay for the sermon, you filed out in the hymn before, and Miss Manifold slipped out too and distributed the small illustrated oblongs. God is love, they said. The Peace that Passeth All Understanding ... I was glad when they said unto me, let us go in to the House of the Lord. You collected these and stuck them in a book and when it was full you got a prize. Emmanuelle was diligent, until the book was almost full, and then she stopped. Maybe it was the bony-faced lay preacher who kept asking her had she found the Lord yet? Bending over her with his corrupted mint breath and the hair poking out of his nostrils. Or perhaps it was the dank smell of the church hall, where the damp climbed the walls and the hymn books grew mould. Once the minister put his hand on her neck and said, Emmanuelle, eh? A most suitable name for a young Christian. He'd beamed at the class. Can anyone tell me why? No one? And what about you, Emmanuelle? You should, you know. Such an important name. It means, God with us. Remember, Emmanuelle, God with us. His hand curled round her neck like a fox fur with little pointed teeth. As he walked away she heard him say under his breath: A surprising name in a godless society. Of course she didn't know then that she'd been named after the pretty blonde girl in the novel who ends up in the sheik's harem after her party is raided by Bedouins, while they're travelling in a caravan through the desert, a situation fraught with danger for a virtuous young girl but she survives and the virtue too, her mother wouldn't have thought the name suitable without that.

Emmanuelle remembering the minister's hand on her neck thinks, perhaps this is something I have to do. Come to terms with being named God with us. However accidentally. Perhaps that's why I left Sunday School when I did. Why I don't go to church now ... Why does Lou go to church? Emmanuelle considers it might be the singing. Remembers a day when Lou and Percy were still living in the big house and she went to visit and there was Lou at the bottom of the garden, singing. Herself pregnant, fit and full of health, the bulge that would be Maud a tiny proud advertisement, not weighty or encumbering, and she stepped with light feet and heard the singing and stopped and listened to Lou's voice welling through the winter air. The voice was a dark contralto and all the words were audible:

I leaned my head up against an oak
Thinking that it was a trusty tree
But first it bended and then it broke
And so was my true love to me.

Lou stood under the oak in the garden and her voice was so dark and rich and full of pain that Emmanuelle shivered.

O love is handsome and love is kind
And love's a jewel while 'tis new
But when it's old it bloweth cold
And fades away like morning dew.

Emmanuelle stood listening to this voice singing these words and lost all sense of her good fortune, her health and blessedness, her pleasure in the growing baby. She was overwhelmed by the death of love. She stood under the bare grape vine with tears running down her cheeks, so that Lou who'd turned and come up the garden to her was so frightened by her look of desolation that she ran the last few steps and grabbed her. Lovey, she said, what is it? What's wrong? Is the baby ...?

Emmanuelle looked at her. Do you think that's true?

What?

About love growing old and fading away.

Oh Em, that's a song. One of those plaintive old songs that get their fun out of being broken hearted.

But somebody wrote it. It must have been true for somebody.

Oh, I daresay. Broken hearts are always happening. Though they're not necessarily permanent. But the song's for the pleasure of the sadness of it; sad songs are lovely to sing when you've got a voice like mine.

Lou made her go inside and sit down and drink a cup of sweet tea. Emmanuelle knew that she thought it was the baby making her feel delicate that caused her to be upset. And maybe it was. Maybe it was being pregnant that made her fear the death of love.

I didn't know you were a singer, she said.

Oh, a singer. I'm not. Not a real one. I sing for myself.

Sing for me, said Emmanuelle.

Lou laughed. And have you in tears again?

It did seem that Lou had a huge repertoire of lost love songs. Love done in by betrayal, or else through death. Like the woman looking out to sea for her lover:

> But my eye could not see it
> Wherever might be it
> The barque that is bearing
> My true love to me.

Such gusto, Lou sings with, every syllable of pain dwelt upon.

She likes hymns too. Emmanuelle on rare occasions sitting in church next to her listens to her belting out the songs of praise. Praise my soul the King of Heaven ... Lou worships with her voice. I wish I could sing, mourns Emmanuelle. Maybe Maud will take after her grandmother.

At the christenings of princesses godmothers gave gifts of beauty and good nature. You could at least wish for the passing on of useful inheritances: the singing voice, the curling hair, the strong white teeth, the intelligence. At Maud's christening Emmanuelle held her daughter in the long dress her father and grandfather had worn before her and wished not that she might be good and a dutiful child of the church but that she might be happy. Though maybe happiness might lie in the church. Or at least comfort for unhappiness. When love died, when despair or danger did for it, then God could come in handy.

She sent her children to Sunday School that autumn. She thought it might have changed a lot since her day, become somehow relevant, though she couldn't imagine how, what you heard of was rock music, and videos instead of feltograph pictures, but it seemed similar, there were even still the little square pictures with their bowls of pansies and roses climbing round cottage doors and the mysterious words: Rejoice in the Lord. Suffer the little children. Come unto me all ye that are heavy laden. That had a picture of a golden-haired man in a nightgown, nursing a sheep. Emmanuelle looked at his rippling curls and muttered: *For only God my dear, Could love you for yourself alone, And not your yellow hair.* She'd have liked to be saying this to somebody other than Maud, who couldn't be expected to know what she was talking about.

One Sunday Maud said, We had prayer today. That's when you ask God for things.

Oh yes, said Emmanuelle.

I prayed for a train set, said Maud.

I prayed for a bike with trainer wheels, said William.

The next week Emmanuelle said, Well, and what did you pray for today? William? Did you pray for a bike again? No, said William, that was last week. This week I said a aeroplane that flies. I see, she said. And what about you, Maud?

Maud frowned. You can't pray for things like that. You have to pray for other people. Or being good.

Did you pray for being good, asked William.

Maud was silent. She looked away. Not yet.

I think Father Christmas is better, said William. You can tell him the things you want.

He doesn't always bring them, said Emmanuelle.

Yes he does, said William. You go and see him and sit on his knee and tell him what you want and he brings them.

Not really, William. It doesn't work like that. You can't always have what you want. Remember when Maud asked for a lawnmower to ride on?

Maud wants a speeding lawnmower, said William in his gruff voice.

But Maud didn't respond. She was worrying about something else. Even trying to explain it was hard. Mum, she said. Mum ... the teacher said that if we're good we can get to sit on the right hand of God. She stopped. Emmanuelle said Mmm. Well, said Maud, the left hand ... She stopped again. Emmanuelle has seen enough Last Judgments to know about the sinners on the left, the scales, the gaping jaws open to swallow the skinny naked people, all the sorry lost Adams and Eves come to this final end, no choices at all any more, just comic-book fiends chuckling as they shovel you in. While orderly on the right line up all the goodies. Serenity on the right, oh yes, but all the energy on the left, even if it is the energy of pain and malice, that's the picture you want to look at, not the orderly smug rows. Maud was turning her head away, watching the toe of her shoe slide along the crack in the concrete path. Stand on the crack, break your mother's back. Well, she said, her voice so soft you could hardly hear, the right hand of God ... but what if you're left-handed? For Maud was like her grandmother in this, she was left-handed. Us artistic types, said Lou, which worried Emmanuelle a bit; what if Maud wasn't?

It's really just accidental, said Emmanuelle. It's the good people on one side and the others, not so good, on the other. It could just as easily be the other way round.

But the right hand of God, it's better. Right hands are better.

No, sweetheart, it doesn't mean that at all. It's like a car, you can have the steering wheel on the right, or on the left, it isn't that one's better, it just happens like that. Halfway through she decided that this was a hopelessly inept comparison. She hoped Maud wouldn't notice. Sending her to Sunday School so she could one day make informed choices about religion wasn't meant to include the elucidation of texts.

Like in France, said Maud.

Yes, said Emmanuelle. And more countries have steering wheels on the left, you know.

But still, it's the right hand of God.

I'll tell you what, when we get home I'll show you a picture.

She got out a book on medieval architecture with large grainy black and white photographs of cathedral tympani. She flipped through it until she found one where the suffering of the sinners wasn't too obviously grisly. Look, she said, pointing to the majestic figure in the middle, there's God (it was actually Christ, Christ in Majesty, but that was the same thing, wasn't it?) and see here's his right side, and the good people there ... How had she got into this? she didn't believe in Heaven and Hell, not like this. Good and evil, okay, but not simple-minded salvation ... But, she said, taking up Maud's left hand and laying it on the book. See? They're on your left hand.

Maud looked at the book, at her hand lying on the smug-faced saved. She frowned, and then she smiled. Sometimes people thought Maud was plain, with her straight brown hair and neat features, pity she missed out on her mother's looks, they said, but she could smile wonderfully. She eased your heart when her brow cleared and her eyes lit up; there was clarity, and beauty, and Maud saw it. She hugged her mother, and then skipped off to tell William that goodness was on her left hand, his sister's left hand, and that was what counted.

Emmanuelle wanted to go and find Lance, to tell him about this conversation. I felt like a medieval schoolman, she imagined saying to him. Chopping logic with a seven year old. But he was down at the pool with Stuart, doing his exercises, and it was not the moment.

Give Us

Maud said that other children's mothers went to church. Every week after Sunday School they went to church with their children. She said this so often, in a poignant voice, that Emmanuelle went. Maud and William sat with their friends in the Sunday School class. Emmanuelle looked round the scanty congregation and wondered which were all the other mothers. Judging by the age of the women, Maud had conned her again. She sat on a hard pew and thought no wonder children pray for train sets and bikes with trainer wheels. She made a list in her head of all the wanting words:

> *Grant us oh Lord*
> *Give us we beseech*
> *Bless us*
> *Save us*
> *Deliver us*
> *Lead us not*

Begging, asking, demanding. Wishing and wanting and sharp with it. Even the requests turned into imperatives:

Accept our prayers
Send to us thine Holy Ghost
Give us grace
Receive our supplications
Keep us steadfast in this faith

The priest had a meek voice that did not make itself listened to. She turned over the pages of the hymn book, finding more evidence of Christian greed. Not a please in sight. Even *may we* sounded like a command. Her own name had the same peremptory tone. God with us. Quick smart, God.

That was why Percy wouldn't go to church with Lou. It's all gimme and handouts, he said. Imagine what we'd think if our only conversation with our children was them asking for things.

Had anybody tried talking to God? Treating him like a husband or wife, that you talked about your dearest thoughts with? Augustine, or some of those subtle old schoolmen, did they have conversations with God, and listen for his answers?

Now there was a droning kind of hymn that Emmanuelle didn't know the tune of. Percy always said the Anglicans couldn't sing, you needed the Methodists for singing. She turned the pages of the Prayer Book. *Lessons Proper for Holy-Days. Tables and Rules for the Moveable and Immoveable Feasts. The Golden Numbers. The Order for Evening Prayer. St Luke, The Magnificat. My soul doth magnify the Lord.* Imagine a soul of crystal, smooth, curved, polished, and the Lord looming very large through its convexity. Distorted, maybe. The Lord enlarged and twisted. Everybody's soul its own particular crystal, with its own flaws and loops and thicknesses in the glass, so that the viewing was always idiosyncratic. But the magnifying was there, and it worked both ways. She read, *My soul doth magnify the Lord*, and then further down the page, *He that is mighty hath magnified me.* A soul like a crystal would be full of light, light would shine in it and through it and from it, there would be looking and seeing, but not always straight.

She went out of the gloomy church into the surprise of dazzling winter sun, still holding the prayer book. You have to leave the book behind, Mum, hissed Maud. People will think you're stealing it.

Emmanuelle was wrong about the peremptoriness of her name. Emmanuel is a name of Christ because he is God born of a woman, and so in him the two natures, divine and human, are united; this is how the name means God with us. But she didn't know this, she believed she was right about its demanding nature, so for her it was true. As for her mother it was the name of the beautiful young woman who was kidnapped by the sheik in a desert romance, and married not ravished by the after-all gentlemanly hero. A young woman the mother always imagined resembling Joan Fontaine, only with more abandoned hair, but Emmanuelle herself grew up looking quite different. There could have been awkward moments when the pornographic movie came out, but by then Emmanuelle was herself and besides nobody they knew actually took any notice of it. And it was only when a churchy smell, damp, powdery plaster, rotting flower water, brought back the memory of a hand on her neck warm and toothy like a fox fur that she wondered if names are more than their intentions.

There are times when it is possible to believe that messages are offered. For instance, Emmanuelle opens a letter and an edge of the page like a razor slits the pad of her thumb and stings like a poison thorn. And afterwards whenever she uses that thumb which is shown to be surprisingly often it stings afresh. The letter is from her mother, in Boston, apparently settled in a life so different from the one that Emmanuelle once shared it is hard to believe in it, though she reads the pages over and over in an effort to do so. Her mother has a habit of copying out quotations that she thinks her daughter might like. Her writing which is always round and regular and entirely legible becomes even more so in these quotations; they are something made, like her embroidery, with the skill of her eyes and hand, and given to her daughter. Often they are provided by her new husband, who is called Carter and has an eye for telling words, quite lucky really considering he was met on a bus-trip to Uluru, and in this case Esther is the mediator, offering the gift from Carter with the affection of both of them.

The thumb-slitting letter has some words from Miss Forbes, courtesy of Carter. Who is Miss Forbes? Esther doesn't say, except that she's nineteenth century, nor does she give the source, she simply puts it in its own small white space and adds, Isn't it wonderful? Yes, it is.

> The sense of being well-dressed gives a feeling of inward tranquillity which religion is powerless to bestow.

Emmanuelle sat at her kitchen table and smiled with delight. She knew what her mother meant by noticing this. That she was a little bit shocked that a nineteenth century lady could think let alone say such a thing, but she was also saying haven't we two sometimes got a certain amount of inward tranquillity from feeling ourselves well-dressed, too, but then maybe if we can see the irony it's all right.

Emmanuelle folded up the letter. It was a nice quotation. She'd have liked to tell it to somebody. Who could she tell it to? Her thumb hurt. It did not bleed but it stung as though poisoned.

Something Old, Something New

Sometimes Frankie the antiques dealer sent invitations to his clients. This one announced the arrival of two container loads of goods from England and Europe, which had to be seen to be believed. Emmanuelle looked at the card. She couldn't imagine that anything she could possibly want would be found in such a consignment, however large or unusual. She looked at the kitchen cupboards with their glass-paned doors and all the things they contained. A number of people had used those things and added to them, had disliked or cared for them, there was the Meissen vase she'd once talked about dropping and smashing, there were things to do everything you could think of wanting and much that you didn't, she didn't need any more things.

Then she remembered that in less than a month it would be Lance's birthday, and that she wanted to buy him something amazing. Something rare, precious, of beauty and worth, that would say to him, these are qualities I think are yours too; you are precious and rare and all such things to me. She had no idea what such an object might be, but it seemed sensible to suppose that it might exist. And that Lance would have time to read its messages. That he would desire too.

Mel visiting him in the night didn't change anything of this. Made it the more important.

She certainly had time to spend looking. From being so busy she never had time to think what she was going to do next she was now for long moments possessed of a limbo-like leisure. Stuart took care of Lance and Maud was at school all day and William went to kindergarten, but it wasn't time she could make plans for, like a job or doing something useful, because she didn't know what was going to happen in the future. Not even on the next day.

One day she went into a room which was called the trunk room at the back of the garage and got out the books she'd had as a student; they'd been packed up in boxes when she got married and she'd never unpacked them, when she wanted to read she bought a new book, browsing in bookshops, reading the reviews in the Saturday papers and remembering the anger or pleasure as books she'd worked on got well or ill-treated, keen to keep up with her one-time world of publishing. She took the old books up to one of the bedrooms, there were more bedrooms than they used. The patriarch of Peppertrees had imagined a large family, not the one son and a daughter who died of polio when she was fourteen. She put the books on shelves, thinking maybe I should become a mature-age student. Or keep on reading the Russians. The course with Brian hadn't got through many. Or go back to Milton. She remembered Brian saying, one day you will be glad you read Milton. Then you can re-read him. What is hard is to start. The Milton was an old foxed book bound in red morocco with gilt lettering and page edges, and the smell books had when they were old and prized, like the second-hand bookshop down the end of Hunter Street where she'd bought it. Liking the idea of a book that other eyes had read and hearts been moved by. Now she thought of *Paradise Lost*, the poem not the cocktail, and its end, with Adam and Eve led out of Paradise by the angel, and they look back and see the flaming sword of God brandished over what used to be their home, and she remembered the lines she'd learned because she so much liked the infinite terrible sadness of them:

> They, hand in hand, with wand'ring steps and slow
> Through Eden took their solitary way.

But when she turned to the end to read them again it was the lines before which caught her attention:

> The world was all before them, where to choose
> Their place of rest, and Providence their guide.

She hadn't thought much of them, being caught up in that marvellous sadness of the last lines. *The world was all before them, where to choose* ... This was Adam and Eve at the worst moment of human history, and they had choices.

Emmanuelle chose the bus or the train for going to town, or fish or chicken to cook for dinner. She chose blue and white plates, or porcelain or earthenware, Castle or Cold Power or Softly for delicates, she chose clothes in natural fibres, not going to church, certain books, having lunch with Susie, or maybe it was Susie who chose that, as Lou did. The television her children watched, the schools they went to, the suitably exacting educational toys. What did Lance choose ...? The Fortunate Fall, said Brian. It gives us a choice. She wanted to talk to Lance about these things, soon there should be a time. Perhaps after an amazing birthday present that said, You are rare and precious, as I am.

It was Lance's day for going to the hospital, so she got Stuart to drop her at Frankie's. He opened the car door for her, held it while she got in, then did the same for Lance, afterwards leaning in and deftly clicking the seat belt shut. So there they were, neatly strapped in opposite corners of the car, a soft bare space of seat between. Lance tipped his head back against the rest and closed his eyes;

once more the thick black fringe of his eyelashes touched her heart. She reached out and took his hand and held it in hers, clutching it in her fingers, like a woman wanting to possess her lover by means of this part of him. It was his left hand, the side he was still neglecting. He opened his eyes and looked at her, as though he thought she might have been doing it for medical reasons, but not minding, leaving his hand there. She picked it up and rested her cheek against it, then gave it back to him.

When she got to Frankie's she wondered how she could have ever thought to find something suitable for Lance. There was a lot of elaborate furniture, mirror polished with inlays and gilt moulding, bombastic stuff with ormolu or spindly carving; she realised that what she wanted was something old and honest and shabby, that brought with it the virtue of all the generations that had used it. One such object was a French kneading trough, of cherrywood, where the bread dough would have been made and put to rise, but when she opened it she discovered that the bottom had been lowered and it was lined with green baize to make it a drinks cabinet, with space for bottles and glasses and in one corner a stainless steel insulated box for ice-cubes.

She wandered about the shop, knowing nothing would please her, though she considered a nineteenth century bronze Hermes of androgynous mien with long curls and a knowing smile and wings on his cap and feet, but not of course wings for Lance at the moment. Luckily Frankie wasn't there to extol his wares, insisting on a tour of prize pieces, and she could easily leave. She was picking her way through the narrow passageways between furniture, the shop was stuffed, when across the room she saw Susie's face, reflected in a mirror. She slipped back behind an armoire; she'd thought of ringing up Susie, who'd have got an invitation too, and suggesting they go together, and decided not to. She peeped again. Susie was smiling in a smug sort of way, looking pleased with herself. She must have found something. Though she seemed to be idly looking still.

Emmanuelle waited until she went behind a row of triple-fronted bookcases and slipped out of the shop. She was a bit surprised at her behaviour. It was one thing not arranging to go with Susie, another carefully avoiding her when she was there. She was thinking about this, and didn't see the man until he stopped in front of her. Hello, he said.

She must have stared at him in a blank way because he then said, Emmanuelle? Hello, she said, though she still didn't remember him, and then the thought came to her of her bare bottom on a cane chair and she knew who he was. Knight.

You were wearing a dress, he said. I don't think I've ever seen such a dress.

The colour of aubergines ...

Yes, he said. Yes. That's exactly right.

She'd forgotten about the dress. When finally she got home that night, the next morning, wrapped in the green cotton hospital blanket, she'd taken it off as quickly as possible, not looking at it, rolled it up and put it on a high shelf in the wardrobe. Normally such a dress she'd have hung up carefully on a padded coat-hanger and inspected the next day to see if it needed cleaning and stored it in a plastic bag with pomander balls.

How is your husband, he asked. Yes, of course he knew, the firms had merged.

He's all right. I'm looking for a present for his birthday. I thought Frankie might have something. He's got a giant new consignment from Europe.

Is that the antique shop back there?

Yes.

I never go to antique shops. Though I pass that one every day.

What would you want, if it was your birthday and somebody was buying you a present?

Ah, that's the trouble, isn't it. We've all got the things we want. Or else we can go and buy them. If they can be bought, of course.

So we should only give presents that money can't buy, then?

Or else things people don't know they want. He laughed. Have you got time for a cup of coffee, he asked. They went into a place that was very dim and had padded booths and no music. You could talk softly and be perfectly well heard. He rested his arms on the table and interlaced his fingers in front of him, which meant he was leaning towards her. His hands were olive-skinned, with pink and white nails and slender fingers. She imagined they would be deliciously scented. I telephoned you, he said.

Did you?

She remembered Mel and the lists of people who'd called, he could have been on one of those. The waiter came and he ordered coffee, macchiato, pronouncing the word softly and very purely. She asked for a short black and a glass of water. Maybe they always brought water here.

Why don't you buy him something modern? Something new, just made. I mean, a work of art. Antiques. There's something tired about them. Overwrought. Overpossessed. Effete.

That's what I thought at Frankie's today. But what I was looking for was something old, but honest. Still having its energy in it.

He shook his head. Something new, he said. Something contemporary. That's where the energy is.

I see what you mean. I'm not very good at modern things, though. I'm not sure I understand them.

Who does? I don't. But I know a bit. I could help if you like. We could have a look at a few galleries.

She leant back on the banquette. It was padded, covered in murky turquoise brocade.

That sounds like a good idea, she said.

They arranged to meet one morning, that was easiest for her. We'll have lunch after, he said. Don't you have to work, she asked.

Of course. I work hard. I choose my own hours. I need some off.

The coffee was good. Life is too short for bad coffee, he said. For bad anything.

Oh, she said, I think that. It's easy to think. But can you make it happen?

The small things aren't a problem. The big ones may take a little trouble. He smiled at her. She wasn't sure whether he was being portentous or just funny.

Do you know what, she said, leaning sideways on the seat so that she was practically lolling, smiling, drawing the words out slowly. She was wearing khaki linen trousers and a fawn-coloured silk jacket with a lighter shirt, so that her clothes matched the stripy blonde of her hair, not hairdresser's striped but naturally fair hair, which fell in a fan across her cheek. The pale colours glimmered in the dark room. He leaned back too. In the crowded restaurant he'd touched her, in this empty coffee shop they lay back and looked at one another. What, he asked, after a minute.

I don't know your name.

Knight.

I know that bit. Your first name.

Oh. He paused again. You can just call me Knight.

It sounds like a title. I'd feel I was commanding you.

Why not?

He grinned, and she realised he wasn't going to tell her. She wondered if he was married.

I've got a wife, he said. You've got a husband. So it's perfectly safe.

I see, she said, not because she was sure she understood his remark but because she saw a pattern of conversation in which he said things designed not for clarity but for puzzling over. She could learn to speak this language too. Though would there be any profit in it? Why am I thinking of profit, she wondered.

He shook hands when they parted, and she walked aimlessly up the street. Thought she might buy something for dinner. There was a good cheese shop here. And a fruit shop. She rehearsed the conversation with Knight. It's perfectly safe he said. She doubted that. Safety could never be depended on. Never be calculated in.

Here's the cat that's got the cream, crowed a voice, and it was Susie, coming out of a dress shop.

Where? Oh. No, that's you you're talking about, I saw,

Emmanuelle said, and then remembered she was pretending she hadn't seen Susie in the antique shop. But she was carrying a big parcel in the tatty second-hand paper Frankie always used.

Yeah? The two of us, then. But what sort of cream, we ask ourselves. Her laugh trumpeted out. Coffee?

I've just had some.

Have some more. Or, why not, lunch.

They went to another cafe and ordered salads and Susie insisted on glasses of champagne too because she felt so good. She showed Emmanuelle what she'd bought, a large vase of faintly milky glass, tall and heavy and folded in a way that suggested lilies. Aren't you clever, said Susie, that's what I bought it for, I'll get some on the way home, some luscious creamy ones for my sitting room.

More cream, said Emmanuelle. Can our stomachs stand it?

You bet, said Susie. She leaned over the table. I haven't told you about Gavin, she said.

It turned out Gavin was his old self again. Still working terrible hours, nights and weekends too often, not to mention the odd business trip but in between, in the mornings, ah that was cream, the cream de la cream, and Susie smiled that secret smile Emmanuelle had seen in the antique shop mirror. Here's to it, she said, waving her glass of champagne, here's to cream in the mornings, yum yum, and she trumpeted her laugh again. Now come on Em, what about you, what's giving you that happy cat look?

Me? Oh, I was thinking about the funny things people say.

Oh yes, said Susie. But she was too full of things of her own to say to find out what Emmanuelle meant. I haven't seen you for ages, she said, there's masses to catch up on. She talked through lunch, and through the trip home, she had her car and gave Emmanuelle a lift, where's the sexy chauffeur today she asked but her heart wasn't in it. Not long now and you'll have wheels again, she cried with a cackle of laughter. How's Lance, she said, stopping the car in a skitter of gravel at the front door. Why don't I come in and say hello?

Emmanuelle was afraid of this and was saying I don't think he's home, but Susie had the engine turned off and was out of the car. Doesn't matter, she said, I'll come in anyway.

Emmanuelle made more coffee, Susie could drink coffee all day, and Lance came into the kitchen, his left arm scraping against the door frame. The smell, he said. It drew me from afar.

Lance, cried Susie. You look terrific. She stepped across the kitchen and kissed his cheek. Lance put his right arm round her, tightly, so that she was almost tucked under his armpit, and his fingers could clutch at her breast. Well Susie, he said. Susie Susie my old floozie. I've always wanted to screw you. How about now?

Susie's laugh trumpeted out. Not right now thanks. I get plenty at home, for the moment. I'll let you know ... her voice faltered as she saw Lance's face. She remembered that he didn't make this kind of joke. Also he was turning to the door, pulling her with him. She squirmed away. Bit early for it, anyway, she muttered, laugh no longer trumpeting; a creaky little apologetic giggle. She squirmed away and sat on the other side of the table.

Are you going to have some coffee, Emmanuelle asked Lance.

He took a cup, poured in milk and five spoons of sugar and sucked up several mouthfuls. You're okay, Susie, he said. Plenty of meat. In fact I've always thought you looked a good juicy woman. Not a skinny bird like Em here. Oh, she puts out all right, but not much to get hold of.

You sound as though you're feeling pretty much on top of things, Lance, said Susie. She turned bright red. I mean, feeling okay.

You think that, do you, he said. His voice was glum, and he frowned.

Well, of course ...

You can't know, he interrupted. He stared at the cupboard behind her. Sugary muck, he said, slamming the cup down, and left the room by the back door, cannoning slightly into the lintel as he did so.

He's not really himself, is he, said Susie.

No, said Emmanuelle. The thing is, Susie, should the question be, who is he? Or doesn't that matter?

Ooh, said Susie, huffing out air. That's a hard one. Oh shit, is that the time? I've got to get Nathan. He's going to Komon. Can't be late.

What's Komon?

It's this Japanese thing. Teaches you to be intelligent. I'll ring you, said Susie. You need to talk about Lance.

Love Me

Do you love me? says Emmanuelle to Lance. The words come murmuring out of her mouth in a soft watery cadence. Do you love me? Like a tiny stream that has almost dried up, but still there is faint music in its flowing, though the landscape is harsh and the terrain forbidding. Do you love me. The faint liquid music.

Do I love you, says Lance. He repeats the words several times, with a different kind of music, quizzical, forming with agile tongue and lips the cool percussive consonants of a Noel Coward character. Do I love you. Each time he tries a different emphasis, on the I, the you, the love, on the I and you both, until the repeated phrase takes on a syncopated rhythm that stretches it far from its sense. Do. I. love. you. Do. you. love. me.

Yes, says Emmanuelle, with plainness and clarity. Yes. I love you. That is why I am here. In her head she says, why I put up with you demeaning me. She'd been in the kitchen when the telephone rang. The middle of the morning, and she was putting away groceries. Hello, she said, and there was Lance saying, Emmanuelle, in an old slow way he had, as though the syllables of her name gave him pleasure, as though far from wanting to abbreviate it, he wanted to dwell on it. Emmanuelle. Yes? she said, on a soft breath. Come and talk to me, he answered.

But it wasn't talk he wanted, lying on his back in the guest room. She was about to say I can't, I've got my period, which wasn't true, but she was thinking of Mel and all the publicity these days, how sleeping with one person was sleeping with all the people they'd ever slept with and so on, but Lance said, Not screwing, we'll have to get some condoms first but that's all right you were always good with your hands, remember.

Condoms? she asked, but Lance said Shh. His voice was soft. Cajoling. Emmanuelle, he said. So she did what he asked, and afterwards lay down beside him and he turned his head and she looked into his eyes. Those thick black lashes and his eyes grey. The colour of pewter. Lou has pewter, plates, from the French side of the family, arranged overlapping on a Welsh dresser, handsome plates of use once but now only for show because of the high lead content, which drives you mad and poisons. People ate off them once but perhaps not for long. There they are on a shelf and you wonder, who were the people that lifted them down, put food on them, washed them, polished them with cloths so they gleamed, were given them as presents or bought them, saved up perhaps, or sent servants to fetch them; there are stories here and touching them you wish you knew them. They are beautiful; worn, even battered, but all the years of use in them making them a pleasure to look at, and to hold. But pewter in eyes is different. The man with the silver eyes, Emmanuelle once called Lance, looking up into his face as it bent over hers; the girl with the moonbeam hair, he'd responded. Sometimes after that he'd telephone and murmur Silver-eyes here. And once she said he had a silver tongue, like a sixteenth century poet, though in truth he wasn't a very poetical person, he found it hard to let himself go in words, was easier with irony and sharp phrases or else saying nothing at all, which was why she valued him saying Moonbeam.

She tries to imagine him murmuring Moonbeam to her now, but cannot. She gets off the bed and looks at him lying, on his right side so that it is his left that she can see, the left that he is learning not to neglect, which seems to have a smooth untouched look, as though he doesn't live there any more, as though it were a room emptied and cleaned, not much of the shabbiness showing, waiting for its next tenant. But she has to admit, it is probably her knowing that sees that. Yes, she says again, yes, I do love you, with conviction created rather than felt. Lance, she says; the man she married once, whoever he is now, Emmanuelle not wanting to go into the idea of life or soul or being or is it simply brain, that organises the molecules of personality into this person, or another. This is Lance, Lancelot Delattre Hugues-Latimer. And marriages are made in heaven.

Rosmarinus officinalis

Lance was lying on the floor on a pile of doonas and blankets while Stuart's fingers stroked his back. He listened to his voice murmuring. Y'supposed to let all y'worries turn into clouds and drift away. Breathe deeply ... in and out ... let them drift away ... Yvette used to say that, she'd have these things she'd say, but I'm no good at talk, said Stuart. But his voice was soft and warm, like his hands. Lance imagined his troubles turning into clouds, slow exhalations of steamy air, as though there were a frost, his breaths forming white and round and then dissipating. He felt light, and at the same time comforted through his skin and deep into his bones by the touch of Stuart's fingers.

Would y'like me to give you a massage, he'd asked, one morning after their swim. Lance was lying in a deck chair, worn out by grappling with a body that only half existed.

Massage. He thought of sleazy parlours where it was a euphemism for sex, and then of injured sporting heroes. The slap of flesh. The smell of bodies sweating in small spaces. Of skilful fingers and languorous afternoons. He opened one eye and looked at Stuart. It came into his head to say, Aren't you the wrong sex, darling, but he couldn't be bothered. In what way, he asked.

100

The proper way. Y'reckon I dunno how? I know how. I had this girl once, she was really keen. And mate, when she did it, she sure was something. She made me learn so's I could do her. She reckoned I was good. She loved it.

Why not, said Lance.

We'll set it up for tomorrow. Y'll have to give me some money, but.

Stuart went to a shop called Aromantics and bought various essential oils, extracted from plants and flowers, and some sweet almond oil to mix them with. Lance's room would be an okay place, he said; pink and peachy colours were the best, it sort of fitted. He made a soft platform of blankets and doonas spread with sheets, and had a pile of pink towels to hand. He half closed the shutters so the light was soft. When Lance came into the room he found Stuart wearing a loose pink cotton tee-shirt and drawstring pants. On the floor beside him he'd arranged a vase of rose-coloured day lilies from the florist.

I thought you'd use a table, said Lance.

Floor's better. That way I can work from the hips, the centre of the body, he patted his pelvis, instead of the shoulders. It's deeper.

Lance took off his clothes except for his underpants, It's up to you, said Stuart, what makes you feel comfortable. He could smell the oil that Stuart was pouring on his hands, then feel its warmth as he began to stroke his back. Effleurage, said Stuart. That's what this is called. Stroking like this.

How do you know all these things?

Yvette taught me. And she gave me a book, so's I could look things up. Like the oil.

Lance breathed in the warm scent. What is it?

Rosemary. It's a waking up one for the morning. And it's good for the memory.

Rosemary for remembrance, said Lance. And those words themselves brought a memory, floating up through the warm cloudy spaces of his brain, of the Anzac days of his childhood, and men with sprigs in their buttonholes. Singing Lest we forget, the words trembling in their throats. I thought that was just symbolic, he said. Standing for it, not actually doing anything.

I dunno, said Stuart. They reckon different oils do different things. Rosemary's memory. But mainly I like the smell.

Lance lay and felt his worries drift away on his breath like clouds, while the odour of the oil brought him the memory of those child-hood dawns and the men, hats to chest, able for this day at least to utter words like sacrifice and bear the full weight of them, without embarrassment or doubt. And for the moment to make their own offering in return. The line from the hymn breathed in his head. *Still stands thine ancient sacrifice An humble and a contrite heart.* Perhaps rubbing the sprigs between your fingers and snuffing the scent into your brain had an actual physical effect. Maybe you did remember better for the odour of rosemary. Coming out of the house in the dark early morning night that you didn't normally inhabit, walking down the drive to the bush by the gate that you didn't even notice for the rest of the year, your father nipping off the clusters of spiky leaves to put in your buttonhole. Percy had been in the war, in the navy, but that was before Lance was born, all the boy knew of it was a photograph in pale black and white, in a uniform with little anchors on the buttons and strips of braid he knew was gilt. Now he wears an ordinary suit, but they walk down the road dressed in the gravity of adult memories, to listen to painful sonorous words as the sun rises.

An humble and a contrite heart. The gliding touch of rosemary that brought him that memory takes it away again. The matter of the heart's contrition is exhaled upon a breath and Lance's mind gives itself to the sensations of his body. Stuart's hands knead and cup, tingle and flow, the blood dawns in his flesh and in the end it is a clarity that carries him into sleep. He has forgotten the loss of his left side.

Breakfast

Emmanuelle wasn't a wimpish sort of person. When she said Condoms? to Lance and he replied Ssh, she complied, but only temporarily. She liked to think about things, to understand them, before she responded. Don't you ever fly off the handle, Susie once asked her, and Emmanuelle got a sudden picture of a crazy blade whirring through the air, and how you would duck. I don't suppose I do, much, she said. But this didn't mean she never got angry, or upset. Only that she was quiet about it, which sometimes meant that she nurtured her anger. A careful observer could have read her calm, known whether it was repressive, or irritated, or beatific, but who was there to take such care? Not prattling Susie, or Lance in his busy times. In the days when he might have observed she wasn't angry often; Lance knew she was a measured person, thoughtful, and it was a bond between them, he valued that quality, and she was pleased that he did so. But what did Lance value now? And who else was there? Her mother was in America, and Lou who could be sensitive to the quality of Emmanuelle's calms had that kind of elderly self-centredness that doesn't always bother.

Because it was her nature Emmanuelle ran an orderly household. She had a sense of the virtue of it, that in orderliness was the good life, offering the pleasure of small moments that strung together may make happiness. Like this breakfast: porridge begun the night before, juice out of oranges, preserved quinces the colour of carnelians from the lumpy tree at the bottom of the garden, milky coffee in big round honey glazed cups, with plates and the right knives and cotton napkins and Maud and William using the Beatrix Potter china that had been daddy's when he was little: two more mouthfuls of porridge William and you'll be able to see Farmer McGregor and maybe he'll catch Peter Rabbit this time. William knew as well as his mother that Peter Rabbit would today and forever escape the furious Farmer McGregor, and yet there was a certain excitement in just checking. It took four spoonfuls to make sure, but William didn't notice; Emmanuelle was deft at this sort of trick. She walked round the kitchen in pale tracksuits that never looked grubby, which fuelled Mel's envy. Emmanuelle always made a pot of tea for her. Mel didn't eat breakfast because of losing weight, just strong tea with no milk or sugar, but sometimes the smells especially if there were croissants warmed up got to her and she succumbed and then felt angry particularly with Emmanuelle who'd made it too hard. Stuart didn't eat breakfast with them, he had a blender and made himself a drink of yoghurt with pureed fruit and eggs to get a healthy start to the day. After that he went in for junk food, sometimes straight after dropping the children at school; occasionally in the car there'd be a whiff of fatty onion and chip grease until Lance said What's that stink? If you don't mind Stuart I think you'd better indulge your food fancies out of the car. Take an extra five minutes, but spare me the pong.

This morning, Mel gone, late and scattering as usual, Emmanuelle could never understand why she didn't give herself an extra five minutes and do things calmly and easily, Stuart off for the morning getting the car serviced, Lance came in just as the others were leaving. She made fresh coffee and sat down at the end of the table, quite close to him. She hadn't cleared up, if she did that he'd go away. She sat in a companionable way beside him, each holding big cups of strong milky coffee in the palms of their hands. In the way they sit cornerwise to one another, elbows on the table, thoughtfully sipping the coffee, there is a whole history of repeated gestures; out of such small acts, comfortable, affectionate, is woven the fabric of their joined lives. It was several days after the shushing incident; Emmanuelle had been thinking about it and wanted to talk, not just about that, of the puzzle it was a tiny piece of. About Mel, for instance.

Delicately she begins.

The other morning ... that business of the condoms. I don't want you to think I'm not grateful, I mean, for thinking about me like that.

Lance stares at her, frowning. You? Grateful? I did it for myself.

She looks at him, and waits. Well? says Lance. You can't be unaware of it these days. Just got to turn the television on. Beds of nails. Beds to infinity. People mown down. You'd be mad not to heed those warnings.

I know. That's why I was grateful.

More sense in suggesting it in the first place.

I was going to ...

Yes, but you didn't, did you. Left it to me. When I think of where that guy might have been.

What guy?

For God's sake, Em. Do you have to make things more difficult than they are already. I just hope for your sake you're making the bugger wear one too.

Emmanuelle's not replying isn't any longer a thoughtful plan. She is speechless.

Do you want me to spell it out, says Lance, pushing his face close to her gaping eyes. I hope for all our sakes that you are making your friend the chauffeur wear a rubber.

Stuart? she says, as though the word is an impediment she has to overcome.

Stuart, he mimics.

Do you think I'm sleeping with Stuart?

Lance pushes his chair back from the table. Let's not go into any detail, he says. It's your choice. I'm only concerned with the health aspects. He leans over the table and glares at her as he says this. His eyes are very wide, the black lashes no more than an outline. Lance's grey eyes, the colour of pewter, pewter hard and thick and leaden, you could even remember malleable, with cruel little dents in them, and Emmanuelle thinks of the danger of pewter, the poisoning, the madness.

What about Mel, she manages, as Lance is going out the door, and not with her usual forethought.

He turns. You mean you think he's having it off with Mel as well? A bit tacky, isn't it?

He smiles with wicked pleasure for the good exit line she's given him and slides round the door, barely brushing it with his left arm.

Ballgowns

Susie was humming round the house feeling like a young bride again, full of house pride and nest-building, not entirely realising that it is all the morning fucking that gives her this light-headed tight-legged wonky blissful feeling. Lolly does the hard work but Susie polishes it all up, placing the silver boxes just so, refreshing the water in the lily vase, waxing the dining table. Scent and shine are her business. The fine-tuning of the elegant life. And the hidden orderliness of closets.

So she hums and hops from room to room with that pleasant stiff-legged juicy gait and decides it is time to do an end of summer drop on the dry-cleaners, mainly Gavin's suits and gets them out and emptying pockets finds a letter from a woman. It is a love letter, explicit enough on the love, more so on the logistics. Times and places. Kisses in crosses.

It is hard to believe the banality of this. A letter in a suit pocket. How soapy can you get. It's even scented. And the woman still draws big round open dots over her *i*s. In *loving* and *meeting* and *hoping* and *dying* and *waiting* and *darling* and *will*. In *imagine* and *infinite*. Who'd have thought there could be so many letter *i*s on one page. And two *joys* with big round spots on them too.

Here are the business trips and the night meetings. The balance sheets and the strategies. The sorry pets I've just got to get this finished. Business must be doing very well ... that was Susie, idiotically innocent it now appears, and Gavin agreeing, oh yes, business is flourishing, four *is* to dot in that, except of course *business* is not this lady's theme. Add an extra dot for *lie*. And a couple more for *conniving*.

Pity this bird didn't think of *indivisible*. Room for four of her silly great spots in that.

Susie smooths out the letter. It reduces itself to one question: Did Gavin mean her to find it? For that's what the magazines say: the leaving of a mistress's letter for a wife to find is always intentional. Though the husband may not be aware of it. But deep down he wants to be found out because he's tired of deception.

Well, and so Gavin was, in a way. Though surprised by this letter. He could have sworn he'd thrown it away. Screwed it up and chucked it in the bin. Always very careful with the evidence. And indeed it did give signs of having been crumpled up and straightened out. Not by me, said Susie, Not the first time. No, said Gavin, nor by me. Not straightened out. No. It had to be Nicole. Taking matters into her own hands. Smoothing it out and tucking it away in a forgettable suit pocket. She could be a pain in the bum, that girl. Susie noted the past tense. She also heard the admiration in his voice. A pity really, to do this, since it was all over. Oh yes, quite surely finished, just one of those things, a fling, no more, he was getting out of it, it was taking a while, only a matter of time. Susie knew how these things were, you had to be careful with these unstable types but trust him, his place was here with Susie and Nathan, they were the ones he cared for, one thing this had shown him was that.

There are a lot of ways of saying these things and Susie over the next weeks hears them all. And for some time believes. Nicole is clearly a mad and dangerous woman, a crazy predatory red-nailed false-eyelashed stiletto-heeled suicidal plot-losing unbalanced grasp-ing moll, and you have to feel sorry for Gavin caught in her toils. And then one day she finds a picture of her, now she goes through Gavin's possessions regularly and ritualistically for though she believes him trust is another matter and knowledge more important than honour, a photograph in his wallet which he's left in his jacket on the back of a chair while he has a shower, a Polaroid snap taken in the office, a cruel draining light but there's Nicole it must be her the capital N in a wreath of red puckered mouths doesn't leave any doubt; she's got long straight hair like Susie's when she was nine-teen and she smiles shyly upward and she's wearing glasses, thin round brown-rimmed glasses as the young favour them these days and when she sees the glasses Susie realises: Gavin is lying. But she does nothing drastic; she simply says, Gavin, are you telling me the truth? Is it really all over with you and her? And Gavin says Yes, with sincere eyes, I told you Susie these things take time.

And there it is, time unwinding, slowly it goes for this is as Nicole needs it, fragile Nicole, time whizzing too fast might fracture her, time slowly spooling out and Susie wanting to knit it up into cer-tainty and finality but left with ravelled threads unwinding untidy and no neat patterns that she can make. Gavin lying on the surface she knows, but still tries to believe the truth deep down is what he offers, he's a kind man and can't hurt a girl like Nicole, he does mean it is Susie he loves and in bed in the morning this seems so. He couldn't be like this in bed and still involved with the other. It's just not possible.

In the meantime Susie finds it hard to eat. There's a hole inside that repels food. If she manages to push some in all her passages and tubes seem to contract and squeeze it out as fast as possible. From being a person inclined to constipation, the original anal-retentive, me, she becomes the opposite. Maybe this is how a lot of people function, she considers, in, out, no time to stop anywhere on the way through. She feels scoured. The idea of cream cocktails disgusts her.

The idea of anything rich and fatty makes her feel sick. All she can manage is occasional glasses of white wine, red is too heavy, or maybe champagne though the bubbles are bloating, and nibbling on a little fruit, nothing chewy, or crisp like apples, melon is good, in little thin crescents, a strawberry, a slice of banana, some cubes of mango, sometimes a piece of Camembert is all right, but not often. She doesn't realise how much weight she is losing because she's trained herself to buy loose clothes and elastic waists. Until the day one of these elastic waisted skirts slips down round her navel. She puts her hands on her hips and feels bones. In all this time the most cheerful thing that happens to her is going through the camphor-wood chest where she keeps folded in tissue the dresses of her youth when she went to charity balls with eligible young men and got pho-tographed for the society pages. They smell of another time and place and even another person, and she can fit into them once again. They are actually slightly baggy, easy at least, in their fit. This is the cheering part. The dresses themselves could be melancholy. She looks at herself in midnight blue brocade with a wide neckline that slips off her shoulders and a skirt bigger than a pup tent; you need space to dance in a dress like that. The narrow black legs of men scissor in intricate patterns with yours, the billowing skirt belongs to them as well, you're a new creature, the dancing couple, how pleasing it is when it works. Of course some stand on your feet and there's hobbling and stumbling. A fuzzy, muzzy time that was, of being seen but not seeing, Susie not wearing her glasses but carry-ing them in small beaded bags, whipping them out and putting them on for an occasional brief gaze at who was there and what dresses were being worn, the rest of the time floating round in a hazy light-splashed colour-blurred daze, where even her close-up partner's face lost its firm edges. That was the time before Gavin, when Susie was working for a charity committee, publicity agent they called it but it was more like dogsbody, but great fun, the lunches and teas and garden parties and balls in splendid houses, and the money, well some if it, after expenses, going to good causes, heart-warming work. Gavin sold them a computer, and came and installed it, it was early days for his business too, he asked her out and she fell in love with him, though he was not at all like the suitable young men at charity balls, didn't even dance. She gave the job up when she married him, all that going out at night, and worked in the business for a while, and then they decided to get pregnant and it wasn't happening so she stopped that job, my wife doesn't need to work said Gavin, and eventually though it still took a while she fell and they had Nathan. And now there is Nicole, working in Gavin's thriving computer business, the young girl with long brown hair that Susie was, not so very long ago, so it seems now she can fit into her dresses again. Her eyes fill with tears, the reflection in the mirror of the blue brocade with its tent-sized skirt blurs like the figures on those not so long ago dance floors. Don't sniffle, she tells herself. Nicole is just a passing fancy, remember? That sort of thing strengthens marriages. Trying not to think of her own father, whose passing fancies kept recurring, and her mother pretending they didn't matter. Susie takes off the blue dress, and the old strapless bra embroidered with daisies, yellowed now, but she's too fond of it to throw it out, it fits again neat round her waist with its whalebone strips flaring up to hold the little snoods of fabric where her breasts sit, a very good strapless bra because it always felt so safe, you could trust it, it never fell off or let you pop out of it, she folds the garment away in tissue paper in the camphorwood box and she hasn't stopped weeping because Nicole has stolen her innocence, the innocence that trusted, that grumbled about Gavin working all the hours God made because she believed that he was.

Nathan comes to the door and sees his mother's reflection in the mirror, that she's bending over an old wooden box and crying. He goes away. It's all either crying or shouting in this house these days, and often both.

Supermarket

Emmanuelle was in the supermarket with the children. William sat in the trolley, and Maud mostly walked along beside it, helping push. There was something wrong with its wheels so it kept trying to turn relentless arcs to the right, and you had to push with all your might in the opposite direction to get it to go anywhere near straight and then it would suddenly veer very fast to the left.

She looked at the long rows of brightly packaged shelves. Receding to infinity. Infinity is where straight lines meet; she wished she could see that happening to these, all the shelves inexorably meeting and all their packets and tins fusing together into one vast unnameable unconsumable. Provisioning a family has turned into a malicious plot against humanity and she resents it.

If she parked the trolley too close to the shelves William would do his own shopping, surreptitiously; she'd suddenly notice she had things like instant pavlova mix and plastic training pants and moth-balls that she had no use for, so she had to retrace her path and find where they came from and put them back. She scolded him in a fierce whisper but he didn't stop. He knew she wouldn't make a fuss in public, and by the time it was private she'd have stopped being angry. Even if she didn't park close to the shelves the trolley could suddenly set off and collide with them, all by itself or through Maud being helpful. Or else William would lean out of his seat, maybe singing, so that he looked like falling on his head and probably he'd upset the trolley and be pinned under it. Break his neck or crack his skull. Turn into a vegetable or a paraplegic. Maud behaved like a grand lady taking pity on outcasts, drifting down the aisles and offering a good home to catering packs of Mars Bars and three litre tins of sliced beetroot. Shall we have one of these, Mum? I think we need those, Mum. Isn't this just what we want? No, said Emmanuelle, not that. No, I don't think so. No. Well, said Maud, in a reproving voice, we have to buy something.

The trolley travelled in a cross-wise arc and cannoned into a display of Mighty Bites dogfood, which collapsed. William was aggrieved because he was looking the other way and didn't see it happen. Be watching next time, said Maud. When Emmanuelle extricated it the thing darted in the opposite direction and collided with another vehicle; the small girl sitting in it began to wail and her mother who hadn't seen what happened slapped her. Someone else's trolley rammed Emmanuelle's leg and drew blood. But despite these distractions hers got full, and William could reach its contents; he was examining a two kilo bag of sugar which he dropped on the floor. Heavy, he said. Emmanuelle walked away, but the sugar grit stayed on the soles of their shoes and crackled as they walked.

She knew the theories of supermarket design. That they must be easy to get into and hard to get out of. This one showed an implacable absence of egress. And an illogic of organisation that exacted a lot of walking up and down looking for things. She knew about the importance of shelf ends, and gondolas. The ploys used to catch children. Sweets at eye level. Balloons. Enticing plastic frippery. All the things that make shopping a kind of hell. Where are you Dante when we need you? Come and guide us through the spirals of despair. They're horizontal instead of vertical, but so what. She was filled with anger that the whole vast edifice was a trick. A snare and a delusion, Percy would have called it. A snare and a delusion, my dear. Percy hated supermarkets. He reckoned he'd like to bomb them all. When they were empty of people, of course. All over Sydney, Australia, the world, supermarkets exploding in the night.

Her mother had known a time without them. When I was a young married woman, she said, ah those were the days, we went to a grocer's shop. It smelled lovely, of spices and biscuits and treacle and clean wood, a dry smell, thrifty, somehow. There were big tins of biscuits and the grocer packed them into paper bags. Sometimes he'd give you the broken bits. Iced vo-vos hardly ever broke. It was usually milk arrowroots. Ted would take the order in, every Thursday on the way to work. The list made over the week of all the things you needed. And on Friday the grocer would bring you all the stuff, in cardboard boxes, coming round the back and putting them on the kitchen table, and tucked inside would be a chocolate, a small slab, or a Violet Crumble or a Cherry Ripe, some fancy thing because he valued your custom. And every so often you paid him.

Wouldn't it be nice, said Emmanuelle to Maud, if I could send you to the corner shop, with the order, and the grocer might give you a lolly. By this time they were choosing a check-out. She knew that the one she picked would go slowly, or stop, or run out of change, or have to get approval for a cheque. Logically it might not be so, but it always was. This time it was a woman querying the price of a packet of Catty Bix. Emmanuelle stared at a sign for Arnotts Biscuits. The cocky-wants-a-biscuit parrot. On his tee the best poll I see. Maud was a bit young to get the joke. Her mother had told her; she'd save it up.

This supermarket chain used to have an ad on television showing it growing out of an old-fashioned corner shop, the shelves and counter varnished golden brown and with a helpful grocer varnished too along with the demure lady he was serving, all golden brown. Rubbish, said Emmanuelle's mother, shops weren't like that at all. Beer, it says it sells beer, the grocer never did. On no, never.

My mother would never have gone to a shop that sold beer. Or me either. Spiritous and vinous liquors, you never got those at the grocer's.

Now Emmanuelle's mother lives in America. Married to the man she met on a bus-trip to Uluru, after Emmanuelle's father died. Every week sending her daughter a letter from her new home in Boston. A cheerful letter but who knows what that means? Emmanuelle's letters are cheerful too. In one of them she will ask her mother what the shopping's like in Boston. Do they have corner stores. Are people dedicated to supermarkets. Are they in thrall to techniques of marketing. Probably, since they invented them. She knows they have delis in New York but that is not the same.

She was still staring at the parrot when she felt the trolley move. Maud was giving it a shove in order to keep up with the queue. But the trolley's sinister steering took it in a sharp arc to the left and it banged into a man who was bending over dusting sugar granules off his trouser legs. He fell over on his hands and knees. Emmanuelle dragged the trolley back and ran round it to help him up. He wasn't young, but seemed quite nimble. I'm sorry, she said, I hope I haven't hurt you. He shook his head in a dazed way. Je vous en prie, he said. Maud picked up his glasses and he put them on. Ah, he said, please do not trouble yourself, madame. Are you all right, asked Emmanuelle, gazing at him anxiously. These hideous trolleys.

Madame, I agree. I have just resolved to have nothing to do with them. It is after all possible to control one's own life. A little bit easier than controlling a trolley, indeed. He bowed, and held out his hand, Emmanuelle offered hers and he raised it almost to his lips and kissed it, but without touching, and turned and slid through one of the crowded checkouts though there was no exit there. Emmanuelle looked at her trolley and the queues which were now longer than ever and their place lost altogether. Come on, she said, lifting William out and the three of them not quite so sinuously as the gentleman but successfully enough slid through the jammed up checkouts in their turn. The trolley stood abandoned with its cargo of sugar and butter and mineral water and toilet paper and nobody took any notice. Except when it suddenly turned in a circle and hit a woman who was smacking her small daughter for helping herself to the child-level sweets.

Free at last, she said. We've escaped. Were we prisoners, asked Maud. Oh yes, said Emmanuelle. Captured by a crazy shopping trolley. But we got away. She rolled her eyes dramatically. Though of course she knew that she wasn't free, that all those goods were waiting, somewhere else, and she would have to go and choose them all again. *The world lay all before them, where to choose.* Adam and Eve didn't know when they were well off; expelled from Eden was one thing but just imagine if the angel had shoved them into a supermarket. Let's have a drink, she said. What about some hot chocolate?

I saw, said a voice. I saw. It was Edith from aerobics, pushing a trolley full of plastic bags. Aren't you the wicked one. How are you, anyway?

Suffering from angst, said Emmanuelle.

Oh dear. It's not ... I mean, can you do anything about it?

Well, you saw. The desertion of the trolley. Though perhaps that is better described as a symptom.

Oh, said Edith. Goodness me. She lifted her carefully blonde on grey hair off one eye, running her fingers through it like a comb in the way young women do these days. She was wearing a lavender coloured tracksuit with matching running shoes and looking very svelte for a woman her age. She was serious about aerobics. She'd also had a face-lift, it showed in the flatness of her eyes. Oh dear, she said, I hope you feel better soon. Emmanuelle imagined her rushing home to look up angst in the medical dictionary. She was about to reassure her it wasn't catching, but then thought that maybe it was. Though perhaps not by Edith.

Edith wanted to leave angst behind. She manoeuvred the trolley so it might offer some protection. Have you seen Susie, she cried. She's lost so much weight. She's looking really marvellous.

Is she still going to aerobics, asked Emmanuelle, who had lapsed.

No, the naughty girl. I saw her in the village. Not to speak to, hurrying away in the distance. That's when I saw how really slim she's got.

She'll be pleased, said Emmanuelle. I must get in touch.

And what about you? Haven't seen you at aerobics for ages, either, have we? Though of course, if you haven't been well ... Edith looked annoyed to see that she'd got back to health again. Did a leap sideways, up to her neck in the subject of sickness, but somebody else's. Mind you, she muttered, with glances over her shoulders as if there might be spies, I did wonder, with Susie, if it might be, well, the Big C ... You never know, these days, Monica, she lost a breast, you can never tell who'll be struck next.

No, said Emmanuelle, you or me, it could easily be. Edith looked offended. Emmanuelle went on: The same as angst, it could strike anyone, just about. But Susie, wouldn't we have heard ...? She began to feel worried. It was a long time since she'd talked to Susie.

People can be very secretive. Edith put her trolley in motion. Must get on, she said.

Who will buy our things, asked William.

Nobody. One of the shop assistants will have to put them all back on the shelves.

Do what we did, back to front.

Yes, said Emmanuelle. I feel a bit mean. Some poor person.

Poor, said Maud. A poor person. Poor poor person. Maud was of an age where she liked to say words over, for the feel of them in her mouth. A word taster. She liked to spit them out, too.

Well what we really mean is unlucky, said Emmanuelle. Though on the other hand I suppose it is the job. Come on, let's go down to the village. Maybe we can sit in the sun and watch the world go by.

The round world, said Maud, with a very round pronunciation. Going in a circle. Round and round.

Would that he were

Do you know what I wish, says Susie. Sometimes. I wish that Gavin had died. If he'd died and I'd been a widow I could grieve. I could go to one of those mourning classes and learn how to do it.

She picks up her glass and takes a small sip of wine. She's having lunch with Emmanuelle but she can't find anything on the menu that she can think of eating so she's drinking wine and pulling crumbs off a bread roll. She hadn't wanted to come but Emmanuelle had said on the phone I hear you're looking really thin, I'm dying to see you, and Susie had started to cry, and Em had come round and said You've got to stop sitting at home moping.

Now at this talk of Gavin dying Emmanuelle doesn't say anything. She nods, because she's recognising her own thought. If Lance had died. Leaving their life together intact. A pure shape. Immaculate. So memory would have held it. And polished it and shone lovely lights on it and marvelled at its luminosity and forgotten what did not fit this polished pure shape. But the thing is she also sees how entirely selfish this view is.

Susie is going on: But being left, you've lost him but he's still there so you've doubly lost him, and he's walking round with all this other life reminding you that you've lost him.

119

He's got himself, says Emmanuelle.

What does that mean?

Well, if he was dead he wouldn't have himself. I mean if you're thinking of love you should be glad for his sake he's not dead.

Oh. I was thinking you meant Lance not having himself, says Susie. Emmanuelle grimaces, but Susie doesn't see. Yes I see what you mean, she's saying. But he's not thinking of me and I've lost him and what's more somebody else's got him and that's why I think sometimes it'd be easier to bear if he was dead. Tears run down her newly shapely cheek bones. She's taken her glasses off, the octagonal gilt frames designed by Armani, she has three new pairs of glasses, all fashionable, she's given up the heavy black ones and the confetti multi-coloured ones and the brilliant red, all those big squarish frames that sat heavy on nose and cheeks and were meant to make her look fragile behind their weight. She blots her face with care, she's got a lot of mascara on, her eyes now look huge. And the purplish darkness of their sockets is only partly due to art.

Emmanuelle pours more wine into her glass. For sympathy. I suppose, says Susie, what I should wish is *her* dead. Susie mostly can't say Nicole, it's a spiky lumpy sticky mass in her mouth that her tongue and teeth can't get around. Well, I do, a lot. Dead. Or gone away for ever might do, though would I believe it.

What if Gavin wanted to come back? Gave her up, fell out of love. Would you have him back?

Oh yes. What choice would I have?

I don't know. What about starting a new life? Doing what you want. Being your own person ... Emmanuelle's voice is wistful. You could get a job. What about the sort of thing you were doing before ...?

I wouldn't want to go back to that. Susie shudders. Gooseflesh shivers up her arms, even in this overheated cafe.

I thought you had a wonderful job in advertising.

Susie gives a sly smile. I said I did. No. Well. By a giant stretch of the imagination. I worked for the Pomegranate Committee, you know, the charity balls and all that. Dogsbody really. Maid of all work. All night and half the day. You have to be young to get fun out of that.

I imagined you writing brilliant copy.

I meant you to. But I didn't.

Maybe you could.

Susie shivers again. She feels the cold now she's thin. The thing is, she says, you know perfectly well and so do I that there's no jobs for middle-aged women with no training or talent. Not that you'd want.

What about a business? A shop, maybe. You've got good taste, says Emmanuelle, not entirely sincere.

Yeah? But no money. You can't start a shop with no money. Maybe I should go on the game. Become a sex worker. They have unions and all these days you know. After all, remember my famous interest in sex.

Yes, says Emmanuelle. I've been thinking about that. What you said about having a chauffeur. I reckon what you wanted wasn't sex, whatever you said, it was love. What we all want.

Susie wraps her arms round her shoulders. Well, I suppose, she says. Though it's pretty cruel to say so, don't you think? She takes another sip of wine. When you look at it, what I should be doing is wishing I was dead.

Susie! You don't, do you?

Her lips turn up in a small smile. No, she says. I don't suppose I do.

Wandjina

Driving up Oxford Street with Stuart, Emmanuelle saw a young woman, rather stocky, with long straight legs, looking in the window of a shop full of dresses hung with chains. That's Mel, she said. Oh no, I don't think so, said Stuart. It was Mel, he was lying because he knew she wouldn't want her employer to know she wasn't at hotel school. Never was at hotel school.

I'm sure it is, said Emmanuelle, craning back, but Stuart was zipping along, changing lanes, and the woman was lost from sight. Probably just looks like her, said Stuart. People do. She'd be at that school of hers, this time of day.

He dropped her along the street from Ormond House. Knight, sitting in the window of a coffee shop, saw her get out of the car, her fine leather shoes and long pale legs, her hair combed smooth and held back by a black velvet band. She was wearing a black suit that simply fitted. She stood on the pavement and looked up and down the street; Knight observed a kind of exquisiteness in her. Everything exactly right, the judgment was intimidating. If it was judgment; maybe it was natural. But if he'd seen her looking like this that first time he might simply have admired her, like a fine carved figure he did not desire to possess. Perhaps it was the

aubergine dress that had revealed her to him. She'd looked exquisite then too, but in a way that he wanted to know more about. He
went out of the cafe to meet her, and they walked along the street.
At the florist he stopped suddenly, and went in and bought a bunch
of violets. They were wildly out of season and had a faded hot-house
smell, but they were in a round purple posy that seemed right. As
she took them from him and stood, smiling faintly, her nose dipped
down to them, he suddenly felt as though he were in a film, and she
some famous leading lady, some movie star from another time when
women wore perfect black suits and their fair hair fell forward from
bent heads. It was quite a violent feeling because it was another
place, another time, the world was quite different when women
were like this and for him to be in it meant some wrench of circum-
stance that suddenly seemed dangerous. But it was after all Oxford
Street in the 90s and there were blatantly up to the minute characters pushing past them, girls in skirts like bandages round their
bottoms, middle-aged mothers with babies, guys striding along with
large overcoats flapping, it was only for a moment they'd been in a
black and white movie of tragic intent.

There was a parking ticket on his car. Oh what a bore, she said,
but he put it in his pocket and shrugged. I never worry about
parking, he said. I put the car where I feel like it. And yes, I do get
booked, but I reckon it doesn't cost me more than legal parking
would. And the hassles saved!

You like to gamble, she said.

Not in organised ways. But yes. The chance part's a lot of fun.

They drove to galleries, with Knight leaving the car wherever he
pleased. Emmanuelle kept hold of her violets, he noticed, as though
this were the natural thing to do, like carrying her handbag, idly
sniffing them from time to time as she examined various works of
art; paintings, prints, ceramic sculptures, even some garden orna-
ments made of found objects. None of them pleased her, not for
Lance. I'm sorry, she muttered, I can't imagine Lance with any of
these. He wasn't even going to look at the Aboriginal arts gallery,

but she stopped at its window display, then went in. There was a large painting on an easel in the middle of the shop. There, she said.

I didn't know you were interested in Aboriginal art.

Neither did I. But this is beautiful. It moves me. I want to stand and gaze at it.

He looked at the three haloed heads, their wide eyes and nostrils but no mouths. He could feel its power too.

I wonder what it means, she said.

A young man with the habit of pedagogy is pleased to tell her. They are Wandjina, he says. Wandjina. Spirit ancestors. A long time ago they lay down in a cave and turned into a painting. There's only a certain number of them, you can't make new ones, you can only copy.

So this is a copy?

Certainly. They aren't always good, but this one is. You can see its energy. This artist is one of the people who keep the Wandjina properly painted up, they have to be ritually restored before the wet season. The caves, you see, the paint doesn't last too well. They're important, the Wandjina; it seems that the fertility of all species derives from them.

What's this on their chests? Knight points to a round object, like a stone.

That's the breastbone. And you'll have noticed no mouth. That's because if they had mouths it would rain incessantly. And see here, the band of red ochre around them, with the radiating lines, that's lightning. And their heads, look at their round heads and shoulders, the shape of cumulus clouds; the Wandjina emerge from the clouds and return in that form.

Emmanuelle stares at the painting. It's not certain that she's listening to the young man. Knight is, and watching her and the painting at the same time.

There's always a number of Wandjina in the caves, says the young man. Big mobs of them, the Aborigines say. They're not alone because Aboriginal life is not made for solitude.

I'm going to buy it, she says. Knight has noted the price. It's not cheap. Have you got somewhere to put it, he asks?

No. I'll have to make a place.

Will it suit your house?

Not obviously. I'll have to make the house suit it. She turns and looks carefully at him. Don't you think I should buy it?

It's your purchase. Do you think Lance will like it?

Well. I'm buying it for him, aren't I? I expect he'll be as enraptured as I am.

Knight imagines this as a test for Lance. What conclusions will Emmanuelle draw if he isn't? He looks again at the painting, at the eyes like black coals, at the oval poignant breastbones, wondering how it is that they demand so much of the viewer. This is what has caught Emmanuelle, their exacting of attention. Of love, even. She has fallen in love with the Wandjina, and so has he, a bit, and so he wonders if Lance will.

The young man is unwilling to let the painting go just yet. It's the centrepiece of his exhibition. The prize. In a fortnight she can collect it. Emmanuelle is disappointed, she wants to possess the painting immediately, but the delay is reasonable, and it's still in time for the birthday.

In the quiet restaurant where they went for lunch she flopped in her chair and let out a long sigh. What a great painting, she said. I'm exhausted. Thank you for finding it for me.

It's the last thing I'd have thought of. You found it for yourself.

I wouldn't have without you.

We did it together.

Together. She smiled.

This restaurant had a clever young chef who had not become fashionable so it was still quiet. The only other diners were two women engrossed in their conversation and a couple who didn't speak. Knight sat in his chair and gazed at Emmanuelle. She gazed back. I'm still excited by that painting, she said. Mmm, he replied.

The waiter brought menus which they didn't think to look at. Do you want something to drink, he asked. When he came back with the wine they picked up the hand-written pages guiltily. Are you hungry, Knight asked. Not hugely, she said, though maybe I am. Shall I order, he asked. She nodded. The prawn soufflé is good, he murmured, the sauce is amazing, a kind of sabayon, you know, zabaglione, only fishy.

There was something beautiful about the way his mouth said zabaglione, the round curves of it, the flick of his tongue against his teeth, the gentle upcurl of his lips at the end, and the long lilting sound of it, zabaglione, it rested in the air between them, she watched it, but then fishy was a good word too, what pleasure it took in the faint pull of the teeth on the lip as they pronounced the beginning sounds and then the quick rush of air to finish, not a word you often thought of, fishy, but there it was with its own beauty.

They call it a soufflé, Knight said, but it has something of the texture of a mousseline. Not too fluffy.

You had to marvel. Mousseline. Fluffy.

And so the meal proceeded. The prawn soufflé was indeed an amazing dish and they savoured it in tiny forkfuls, tasting it with tongue and palate at the same time as they formed their beautiful words for one another's delectation, sipping the wine from large round bubble-like glasses that they held delicately as though they were the moment blown solid, but fragile, while they listened and looked, not at the meal, they ate the food without needing to see how they did it, looking at one another, and this gaze changed all the values of the things around them, they bent or fractured or melted or slid aside and the only inviolable space in the room was that which their two selves created; here seeing and hearing were true and clear and entirely sufficient. This gaze, it was like a gentle magnetic beam, they were held in it, could move, sideways, back, forward, but not escape, it was its power that created their space. The gaze it was that each saw, and partly understood. How it changed the rules.

Looking, said Emmanuelle. It's what being in love's about. Lovers looking.

Yes. That's why you fell in love with the Wandjina. They looked at you.

She smiled, like lucidity dawning. Of course, she said. Those eyes. The colour, did you notice, indigo would you call it, bluish greenish black ...

And their breastbones the same colour.

Perhaps they see with them. Perhaps they aren't bones, they're hearts, and they see with them.

I think your eyes are the same colour, he said. In this light. Indigo.

The word was almost too beautiful to bear.

And do I see with my heart too, she asked.

I'm beginning to think that maybe I do.

Knight had organised a place to go so they could spend the afternoon in bed but he decided not to. The sitting and looking seemed too important. They had dessert, to prolong it, ice-cream in silver goblets with little spade-shaped spoons. I do believe it's passion fruit, said Knight, and Emmanuelle leaned back in her chair and laughed so much her eyes ran with tears, and he leaned over and patted them dry. With a handkerchief. He carried a handkerchief.

Then there was coffee, two cups each, macchiato, he said softly to the waiter, two macchiato, the afternoon passing, the restaurant empty, the waiter no longer putting his head out of the kitchen to see if they needed anything, until finally they went out into the street where it seemed strange to discover the sun still shining and she got into a taxi. It took off quite fast but almost immediately stopped again; the traffic ahead seemed to be knotted up.

The traffic's bad, said Emmanuelle, with a small sigh, not because she cared at all but because she expected the taxi driver would.

That's not bad traffic, he said, that's just a few drivers being silly. Bad traffic is a lot of cars not able to move. This is a couple of idiots not knowing where they're going.

The taxi driver spoke in a grim way, but with beautiful phrasing. He spoke like a skilful speech-maker, or sermon-giver, one who considers the sense and weight of phrases, their rhythm and heft, and is determined to do them all justice. Or else not talk at all; he said nothing on the drive home until almost at her turn-off from the Pacific Highway several cars weaving in and out of the traffic, overtaking and cutting in caused him to swerve and then he had to brake suddenly to avoid a woman with a pram. There you are, you see, said the driver, that's the danger. You fight with monsters, you've got to watch you don't become a monster.

That's very neatly put, said Emmanuelle.

Not mine, of course, a greater mind than mine. A man who knew what he was talking about. You gaze for long into the abyss, the abyss gazes into you.

Who, she asked, who said that, but he was saying Where now, madam, and she had to give directions and they were at her house and she was paying and there wasn't a chance to ask him who it was he was quoting, in that grim voice so mellifluously cadenced.

Giving Mel a Lift

When the day came to pick up the Wandjina painting Emmanuelle drove herself because the time of the ban was over. She was a licensed driver again. She took the Mercedes in case the painting didn't fit into her smaller car, and awkward at first soon remembered that the thing about driving is not to think about it, and was quite quickly zipping down the highway, humming scraps of songs, what a pity to have to stop I could drive and drive forever. Like a road movie, and she disliked road movies. Maybe doing it was different from watching it. And then when she had the painting in the back she couldn't wait to get it home, and anyway she shouldn't leave the car in case somebody broke into it and stole it, a painting in a Mercedes would not be safe.

She was driving down Oxford Street just before turning for the Cahill Expressway when she saw Mel again. The young woman was standing on the concrete island in the middle of the road, taut and on her toes, waiting to finish crossing; they saw one another at the same moment. Emmanuelle was hardly moving, she stopped and beckoned, Mel hesitated, then ran round the front of the car and got in.

You might as well have a lift home, said Emmanuelle. She knew

Mel would be going in this direction because of having to pick up William shortly.

I was just going to catch a bus down to the railway, said Mel.

But the hotel school isn't near here, is it? I thought it was at Chatswood, somewhere in that direction, isn't it?

Mel looked embarrassed. I'm playing hookey.

Oh.

Emmanuelle with her habit of staring out her bedroom window when she couldn't sleep had again seen Mel flitting across the lawn from the direction of Lance's bedroom. She'd been wondering if she should say something to her.

How are you getting on? At the school?

Oh, all right.

Emmanuelle could feel Mel's reluctance. And something stubborn, tenacious, that would hang on to what was hers even if it was failure, or unhappiness.

I suppose you'll be graduating soon.

Not just yet.

Well, when you do ... you'll be going off to a job?

I don't have to, said Mel.

Surely ...

If I like where I am, I might as well stay, said Mel in a hurry. I mean I don't have to get a hotel job straightaway, plenty of time for that, I might as well stay on with you. While you need me, I mean.

It's just that it doesn't seem much of a career, said Emmanuelle. But I'm glad you like being with us. We like having you.

This was true. Mel did a good job. But Emmanuelle had to wonder why she wanted to stay. She took a deep breath.

Mel, I feel I should say this ... I've been thinking for a while ... I mean, I don't think you should let yourself get pushed into something that ...

Mel was staring through the windscreen. So was Emmanuelle,

with quick side glances at the girl's unyielding profile. She went on: I mean, sexually ... of course, you're free, I'm not making any moral comment, nothing like that, but girls in your situation, I just want to be sure you're not being, well, that it's not something you don't want ...

Emmanuelle is talking about Lance. Mel thinks she's talking about Stuart.

Oh, I want it, of course I want it. Why shouldn't I?

I just thought, maybe you felt a bit, coerced, perhaps.

Coerced? Why? I like sex, I like making love, it's great.

Well, yes, I suppose it is fun, for the moment. In these very peculiar circumstances. But you can't expect it to go on ...

Why shouldn't it? Maybe he loves me.

Emmanuelle is silent. She wonders what Lance can have been saying. Mel must know how he is. How unstable. Not himself.

In the circumstances, she says, you must admit that doesn't seem terribly likely. Please, understand, I'm not speaking about me, or worrying about morals, I just wanted to say, you should see that you don't have to ...

I'm not doing it because I have to. It's because I want to.

I thought you might see it as a ... duty ...

Duty? Sex?

Well, with a man ...

He doesn't belong to you, says Mel in a small tear-tight voice. He doesn't belong to you! What right ...

Well, in a way he does. As much as he belongs to anyone ...

This isn't the feudal era, howls Mel, crying now. What are you trying to say? That only beautiful people like you have control of anything in the whole world? Why shouldn't I have him? If it lasts or not is it any of your business?

My business? How can it not be my business? Emmanuelle tries to see Mel's face but she has her hands over it, hiding the crying. The whole situation was a hideous mess. She said, I'm beginning to think there's no point in talking about it. I'm sorry I brought it up. She spoke coldly. Mel was making little gulping sobs.

I suppose you want him for yourself, she said in a sneering sarcastic way.

Well, it would hardly be unusual.

Mel gaped, but Emmanuelle didn't see, her head was turned, watching for a gap in the traffic. Look, she said, let's stop talking about it. You must admit it's not very nice for me, but then a lot of things aren't these days. I get by through not thinking about the future. I suppose you're doing the same thing.

Not all of us have very wonderful futures to think of, or not, muttered Mel. Everything's always been pretty makeshift for me. Why should it ever be any different? She felt intensely sorry for herself. And shocked by the greed of this woman in a way that was a kind of revelation. Did having so much make you feel everything was yours by right? Everything? Other people's lovers too? Mel recalled Lance's remarks at that lunch. Accusing his wife and Stuart. At the time she'd thought that was part of his illness. But you had to think now that he knew what he was saying, warning Stuart off like that. You'd never have thought, to look at Emmanuelle, so cool and smooth and perfect, but it sounded as though she was as itchy as a dog underneath. They must be doing it in the mornings, when Mel wasn't there, out pretending to be at hotel school, couldn't even get a place in a crummy outfit like that. What chance did she have.

Mel wanted to vomit. She tried to breathe in a way that would hold it down. When the car stopped under the porch she jumped out and bolted round the corner of the house. Out of sight she leaned against a tree and breathed the sharp leafy air, cold against her clammy face and neck. The desire to vomit passed, but her insides were still in a mess. Rotten. Rotten and stinking. Poisoned. Emmanuelle like. Like the wicked witch with the mirror, beautiful on the outside, the fairest one of all, but inside poisonous, and poisoning. Mel's misery welled up like the vomit. So cynical she believed herself, and yet she hadn't known the world could be such a wicked place.

Emmanuelle was sitting in the car feeling too chilled to move. I don't understand the young, she thought. I didn't know values had changed that much in a space of ten years. So cool about it all. I suppose I should sack her. For the sake of the children, probably. Or maybe she means to sack me. She wondered if it was something she could tell Knight about, in their lunches which were becoming a habit, when they sat and gazed at one another still, marvelling at what eyes could do, both reluctant though they never spoke of it to move on to the next stage but sure also that soon it would come, after they had spent long enough paying their eyes attention.

If Mel thought she was in love with Lance, and he with her, well, that was the future, and it would come. In the meantime there is the Wandjina. In a parcel large and solid and sharp-cornered in the back of the car. There is a place to be found for them. The spirit figures who long ago lay down in a cave and turned into paintings. She will find a place for them in her house, where she can look at them and be comforted, by their round wise eyes that take in so much and the oval breastbones that Knight wondered were they hearts that could see too, the same indigo colour as their eyes. And the no mouths. Is that because they have passed beyond desire? The eyes to see and gazing understand but no mouths to gobble or gabble, to suck up flesh and spit out words, greedy gobbling grabbing mouths, how serene and full of pleasure to be beyond that wet fleshy sucking flapping. There's probably a prayer for it. Lord help me to be beyond desire. It is simpler to look at these infinite wise eyes and feel that they understand. Probably that wasn't what the Wandjina meant to the people who made them. She hopes they'll forgive her borrowing.

Clouds

The day after the first massage Lance was taking his morning swim. The air was cold but the water in the pool was warm, and perhaps it was the salt in it that made him feel buoyant and not too unhappy inside the awkward envelope of his body. He rested his hands along the ridge just below the waterline so that he floated and only his nose was out in the cold. Another massage this morning, he said to Stuart, taking it for granted, but Stuart said no, it wasn't a good idea to have them too often, it could have a sort of poisonous effect if you absorbed too much of certain oils through the skin. Tomorrow, but, he said, tomorrow should be okay.

He wore the pink cotton trousers and the tee-shirt. He looked wholesome and cuddly in these clothes, like a large and muscular baby, with his pale brown hairless skin and his downy hair; you imagined somewhere a giant madonna whose arms he'd just slipped out of. First of all he stood on the terrace and cut his fingernails with snapping nail clippers. It's important to have short nails, he said. Wouldn't want to scratch you, would I.

Lance lay on the nest of blankets and doonas. This time his boxer shorts felt clumsy, so he took them off. He lay on his stomach and closed his eyes. The oil was warm, Stuart's hands stroking it were

134

familiar on his body. May your thoughts become clouds, said Lance to himself, and float away. Rolling rosy-coloured clouds they were this time, like cherubs on a painted ceiling, those fat boys of love, pink and fleshy. And static. He blew out his breath in a deep sigh, thinking to release them, to liberate himself. They began to billow and boil like clouds seen from an aeroplane, tumultuous columns of them climbing through a dawn sky. His head swam with their pinkness.

What sort of oil is it today? It wasn't rosemary, he could tell that.

It's a mixture. Rose and jasmine.

Flowers, he said. His body felt as though it were flowering. Yeah, murmured Stuart, with a bit of evening primrose and all, mixed up in some sweet almond oil. Your sweet almond's the base, see, and the rose and jasmine are the essential oils. The essential oils, that's what counts. His hands moved in the long gliding strokes that he named effleurage, gentle but pressing too, finding out the secret places between his muscles. It was good to feel yourself found out like that.

After what might have been a long time Stuart turned him over. He massaged his chest, his shoulder blades, his neck, slowly, the languor of it enchanted him, the hands moved down to his ribs, his waist, the skin sliding over the sharp bones of his pelvis, the movements repeated, varying, developing. Flowering, he murmured. Stuart moved down the thick muscles of his thighs where the black hair grew thick, up the insides of his legs, traced gentle circles on his belly. His body was relaxed on rosy clouds but all his flesh was zinging.

Turn your thoughts into clouds and let them float away. He'd turned them into clouds, oh yes, but they hadn't floated away, they were here and he was floating on them. On a painted ceiling with amorous cupids and what would happen next. The painter never painted what would happen next but that's what the painting was about. He had an erection now, and Stuart was massaging it. Or maybe massaging wasn't the word. It was just not more than he could bear. Every tiny vessel in his body was straining to send its blood there, where the touching was; from his curling brain to his flickering toes every inch of his body hummed and tickled with darting rills of blood. And yet he lay there, floating, still, with his flesh dancing and singing inside itself. And a kind of amazement in his head. So this is what it's like.

After a while his eyes fluttered open and he saw Stuart kneeling beside him, without the pink tee-shirt and trousers now, and he reached out and touched the smooth firm curves of his flesh. Stuart poured oil into his palms, and Lance's, and they explored one another's bodies. Roses and jasmine, muttered Lance. He felt wild with the scent and the excitement of the other man's touch, desire flowed through him, and the longing to possess and be possessed, he was possessed but it wasn't enough, it was exquisite like pain and ecstatic like pleasure, he wanted anger and rage and abandon and languor and yet there were no thoughts or words for these things. Just roses and jasmine. Roses and jasmine.

Finally they lay, panting, exhausted, sticky, in the tumbled and greasy wreck of the nest so pretty and proper and of medical intent, and heard the faint rumble of Emmanuelle's car driving into the garage.

Stuart slipped on his pants and shirt and made a bundle of the sheets. The room stank of the oil, with other odours of semen and sweat sliding uneasily through its blowzy sweetness. He leaned against the door of the bathroom where Lance sat on a small plastic stool taking a shower. Stuart's lips pinched into a little smile. Roses and jasmine, he said. Takes kilos and kilos of petals to make a teaspoon of oil. Whaddya reckon, it's worth it, ay?

Afternoons in Dull Hotels

I thought we could have an affair and just be bodies, says Knight. Bodies without pasts or even presents; no attachments, no encumbrances, just us, sometimes, in a room, fucking.

Knight says, I wanted us to have an affair out of time and place. I had an idea of free spirits, no baggage.

He says, I thought we could meet, then leave one another, go home, out, away, forget until the next time.

These things are said in surprise that he could be so wrong. For this affair is made of talking. Bodies in a room, yes, who touch each other, and Emmanuelle remembers how the skin of her thighs feels soft, like satin, no, not satin, a marvellously silky thing there is no word for, they lie and touch and their fingers marvel at the gift of this other body. It is not frenzied bonking they go in for, but sweet dying in one another's arms. And afterwards still the touching, and the talking as well.

Emmanuelle starts it. She tells him about the grandfather who named his house Peppertrees, because he loved them, but not well enough not to cut them down. Who had a daughter called Venetia who died of polio when she was fourteen, and maybe Maud should have been given that as a first rather than a middle name, only it seemed grandiloquent. About Lou not marrying Sunny Bell because suddenly she fell in love with Percy Latimer. About her own father who was called Edmund Parry and went to war when he was eighteen and it half over, she knows it was in New Guinea but that's all, he'd never talk about it, and then spent the rest of his life working in the bank, never getting to be manager because he would have had to go to the country for that and he did not want to take his wife away from Newcastle where all her family lived at stone's throws from one another, she's called Esther and was a dressmaker in an occasional way, making exquisite clothes for just a few customers, embroidering posies of grub roses on the facings as a trademark, only the wearer would ever know, and Knight thinks of Emmanuelle as an exquisite piece of needlework come to life. A daughter who was a gift to her mother to embody this talent. The mother who got her daughter's name out of a book she was reading, says Emmanuelle, and she finding out from a hand on her neck like a fox fur that it means God with us. She tells him about Maud and the right hand of God, and showing her the book of cathedrals and when you look at them the left hand is the side of the saved, comforting for Maud who may be artistic but you wouldn't want to expect it, her grandmother on her father's side is left-handed and so was her maternal grandma but they trained her out of it, you can't sew with your left hand it's wrong, they said, and Esther still resents it, while her right hand sews perfect minuscule stitches, always embroidery now, now that she is sixty and widowed and married again to a man she met on a trip to Uluru and gone to live in Boston. She tells him about Brian reading aloud Milton, *Of man's first disobedience and the fruit Of that forbidden tree*, that was when she fell in love with him, his thrilling voice, and the ledge on the cliff above the sea, the glade he called it. She doesn't tell him about the way his wife's heart gladdened when he sang *Where'er you walk* about the house so she could think Thank heaven he is not in a bad temper, because she doesn't know this, though she's often wondered about the wife, is she still married to him, and Brian, I expect he's still having it off with female students, she says, cynically relegating herself to one of a habit, though she doesn't really believe this, cynically she says to herself of course I wouldn't have been the only one but in fact in the bottom of her believing heart she is the only one, maybe not in fact, but in love.

They lie, Emmanuelle and Knight, on a bed in a plushy dull room with a wide window looking over terrace houses stepped down the valley and flats and other hotels, their bodies gently enlaced, their eyes and hands touching. I bet you were a good little girl says Knight, but No, she answers, her lips curling, people thought I was, but I wasn't, I just didn't get caught. Never carelessly wicked. Not that naughty really, but doing what I wanted. Quite politely. And kindly, you have to protect your parents. They're the innocent ones. I'm sure Maud will do the same for me.

Emmanuelle's an only child though there was a miscarriage when she was eight, not that she knew at the time, just that her mother had to stay in bed and her father brought chocolates and half under the pillow was a packet of white padded things that looked like hospitals. It was years later she found out why, but what it meant of hopes or intentions she has never discovered, nobody tells you not to ask but somehow like the white pads you know you don't. The silences in families can be resounding.

Not in mine, says Knight. He has five sisters and two brothers. The noise. But the effect the same. There are secrets which will be safe forever. And why not. That's the way I want it for me, says Knight.

I think you owe people their stories, says Emmanuelle. They give themselves to you in their stories and you should accept them. Her hand on his shoulder blade is soft, and yet there is his shoulder-blade as he's never realised it before. I think we have a duty to the past, to talk about it, she says. To explore by finding words for it.

For her father going to the bank every day in a navy blue suit with pin-stripes. Carrying a briefcase though there was not much to put in it, sandwiches, a newspaper. Walking down to the waterfront at lunchtime, crossing the railway line, watching the pilot go out, the tugs, the big boats brought in. Maybe not minding not having his own bank to manage, since he is part of a quite magnificent edifice of coffered ceilings and Corinthian columns, filled with the orderly silence of money. And what about Knight's father? The butcher with a fine marble shop in Cowra, the sharp knives that curl the meat from the bone as though helping it find what it truly wants, knives sharpened thinner and thinner, the mild *thunk* as they are slid back into the hard leather pouch that holds them. And Knight the small boy, you must have had another name then, says Emmanuelle, walking home from school, stopping at the shop, warm with pride at the sight of the burly father master of his domain, the meat, the other butchers, the conscious ladies to whom he says Tender? Tender as a woman's heart, and they all smile inside the safety of the old jokes. And the growing up, and the misprizing of the skills with meat, okay for the rest of the family if that was what they wanted, the brothers could follow the trade, the sisters could marry it, or some other, though one of the girls did catch the local chemist, had caught he'd have to say, they were older than him, his eldest sister was born in 1932 which makes her about the same age as Emmanuelle's mother, he was the child of his mother's forty-second year. Butchering not the job for him, he was going to grander things, study, accountancy, a life in the city, and look, here I am to prove it. And it's only now I'm thinking, says Knight, how good my father was with meat, no, not that, I always knew that, how valuable it was to be so good. How valuable.

I see, says Emmanuelle. She thinks of her own father, Edmund Parry, Ted they called him, going to the job he knew he did well, the figures running smooth as ink from the fountain pen that formed them, and then one day the bus starting again before he'd quite stepped off and him flung against a green iron lamp post. She

was pregnant at the time, and she remembers that part of her
sorrow was that he would never see her children. Did I value, she
wonders.

And the stories of the present? Well, there is Emmanuelle, but
she wants her present to be past before she begins to think about it.
Lance ... And Knight? No, he has no children. His wife is a merchant banker. She is called Fiona and she's thirty-eight. She is
leaving children till the last minute. She hears the biological clock
ticking; she is like a woman lying warm and tucked up in bed,
hearing the ticking, knowing the alarm will go off soon, but there's
a bit more time, make the most of it. Knight has been married to
her for eleven years. They are good friends. And when she is ready
there will be children. Fiona has sisters, to whom she is close; nieces
and nephews, parents in Brisbane, she wears suits with broad shoulders, she's very thin, it's time-consuming, merchant banking, the
place of children in such a career is not evident. But we intend to,
says Knight. Oh yes, children or maybe I should say a child is on the
agenda. I hope I'll be good at it. I worry.

Time, says Emmanuelle, will is important but there needs to be
time; remember that.

Time, he sighs, time. What I want is to be out of time. Like this.

Her knee nuzzles his hip. His hand curves round the small
muscle of her calf. It is warm enough for nakedness, a sense of sun-
shine blooming outside; there's the room, the bed, the lovers, and
the long close languor of the afternoon. Which will not be achieved
again very soon. They lie with such leisure in their touching and
speaking, as though endless time were theirs, but soon this
allowance will be over, and the next might not be for a week, or
nearly, or longer.

You might have thought that the telephone would be an important element in their affair. That they might have spent hours in
conversation thus. But the telephone is no more than a brief tool.

142

Their stories need flesh; their bodies need to be there, delicately touching, though this may be a matter of their eyes alone, before any conversing can take place.

And it isn't safe at all, this affair. Knight was quite wrong about that. They don't leave one another and go home, out, away. Their bodies do, but their minds are not so resolute. Sometimes I wish I'd never met you, says Knight, his tender hand smoothing her cheek, his eyes fixed on hers. Sometimes I do, he says. But really I mean the opposite.

What is the opposite of never meeting, asks Emmanuelle.

Knowing you forever, says Knight.

Inexplicable Moments

Lance no longer woke up in the morning in dread of another day to be negotiated. Consciousness came with a little flutter of pleasure. His body that for so long had been miserable with failure remembered before his mind did that there were good things waiting. He thought of Stuart and his big splendid body that he tended so carefully, his pale blue eyes and downy hair short against his skull, his rough voice that murmured sweetly that it was no good with words. Lying in the softness and warmth of his bed he remembered the pleasures of the day before and anticipated those to come; he imagined what might take place and smiled with secret delight because what he imagined was never as good as the things that happened. But he was in no hurry to get out of bed and begin, it was here with him, it had already started. He realised that a body can get so much into the habit of making love that it keeps going on secretly inside itself even in lovemaking's absence. The blood knows, and the flesh, they remember all their hidden quivers of joy and the remembering is it happening all over again.

He no longer went and had breakfast in the kitchen. He preferred this solitude and the recall of love. At first Emmanuelle had brought him coffee, and offered toast, then he said she should stop.

143

He would get his own, when he felt like it, maybe have something with Stuart. It was better not to eat too much before exercising, he said. Emmanuelle stood in the doorway watching him while he spoke. He was lying on his back, his head on feather pillows, the doona scooped around his chin and up to his ears. All right, she said, if that is what suits you. She nodded gravely, then went away. He thought of her with benevolence and irritation. In the same way as he thought of the children. With immense good will, but not wanting to have to do anything about them. They all had dinner together in the evening, Mel and Stuart quite often too, you might as well, Emmanuelle said, it's no trouble for me. She made soup, or pasta sauces, and went to a deli called Mr Pymblecharc and bought cheeses and cold meats and fancy breads, and there was always fruit. She ladled the soup into deep bowls and passed them out to this motley family. She liked the mundanity of it, the homely food, the cheerful conversation, Stuart would ramble through long incoherent stories about the people he'd had dealings with during the day, and so would Maud and William, and she'd try herself to make offerings of this kind. Even Lance would make an effort. Shortly after dinner he'd go to bed and read, he was making his way through the complete works of Dickens, the volumes that had belonged to Emmanuelle's father: I think you should have those, Esther had said after Ted's death, and Emmanuelle had put them on the bookshelf in the guest room and meant to read them one day. Now Lance had started, and his contributions to the meal-time conversation were odd facts about Victorian London and people and habits that he'd describe in a careful detailed manner, quite dry, but the facts were interesting. Only Mel was quiet. Asking her did no good, she never found anything to say.

At some point during this meal they would discuss what was happening the next day, and make sure everybody's activities fitted, Lance going to the day centre, or the doctor, Emmanuelle's plans, who was picking up the children. Lance's terrible sneering

lasciviousness seemed to have passed; he'd ask Emmanuelle about
the plans for her day and seem interested in the details. Are you
going to town in the train, he'd ask. Are you seeing Susie? Will you
be home for lunch? There was a calendar on the pantry wall where
they wrote up things like dental appointments. Is this accurate,
Lance would ask. Are you keeping it up to date?

I know what I'm doing, she said. Ah, said Lance, but do the rest
of us?

She wondered if he was checking up on her. Whether he suspected her of liaisons and was trying to catch her out. Not Stuart, he
seemed to have stopped making that connection, but somebody
else, and since there was somebody else his questions worried her.
She tried to offer him quite complicated everyday outings, so that
when she did want to meet Knight they would have formed alibis of
habit. But Lance didn't seem interested in what she did, only that
she was doing it. She wondered if he wanted to be sure of his own
time for seeing Mel, but her days were quite strictly mapped, there
wasn't time for Lance in them. And it was in the night she saw her
slipping out of the shadows of the guest room terrace and across the
back lawn.

One of the things she did was go to art galleries. She started off
with the New South Wales Gallery, and worked steadily through the
special exhibitions and the general collections, buying the cata-
logues and books from the shop that would help her understand;
she walked slowly and sat down often, immersing herself in these
works of art that people had made out of the world around them,
celebrating it, perhaps, or imitating, making fun, satirising, coming
to terms, all these different approaches their ways of making sense
of the world they found themselves in. Even a Lambert portrait, she
sat looking at its life-size smiling woman, pretty and fashionable,
with pearly skin and silver-fair hair, so rich and happy she looks, so
comfortably frivolous, and yet this is just a moment, and it's the
painter's gift; there'd be a husband cruel or loving or inattentive

perhaps and making up for it by paying Lambert to paint her and the artist glad of the money; even this portrait, when you look into its sitter's blue eyes, tells you that life is uneasy, and not simple. And when you look at a set of painted fibreglass fruit bats hanging from a Hill's hoist, surrounded by droppings in the shape of flowers, or perhaps stars, you can stare at it and feel your heart ache.

Emmanuelle felt she was leading another life through her absorption in these things that people had made. She felt hollowed out, and slightly breathless and choking, she needed to take care of herself. Hold herself delicately as the container of all this seeing. She sat in the cafeteria with coffee and a sandwich and looked out across the derelict wharf that people wanted to turn into a work of art also though they were arguing about the best way, and the money of course to be made and spent lent rancour to their divisions. The harbour was winter blue, slopping into little waves, sparkling, as it had offered itself to Kooris and convicts and anybody else who'd tried to make a life here. She imagined the old inhabitants standing on these shores, and their spirits cheered by the beauty as well as the comfort of the storehouse they knew it to be.

After this art gallery she would start on the Museum of Contemporary Art. And there was the Powerhouse, and the Ervine gallery, and all the commercial places with their exhibitions of new work. By the time she'd done all that she should know more than she did now; should be able to work out where she was going, with her new knowledge plus the mere passing of time, in which outcomes might begin to reveal themselves. So she told herself, but she didn't want the process to end.

Emmanuelle knows you can smile with painted coral lips like a Lambert woman, and wonder what the hell is going on.

At night with the children in bed and Lance too, reading his way through Dickens, and Mel and Stuart out, or watching television, whatever they did in their own time, Stuart body-building often, she heard the creak of the machines if she opened a window,

Emmanuelle sat in the spare bedroom that was now her room. She'd given it a name, she called it the bookroom, or my bookroom, because it had started off with the books from the time before she was married, and she kept adding the ones she bought as she wandered through galleries and bookshops thinking of the making of art. She'd furnished it with things from the rest of the house that seemed particularly suitable, mostly old things, a porter's chair that enclosed you in a room of your own, a small ornate secretaire, a Georgian table, most of them out of the drawing room where nobody went much any more, now there were no parties or dinners. Stuart helped her move the furniture, and apart from him, and Magda who cleaned it, nobody knew it was there. Not because she was secretive, but because they weren't curious. At night she sat reading her books in her own world.

The Wandjina painting was on top of the secretaire, propped against the wall. When she wasn't in the room she covered it with an old piece of velvet that had once been a curtain, but when she was there she uncovered it and often looked at it. The Wandjina were good company. Their friendly eyes understood what was going on, as though being so large they took everything in.

One morning she set off on what she thought would probably be her last visit, this time round, to the New South Wales Gallery. She was taking her car to the station, and then the train; she'd walk up through Hyde Park and past the cathedral. So much for having a chauffeur, to drop you at the door, as she and Susie had fancied it. Stuart was nearly always busy with Lance now. Emmanuelle thought it was interesting how well they got on, considering they were rather unlike, Lance lean and ascetic, not interested in sport or physical activities, Stuart the opposite in just about every way.

She was driving down a suburban street when just ahead of her the front door of a house opened, though she didn't see this. What she did see was a small white dog come hurtling out of a gateway and across the road, but not in time to stop. She stepped hard on the brakes, but there was a thump under the wheels. The car came to a halt a few metres past the gate, and when she got out and ran behind it the little white dog lay in the gutter with blood sliding from his mouth and his brown eyes sightless. She squatted down beside him, not knowing what to do. The air was very still around her, the sun of this brilliant autumn day shone hot on her back, the sliding blood was already sticky. An old man was shuffling down the path in a kind of bobbing difficult run. As he reached the kerb Emmanuelle stood up, her eyes wide with fright. I'm so sorry, she whispered. The old man didn't look at her. He stumbled down the gutter and sat on the edge of it by letting himself fall. Emmanuelle felt in her own bones the jar and wrench of it. He picked up the dog which was certainly dead, Emmanuelle didn't know how she knew this but she was sure of it. She had been going to say, Get in the car, I'll take you to the vet, but looking at that little body she knew it to be beyond any aid. There was no mark on it, no sign that it had been the terrible thump under her wheels. The blood had stopped flowing. Robbie, the old man said. He looked at her. He's a Sydney Silkie. That's what he is, a Sydney Silkie. And then he said, You are a murderer, so softly that she almost asked his pardon in her polite way, but then she heard the words. He said them again, in a sort of deadly voice. You are a murderer.

I'm sorry, she said. I tried ...

The old man began to wail. He held the dog high in his arms and rested his head against the long greyish white hair of the little animal's belly and wailed. The sound was so desolate Emmanuelle began to cry. She said, Let me help, won't you go inside, but before she finished he shouted, Murderer. Get out of my sight. Out. The sound came out as a howl. An old woman came through the open door of the house and down the path. She looked at the man, the dog, Emmanuelle, with an expression on her face almost of satisfaction, as though she were saying, Yes, I know this is how life is, and it is terrible. You better go, she said. And Emmanuelle went.

She went home. She wanted to tell Lance about it and have him comfort her. She kept hearing the thump as she drove back through the suburban silences. The thump, and then the quiet, the old man's flat voice, He's a Sydney Silkie. Emmanuelle didn't care for little dogs like that much, the people over the back had one when she was a child and it used to bark in a frenzied indiscriminate fashion whenever she went near the fence. You'd think it would know by now that we live here, she said to her father, that we're part of the scenery. But it always treated them like enemies. Her cat used to walk daintily along the top of the fence, just to enrage it, pausing to stare down at the silly creature throwing itself at the fence in furious darting flurries. Somebody killed it by taunting it through a side fence that was falling down and full of gaps and then thrusting a broken bottle in its face so that it rushed on that. Not the Parrys' section of the fence, and all the neighbours denied it. Emmanuelle felt sick then and did now. The old man's heartbreak hurt her heart in turn. The silly dog had rushed out under her wheels and she hadn't had a chance of stopping, but that changed nothing of love or loss. She was still the dealer of unbearable grief.

And then there was the selfishness of her sorrow; she wished it hadn't been her who killed the old man's dog, she resented the guilt laid upon her for the mad coincidence of driving past just at that inexplicable moment when the door opened and the dog rushed out. There was a gate, she remembered, the woman had stood with her hand resting on its curved wooden top, a gate and a brick wall, probably meant to keep the dog in, and someone, some inadvertence had left it open. Her heart ached for the frailty of all human intention; you tried to keep those you loved safe but idle wicked chance was always sidling by to mock you. Children, pets, husbands, fathers, you couldn't keep anybody safe.

She left the car in the driveway in front of the house and let herself in the front door. She looked in the kitchen though she didn't expect Lance would be there and then crossed the back lawn to the guest room and knocked at the door then put her head in. Not there either. The bed was tumbled as though left after some thrashing dream. He should be down at the pool doing his exercises. Then she was suddenly afraid that he might not be home. She ran down the paved walk that dropped in shallow steps to match the lawn's slope. It was thick with moss, the bundled twigs of the wisteria kept it shady even in winter, and she had to tread delicately for fear of slipping. The pool seemed quiet, and she was more afraid that Lance would not be home. And then she heard a low chuckling sound, not exactly a laugh, nor a moan, a strange little exhalation of breath that was mysteriously familiar. She stopped to steady herself for the words she wanted to say. The lattice gate of the pool fence was open, and through it she could see the two men, framed in the cloister of the southern end which caught the warmth of the low-shining sun.

At first she thought they were practising some kind of martial arts, kung fu, would it be, or tai chi. They were naked, Lance's body lean and slightly paler than Stuart's with its curves of muscled flesh, both gleaming as though they were oiled. Wrestling, maybe, or a kind of dance, their hands moving over one another's bodies with choreographic slowness. They seemed to fit together in a tension partly aggressive, partly complicit, wholly rehearsed. She stood puzzled, loath to interrupt what must be some new treatment, some exercise, she could see Lance's body was already tauter, more sure in its movements, not an invalid any more. He even looked all right beside Stuart's highly cultivated body, which always made her think of some hothouse plant in its lushness of flesh and muscle.

They were about the same height. Their heads moved slowly together, and their mouths met. The kiss was open-mouthed and dreamily greedy. She saw what they were doing with their hands, and realised that this was no dance, no wrestle; or rather, yes: it was the oldest dance and wrestle of them all. Copulation's antic measure. Jig-a-jig-jig. If she stood here much longer she'd see its grand finale, its ultimate pas-de-deux, the elaborate and long-desired mutual fall.

So she turned and went back up the path and across the lawn and into the kitchen and sat at the table for a long time. Then she got her car keys and went out the front door and started her car and drove it round to the garage.

As she was walking from the garage to the house Lance stepped through the gateway to the pool, lifting his hand in a lazy wave. He was wearing a towelling bathrobe, and his face was softened by a naive warm smile that an hour ago would have drawn her to him to tell her sorrow and expect comfort. She waved back, and continued on her way.

The Yellow Chair

She went up to her bookroom and sat in the porter's chair. It was designed to keep the servant safe from draughts in vast chilly halls. Its fabric was a sort of tapestry, with lemons, and yellow flowers, and honey-striped bees, faded but still beautiful; the porter could have sat and traced the patterns with his finger through the long uneventful waiting for people to come and go. She sat and thought, staring at a trumpet-shaped flower without registering it, seeing instead that dance which seemed now to have a stately and hieratic power that fixed it immutably, not just in its moment of time and space but into the future as well.

If I hadn't run over that man's dog I wouldn't have seen this, I wouldn't know about it, it wouldn't exist.

But she has, the dog is dead, the seeing has happened, the dance will describe its measures through the pathways of her brain, as indubitable and as viewable as a picture on the wall; more, for she could close her eyes against that. She can hide the Wandjina painting under a piece of yellow velvet that used to be a curtain, but Lance and Stuart and the acts of their hands and mouths she can neither close her eyes against nor cover up. It's a moving picture etched in acid on her brain, and like acid it burns.

What she has to do is decide how she will live with it. It's interesting how it isn't like the business with Mel, which could be dismissed as the aftermath of the stroke, a phase that can be expected to pass. Like the public lasciviousness, and the private. Though had they disappeared; weren't they rather changed into something else? What Emmanuelle sees in this conjunction is its seriousness. What she cannot see and all her thinking in the yellow chair is not yet showing her, is her response.

She heard Mel and William come home. They didn't look for her, since they expected her to be out. She heard the Mercedes drive away. Then Maud come in. She was a secret observer in her own house, listening to the voices of children, Maud being bossy, William's gruff tones, the deeper thread of Mel's words, the shutting of doors, the shifting of air as people moved about sending its currents through passageways and stair wells, and underneath the breathing of the house, the faint exhalation of its own life which was older than any of theirs. Emmanuelle imagined the house as if she were it, still, settling, aging, patient, not lonely because of all the company coming and going but with no role other than to shelter and observe. Not able to help or save, and understanding that.

The telephone rang several times, and once was answered. She realised that she was thirsty, and suddenly her throat was so dry she could hardly breathe. She went into her bathroom and drank glass after glass of water, then washed her face and put cream on it and painted her eyes a little and went downstairs. The children were watching 'Playschool' but when they saw she was home they left that and after the usual afternoon cuddles and news followed her into the kitchen.

Would you like a cup of tea, she asked Mel, who said okay. She wasn't very friendly these days; Emmanuelle wondered if it was the terrible gloom of youth or something deeper. The children had had their afternoon tea but wanted more, and then Emmanuelle said Let's make cheese biscuits; a good recipe because William could grate the cheese and Maud break the eggs and check the weights, and they both could stir, and roll them in coconut at the end. It made the kitchen smell of baking. The scales were iron and brass with weights that you had to balance; William weighed everything within reach which would have included the cat if she'd allowed it. Mel sat at the end of the table reading *New Idea*. She tried to do the crossword every week, in order to win the thousand dollars prize money. She'd ask Emmanuelle's help in her glum way. The intent children, pink-faced and tongue-biting, the big table with its spills of flour and coconut and lolling slippery eggshells, the women drinking tea and letting the mess happen, the last low sunlight yellow in the flour-dusty air: click, and the contentment is fixed forever. Like the woman in the Lambert painting, smiling with coral lips, and who knows what the hell is going on.

Mel looked up from the magazine. There's a message, she said, I've written it down. Emmanuelle picked up the telephone notebook and read: *Squire Antiques rang, consignment has arrived, auction 4.30 Thursday, usual place.* Mel watches her reading it and says, and maybe her voice is mocking, He reckoned you'd know what it meant. Yes, I was looking for something, says Emmanuelle vaguely. She knows what it means. One of Knight's codes. He devises innocuous messages for use when she doesn't answer the phone. Which he trusts her to understand. Once he was a doctor making an appointment for a gynaecological examination, Doctor Butcher he called himself, out of family piety, a good joke eh, he laughed about it, and she imagined him putting on different voices to go with the characters. Another time he was a bookseller letting her know that 'The Three-thirty from Paddington' by Mardi French had come in. Emmanuelle wasn't frowning at this message because she didn't understand it but because she's thinking how improbable it is that she and Knight should ever dance in the sun naked beside a swimming pool.

While the cheese biscuits were cooking she made some soup from the vegetables in the fridge and a tin of tomatoes. The mixed little family sat down to dinner, as on other nights, and it seemed a night like any other, but this time Emmanuelle knew what the men knew, and looked at them sitting calm and wise and quite without reference to one another and had a sudden desire to pour the bowls of soup over their heads. She imagined how their gentleness, this beatific munching on buttered toast, this spooning of broth and sipping of wine, would turn into yelps as the hot lumpy soup ran down their faces and inside their clothes.

The children were in bed, stories read, nightlights on, and so was Lance. Mel and Stuart had disappeared. Emmanuelle was giving the kitchen a final tidy, for Magda coming tomorrow. The phone rang. It was Susie saying, Em, Em, can you come.

Bianca's Advice

Mel spends long evenings on the telephone to her friend Bianca. She's nanny to the daughter of a Liberal politician and has to baby-sit most nights, but provided the baby doesn't cry she can talk on the phone as long as she wants. Mel and Bianca met when they were both new in Sydney, staying at a backpackers' hotel in Kings Cross with a lot of other New Zealanders. They both got jobs at much the same time and less than a week after they'd moved out the place burned down. It was old and flimsy and the curtains and furnishings so thin and greasy they flamed like torches, the paper said, and there were bars on the windows which stopped people escaping. Eight of the residents died. Bianca and Mel telephoned one another and said It could have been us. With wonder in their voices, and fear too, remembering Danni, who nearly got a job at the same time as them, but then it fell through so she had to stay on at the hotel and keep looking, and Bert and Steve who'd sat around and drunk beer and talked about travel and the world and what they wanted of it. Mel and Bianca said to one another, We were so lucky, and heard the nervousness in one another's voices because why should they be, but the elation too because they had been. Bianca was simply a nanny, a child-minder really; she didn't pretend to be doing any studying. Mel sometimes went to visit her in the politician's house in Woollahra or met her in Paddington when she was supposed to be in hotel school. You should tell her, said Bianca. She won't mind. Tell her you didn't like hotel school and stopped going. You don't have to say you never went.

Mel had been thinking she would when Emmanuelle gave her the lift home from Oxford Street. She told Bianca about the conversation. What do you think of that, she asked her, warning me off so she can get on with Stuart. Is that disgusting, or is that disgusting? Mel lay on her bed with the television on, Bianca on a couch in the family room, the televisions hummed and flashed like a painting that moves and mutters and decorates a space but rarely gets properly looked at. They rotated their ankles or stretched their arms or made bicycling movements with their legs at the beginnings of these talks but then they got tired. Mel had become stuck on peanuts; she tried to eat only a small handful but she always scoffed the whole packet and licked her fingers and pressed them into the crystal glitter of the salt that remained until all that was gone too, and then felt guilty and wished she hadn't, even not eating lunch the peanuts were wicked. Ooh, she groaned to Bianca as if her stomach ached with the guilt of them, Ooh why did you let me, and Bianca who would be eating what she could find in the house, biscuits or cake or chocolate and was quite skinny though she did get pimples, Bianca said *Far niente bambino*, why worry, fat is politically sound.

In general they always have the same conversation, Emmanuelle and her disgusting behaviour running like a chorus through the endlessly replicating dialogues of their days, the children, the job, what they will do when, there is always a when that will change everything and make that doing more interesting, exciting, significant, and yet the indignation and anger and bafflement that curl through and through these dialogues are of a significance that overwhelms them and leaves them stonkered on bed and couch, fit only for sleep.

You wouldn't believe she could say that, says Mel, it's gross. Yeah, says Bianca. Are they all like that, asks Mel. Is it because she's good-looking, or because she's rich? Yeah, you'd never think she'd be like that, to look at her, says Bianca; What do you reckon Stuart thinks? I dunno, says Mel, who doesn't see as much of Stuart as she used to. I reckon she's using him up, says Mel. Disgusting, says Bianca. Doing it's one thing, but coming out and saying it to you like that. Yeah, says Mel. There's a kind of sickening pleasure in all this, like sticking tongues in smelly tooth holes, you hate what comes out but you can't stop doing it.

And you know what, says Mel. She looks at me and she goes, You all right, Mel, don't you feel well Mel? Yuk, well, at least mine never notices me, says Bianca, she's a total airhead. Got a nose like a parrot but at least she doesn't stick it in my business. Yeah, well mine says You all right Mel? and she looks at me with this kind of frown and I go Yeah I'm okay and I have to say that's that, she looks at me as though I'm growing a second head but she lets it drop, she does respect your space, I'd have to give her that.

Yeah, well is that enough, says Bianca. Tell you what, you're always short of cash, why don't you blackmail her? Oh yeah, spot on, says Mel. No, I mean it, you're always talking about money, why don't you get some of hers? Threaten to tell her old man, or something. Why would he worry, says Mel. It's not whether he worries, says Bianca, it's whether she's worried he'll worry.

Mel licks her lips. They're cracked and dry, the salt grains sting. From the television a fat woman glares at her. Fat may be politically correct; it's also ugly. This fat woman is for laughing at. In horror that she shows herself. Isn't she brave. Ha ha ha, what a joke. Bianca's voice sidles on: If that Emmanuelle of yours is as gorgeous as all that why does she need to bonk the chauffeur, says Bianca. Ay? Tell me that. The conversation winds backwards and forwards, plaiting and knotting and fraying the familiar threads. The girls lie on their backs, exhausted.

At the end of these conversations Bianca always said Ciao. She didn't pronounce it very well, since she'd learnt it from her employer, who didn't either. Ciao, she said, sometimes Ciao bambino. Mel usually said Bye in a long-drawn sing-song way that could turn ironic if she hardened her voice just a little. By the time she'd got to these fashionable farewells of Bianca's she'd feel surfeited by the conversation but she was always too tired to want to think about it. Anyway, it could be the peanuts. Next time she started off enthusiastic and afresh. Bianca was her friend and there were rules to friendship that shouldn't be broken. She'd thought there were other rules too, like the way employers behaved, or rich people, rules mostly not kind or just but dependable, so you could learn how to live with them. Like your father being gone away, and your mother miserable; you knew where you stood, you could make your own plans. Now she understood that there weren't any rules and that turned into panic, a chronic kind of panic like a pain that you sometimes forget about but is always there. If you're happy and having a good time or even just interestingly busy you don't notice it, but a moment's pause or a sad thought or loneliness and you remember that it's been there all the time.

Why don't you ask Stuart, said Bianca. See if he can explain. Good old randy Stuart-the-chauffeur. She put her employers into pigeonholes by means of slighting words. The parrot-nosed brainless wife, the politician who looked like he was carved out of pink soap and left in the bath too long, all soggy edges, the baby who was gorgeous but Bianca had no intention of getting fond of it, one day she'd up and leave, overnight. If I were you, said Bianca, I'd talk to Stuart.

She found him working out under the bench press, blowing out his breath and pushing with his arms. The noises were uncanny in the cold night. It's freezing, she said. I'm not cold, he replied. Why don't y'get on the bike, she'll warm you up. Not much fun for a chat, said Mel. Another two sets, that'll do me, said Stuart. How long's that? asked Mel, pedalling. Ten minutes, give or take, said Stuart.

She set the bike at its easiest point and pedalled furiously, and it did warm her up. Not as much as Stuart, whose face was shining with sweat. He stopped and did some warming down stretches. Now what we need is a quick dip in the pool, he said, and laughed noisily when she protested. Nah, I didn' mean it, he snorted, though it's warm, y'know. Cold getting out, but.

How about a drink, he asked, when they were in his flat. I've got anything you like, provided it's bundy and coke. She wrinkled her nose: What, no Bacardi? but not seriously, and Stuart was so brimming with good humour he didn't notice. Probably that was screwing Emmanuelle; whatever she was like in bed there'd be all the other things, the looks, the money, her being his boss. Mel tipped back her drink as though it were coke without any rum, and held out the glass for more.

She scowled at him, so puffed up and sleek. So well cut; even under the sweat shirt he'd pulled on you could see the definition of his muscles. She wanted to say something hurtful, but everything that came into her head just sounded sour. She muttered, You're looking extremely pleased with yourself, in a sarcastic way, and he grinned, and looked even more smug.

So, she said then, and he said So? back, and this drink was going down too. There was a book on the coffee table. Don't tell me you can read, she said. *The Gentle Science of Aromatherapy*, it was called. She flipped over the pages. I been giving Lance massages, he explained, in his earnest way. Essential oils, y'know? My girlfriend Yvette used to do me. She had this black pepper oil, for when you might get muscle fatigue. Great. Really warming.

What are you using on Lance?

Well. I started with rosemary ...

Mel's flipping found the alphabetical list of oils, and their properties. Rosemary, she read aloud, has a pronounced action on the brain. It will clear the mind of confusion and doubt. Did it, she asked.

What?

Clear the mind of confusion and doubt.

Stuart grinned. Well, maybe. In the long run. He sure did feel good afterwards.

Oh it makes me feel sick. All this talk about how they feel. He stays home and gets spoilt rotten and the money keeps rolling in. It's not fair.

He did have a stroke.

Yeah. People do. But money makes even strokes all right. What if it was you or me?

We're fit.

Remember that talk we had? About being rich.

Aw, yeah.

Not getting any closer, are we. Or maybe you are. I'm not.

Me neither. But I gotta say I hav'n been worrying much lately. You got any ideas?

She bit her bottom lip so the marks were startling yellow in the pink flesh. Ever thought of blackmail?

His smoothly smiling face stiffened into seriousness. Blackmail, he said.

She looked at him, pleased to have wiped away the smug grinning. Yeah.

Blackmail ...

I know, and you know, oh yes, you know, a person not a million metres from here that's up to the sort of thing they could well pay quite a lot of money to stop another person also not a million metres from here not to mention the rest of the world from finding out.

Mel hadn't intended to say any of these things. It was Bianca's other advice she'd meant to take. But as she spooled out her cryptic warning she smiled with the pleasure of it. There was a comforting solid sense of familiarity in the words. Like a formula, or maybe a spell. A shape of words to make something happen. Much more satisfying than simply asking for humiliation to be confirmed. You could attack, not just sit back and suffer. Stuart's face was still glum with surprise. Mel's smile glinted like a knife. Of course, she went on, you are involved with the person not a million metres, etcetera. But then who better than the one involved to do the dirty work?

She smiled a smile of killing sweetness, drank the last of the rum and coke, and ran up the slope and across the back lawn to her own room. He obviously thought she meant it. I'm quite clever, she said to herself. I should do more of it. Rum and coke and wicked words sure beat peanuts on the telephone with Bianca.

Whisky Glass

Susie sitting in her white sitting room. White and white and white. The yellow whites of cream clotting, the blues of milk, the pink-tinged hidden flesh of magnolia petals. Without even the contrast of wood. Instead, disguise. Various tables covered in skirts too long for them, so that at their feet swathes of taffeta pile up like foam. The coffee-table glass, hard, but entirely open to the whiteness. And where wood is undeniable it's limed, so that it's pale coloured but the softness of its grain shows through as though it were moire, like watered silk, or clouded. A room for picturing in *Belle, House and Garden, Vogue Living*. Living in *Vogue* is not quite like living on earth. The room does not take kindly to mess or tantrums. Even sitting, even breathing in it, is a faint distress. Some tall white lilies, as purely white as it might be possible to be, Mary's flowers out of a painting of the Annunciation, have dropped pollen yellow as butter on the satin stripes of the sofa, and it will stain. The television is in a cupboard, and the pale volumes carefully fanned on the coffee table have been chosen for their covers not their contents. It is a room for a picture book, not people.

Yet Susie is sitting in it. She is wearing a black dress that makes a statement in the white room, a statement whose meaning is ambiguous, but that is the nature of art. The dress is silk, a marvellous construction of folds and pleats that cling and sway against her now slender body. The newly slim Susie has reinvented the delight of buying clothes; she never lost a perception of it but now she has fully entered into the fact again. She has bought a lot of garments, that demand to be worn, and treated well. When she was a plump person she sat in the family room, a place of polished wood and sunflower chintz, she wore tracksuits and lounged in big foamy chairs and drank cream cocktails. But the new significant slender Susie demands strict and elegant rooms with clothes to match. They exchange energy between them; there's no rest. This silk lies against her legs and floats with the stir of her movements, its delicate flutter against her bare legs is a cool little wind of desire. Her calves arch in high heeled sandals, her hair is shapely, her wrist bears a heavy gold bracelet. Wearing these clothes in this room is a performance, the sense of which must never be lost. She is sitting in a high wing chair, pointed knees crossed, the television cupboard open and playing something unregarded, a glass of whisky in her hand, and she is full of anger. Here she is, thin and glamorous, a work of art within a work of art, and still Gavin is leaving.

Sometimes she walks up and down the room and her heels make sharp stabs in the velvet carpet. She finishes the whisky and twists the glass between her fingers. She needs to wait as long as possible before putting more whisky in it. She rests the glass on the palm of her hand and holds it up to the light. It's made of crystal, very heavy and deep in the base, tapering to a fine thin edge. There's a last lemony daylight in the window; the heavy base, patterned with its own glass being, pulls the light into itself. A New Age person could suspend it in the window, to turn and refract the light; a little net of fine cords and within a whisky glass, turning in the breeze, drawing in light and making meaning in a beautiful room. And more than meaning, happiness, good fortune, the crystal energy healing hurt and harms and making everything well. So they say.

Susie is waiting for Gavin. Gavin doesn't live here any more. He's coming back because there are things to talk about. They'll be things to fight about. She's taken Nathan round to her mother's. She doesn't want him to hear the arguing.

The white room is threatened. Not just by loud voices and abrupt gestures and stabbing feet. By money. There is not enough money for her to go on living in this house, not if Gavin is going to live in another equally pleasant with his new lady. But that hasn't been spoken of yet.

When she hears him coming she turns off the television and shuts its cupboard doors. She stands by one of the foaming taffeta tables. He knocks but lets himself in with his key. Hello, she says, opening her eyes wide and her mouth a little, like a woman about to be photographed. He stands in the doorway, aware that she is offering herself as a picture for him to look at. Whisky, she asks, holding up her own glass, moving sveltely to the cabinet which matches the television. She pours generously into another tumbler like her own and carries it across the room to him. Anger can be charming. Cheers, she says, but here he has to suspect irony. Your health, is his response.

A husband and wife, in the room they've made to live in. A handsome pair, standing a little apart, the woman looking at the man with wide open eyes, the man staring down at the coffee table, maybe thinking that now he would never read the books on it. If they were in a movie there's a chance that they'd get back to together again; we'd know for certain, if they were the hero and heroine and it had a happy ending.

I'm sorry, he said.

What about, particularly?

Well, the house. He gestured at the white room. I know you're fond of it. But let's face it, you do know, don't you, it's ludicrously big, I mean, for you and Nathan. It'd just be a burden.

Oh yes.

Whereas when we sell it, you can find a small place, really nice, I don't mean small, I mean not too big, of course spacious, you don't want to be cramped or anything ... I was thinking maybe closer to town, some really nice apartment, or a townhouse, that would be good, not such a worry ...

I've never found this house a worry.

Well, not in the past. But things have changed.

Things, said Susie. She turned her head, examining the room. Things look much the same to me.

You know what I mean.

And there's me. I'm not changed.

Well, I don't know about that, said Gavin, with the sketch of a lascivious smile.

Susie's brain swelled with fury, as though it were being stung by bees. It pressed on her skull and strained against her eyes. She took a sip of whisky and spoke with meticulous calm.

If it were up to me I'd be happily married to you and we'd go on happily living in our lovely home.

I'm sorry. These things happen. I didn't choose it. I tried not to. His voice whined. Pity the hapless man, it said.

Just for a whim, she said. A whim for another woman and you destroy all our lives.

I'm sorry.

So, we sell the house. And then?

Well, it's in both our names, so it's half each ...

Half? Is that all?

Should be quite a goodly amount.

Minus the mortgage. I won't be able to buy anything for half this. Not when the mortgage's paid.

Gavin was opening and shutting some little silver boxes that made a collection on one of the taffeta tables, and didn't say anything. He was putting them down in a messy way, not back in the artful arrangement Susie had made of them.

I think it should be at least two thirds. What about Nathan? A third for me and a third for him. It's not much, considering what

I've put in. Ten years. You owe me more than half. As she spoke Susie was fiddling with her glass, now empty again. Gavin got the whisky and poured more drinks. They both liked their whisky straight. Susie took a gulp. She squeezed the glass between her hands, her body was so full of tension from the anger she was trying to contain that when she pushed against the thin rim a crescent fell out of it, into the glass. A clean break. She could drink from the other side.

It's the usual arrangement, said Gavin. Don't forget I've got the future to think of. I mean, Nicole, and maybe children ... I'll do my best, heaven knows, I don't want to hurt you, Susie.

She laughed, not the old trumpet, a laugh like a woman whose brain is being stung by bees.

Gavin didn't look at her.

I want to do my best for you, please see that. And Nathan, of course I'll look after Nathan. But you'll have to ... there'll be changes. I mean, I suppose you'll have to get a job, or something. You won't be able to ... I've got other responsibilities now, you know.

When is all this going to happen?

Well, straightaway, really. Soon as possible. You won't be wanting to muck around. And Nicole's got her eye on a place, we want to get settled as soon as possible.

This calm sentence was too much for Susie's fury. It wouldn't stay contained any longer. She lunged at him, and he standing reasonable and considering, whisky in one hand, frail Meissen teabowl he might have been valuing in the other, saw her movement from the corner of his eye. He turned, to duck and distance himself from the brown slop of the whisky, but his foot caught in the table's taffeta skirts and he stumbled and fell sideways towards Susie. The glass she was holding tight in both her hands crashed into his neck. The crystal sharpness of its broken rim cut into his carotid artery. A great spurt of blood came out. He continued to fall, until he lay on the carpet at her feet, his blood pumping out in a fountain. The white satin-stripe sofa, the taffeta table, the carpet like clotted cream, and over them all blood. A white sitting room shows the blood.

White Taffeta

Susie knew she had to stop the blood flowing. She dragged at the taffeta table-cloth to disentangle it from Gavin's feet and the tipped-over tables. A shower of little silver boxes fell out and tinkled against the shards of Meissen. She bunched up the papery silk and pressed it against his neck. The blood stopped spurting in a fountain but it still flowed through the taffeta, however hard she pressed.

The telephone was out of reach while she was kneeling on the floor. She stood up carefully and put one foot on the balled-up cloth to hold it tight in place and teetering on the other inched heel and toe towards the phone. She overbalanced as she reached it and knocked another taffeta table over, the one with the vase of lilies, but grabbed the cord and pulled the phone with her as she scrambled back to Gavin and the saturated ball of cloth. She pressed again with one hand, using her knees on the other side of his head to get a good grip. One-handed she dialled. She wasn't good with numbers. Was it 000 or 999? When a voice answered her own failed; she cleared her throat and it quavered out. Hurry, she said, hurry. A patient voice asked questions, careful, soothing: which service did she want, the address, the problem. As soon as possible, the patient voice said, and hung up. She listened to the mournful signal for a moment, then cut it off and pressed the button with Emmanuelle's number. Em, she said. Em. Can you come?

Emmanuelle heard the dangerous quiet in Susie's voice and came. Grabbed her handbag, wrote on the pantry noticeboard Gone to Susie's, got the car out and was there in four minutes. She knocked on the door but didn't wait, pushed it open and went in.

At the sitting room door she stood amazed, unable to understand the messages the room was offering her. There was the blood, the white room all blotched with blood, turning brownish now and crusty on Susie's arms and face, except where cuts on her fingers welled freshly red. There was Gavin lying wide-eyed, a sheaf of lilies across his feet and a swathe of taffeta like a shroud pulled awry. There was Susie kneeling with fierce devotion to her plug of saturated cloth. And over the floor a sprinkling of little silver boxes and glinting shards of porcelain. It seemed to be a scene of ritual, a wedding, a funeral, its rules skewed and mysterious.

Gavin, said Susie. I've got to press to stop the bleeding.

Emmanuelle knelt beside her. What shall I do, she asked. Then there were ambulance people in the room, saying Leave this to us. Gently pushing Susie aside. You have to keep pressing, she said. We know what to do, a young woman answered her. Emmanuelle drew Susie away. You've cut your fingers, she said. Let's go and find some band-aids.

She took her into the bathroom and sat her on the edge of the bath. She unzipped the silk dress, all slimy and stained, unstrapped the teetering sandals and with a washer wrung out in warm water carefully sponged the rusty stains from her face and arms and legs. The cuts on her fingers were instantly threaded with blood again, and when she washed her knees the same thing happened. The only band-aids Emmanuelle could find must have belonged to Nathan. They've got Mickey Mouse on them, she sighed, and might have giggled, but Susie sat staring at nothing, obediently limp when Emmanuelle lifted her arms or feet as she washed her and dabbed on some ti-tree oil that she found in the medicine cupboard, like a child in the habit of letting her mother look after her.

He'll be all right, she said, with a quiver in her voice.

Emmanuelle doubted it. She'd never seen a dead person, except her father in his coffin, a waxy and not quite true image of himself, but remembering Gavin's wide-open unseeing eyes and lolling mouth she thought he was probably dead. The ambulance people will look after him, she said, they know what to do. She considered how much time had passed. They didn't appear to be in any hurry to get him to hospital. No sirens racing against time to get to healing.

Have you got a lawyer, she asked.

Susie looked at her. A doctor, she said. He needs a doctor. Emmanuelle wrapped her in a bathrobe and went into the bedroom. Latimer Hallett Knight had lawyers. She rang Donald Slatkin, who listened and said, Okay, I'll handle it. I'll get her a lawyer. But what she needs is a doctor. Fast. I'll get a medico over there, get her sedated. No questions till tomorrow, that's the strategy.

When Emmanuelle looked into the sitting room nothing had changed. Gavin still lay wide-eyed in all his bloody finery. The body, was what he would be called now. The ambulance people were in the hall. Susie still sat on the edge of the bath. Emmanuelle went into the kitchen and heated a mug of water in the microwave, dunked a tea bag in it, put in lots of sugar and milk and gave it to Susie to drink. Still the obedient child she sipped at it. Is the doctor coming, she asked. Yes, I've fixed all that, said Emmanuelle. Susie shivered, a long shudder that made the tea slop. Emmanuelle went through her drawers until she found underwear, a tee-shirt, a track-suit of pink fleecy fabric. These are cosy clothes, said Susie, in a little flat voice. Emmanuelle put her arms round her and rubbed at her arms and back. Cosy clothes for a cold night. She sounded like a doll talking. By this time the sitting room was full of policemen.

Intentions

Donald Slatkin had been right about the doctor. He'd come quite soon, a small man in a green tweed suit, pronounced that Susie was suffering from severe shock, and that he planned to sedate her and order her to bed. Questioning could wait till the next day. The police seemed quite happy with that and allowed Emmanuelle to take Susie back to her house, as long as she didn't leave the country, of course. Yes, said the doctor, it is better she not be on her own. She is gravely shocked.

Since Lance was in the guest room she put Susie in her own bed, which she'd slept in all these months alone. She dressed her in one of her own nightgowns and thought it might have been a mirror image of herself in bed beside her. Or a sister out of a fairytale: a dark sister and a fair sister, Snow White and Rose Red were names that came to her; they were kind to a bear and a dwarf and got to marry kings' sons. What happened to these girls after their princes came and carried them off into the happy ever after? Were they sisters still? Did they stay friends, parcelling up their world in gossip, comforting in childbirth and afterwards in the frail business of child-rearing, offering loving presences when husband-princes strayed after the more childish beauties they had been once? Did princes ever get interested in the bodies of men, in the cut and fold and hardness of male muscle, and forsake the softness of wives? For a long time she lay awake and listened to Susie's breaths dragging up out of her sedated sleep, wondering what had happened in her pretty white room this night, how Gavin came to be lying staring at his own death amidst so much blood. A welter of blood. To think the human body contained so much.

But when she asked her, which she did though it was hard, Emmanuelle was no good at asking blunt questions and usually avoided them but in this case she thought Susie could do with the practice, the answer wasn't clear. Susie sat up in bed, sedation and bewilderment and short sight making her eyes large and tremulous. I don't know, she said. Em, I don't know. I killed him. It was me. Without me he wouldn't be dead. I kind of ... threw the glass at him, but holding on to it, and he sort of tripped and fell on it and cut his neck ...

Tripped? said Emmanuelle.

Mmm. His feet got caught up in the table skirt, I think ... and he ...

Tripped, said Emmanuelle. We'll stick with tripped.

But the thing is, Em, what did I mean to do? Was I just throwing whisky in his face, or was I trying to hurt him with the glass? Cut him, wound him, mash it in his face ... I think I had murderous thoughts. The glass was broken you know. I'd been fiddling with it and a big chunk came out of the rim, a clean big chunk like a bite.

Had you had a lot to drink?

That was the third glass. I hadn't had much of it, I remember seeing all this liquid, like pee it was, yellowy brown, seeing this sheet of liquid fly out in his face as I jabbed ... jabbed you see, that means damage.

Two glasses of whisky and a bit; it's quite a lot.

Not for me it's not, not really. Good old Susie the lush. I don't think you could say I was drunk. Susie put her hands over her face. I did kill him, Em. The question is, the intending; I can't work out whether I intended to. That's the question.

No it's not, says Emmanuelle. It's not the question. It's *your* question, and I see you need to ask it. But maybe you'll never get the answer, and that'll be something you'll have to accept. But it's not *the* question, now; you don't have to offer the ... the authorities any questions. Just facts. You threw whisky in Gavin's face. He tripped and fell on the glass.

Emmanuelle stood up. This is how it went. I'm Gavin, she said. You're there, pretty annoyed, and who wouldn't be, throwing whisky at me. Naturally, I duck, or side-step, or something — Emmanuelle did a shuffle with her feet — my foot gets caught in one of your dinky little table frills, and bingo, I stumble and fall on the glass which unfortunately is broken, and probably it would have smashed if it wasn't already anyway, and there you have it, a terrible accident.

Susie, sitting up in bed, Rose Red in a sister's nightgown, watched Emmanuelle's reconstruction of the scene. How do you know? she whispered.

It's the logical thing. It's what must have happened. It's what you're going to say when people ask. And the matter of your intention ... it's for your conscience. But I wouldn't let it trouble you too much.

Susie's wondering face quivered in a moment's smile, then withered. Poor Gavin, she said. Emmanuelle put her arms round her so that Susie's head rested on her shoulder. You can cry, she said seductively. Cry now. And Susie wept, her tears damp in Emmanuelle's neck and wetting her collar. Emmanuelle stared over her head, at a pattern of bare branches in the sunlight on the wall, faded and intermittent on this cloudy morning. She felt sadness welling round her. Neither she nor Lance had liked Gavin much. His death was a shock, a loss like Donne's bit of promontory falling into the sea, a manor of my neighbour, but not a particular grief.

Her eyes filled with tears for humankind being born and dying, not for Gavin. And the hope that for the moment Susie's sorrow might be unambiguous. You need to grieve for a husband, for ten years' habit of a husband. Even if you'd felt like killing him.

Like the Movie

Mel heard Emmanuelle drive away. Unusually late in the evening, she noticed. Maybe she had another lover as well. Stuart for the mornings, someone else at night. Next day at breakfast Emmanuelle had purple shadows under her eyes, like too much make-up put on upside down. Her skin had a fine shiny stretched look in the mornings, you could tell wrinkles weren't far away. Mel watched the light fall sideways across her cheeks, looking for the wrinkle-webs fanning out from the corners of her eyes. Laughter lines people called them. Ha. Not much laughing going on in this house. Not since the stroke. And not a lot before. Mel remembered the backpackers' hotel and how they used to laugh all the time. Sitting in the hot barred rooms with their feeble light bulbs that cast strange shadows, drinking beer. You weren't supposed to bring in beer, but people did. But the talk was the thing. Being in a foreign country, laughing. Perhaps it was families. Her own had been pretty glum. She got a picture in her head, suddenly, of streams of sunlight and people laughing. She heaved a sigh. The sun was okay, even the winter was often sunny, but the laughing; how could you imagine the laughing into a real happening? Wanting to be a person who laughed wasn't enough. You needed some help.

Mel, said Emmanuelle, won't you be late? For Mel was sitting over her tea, not gobbling it up and rushing out the door, as usual.

I'm feeling a bit crook, said Mel. I thought I wouldn't go today.

Good idea, said Emmanuelle, but absently, Mel could tell she wasn't really thinking about her. Probably thinking of her own style being cramped. Have a good rest, she went on, vaguely, and left the room, though the kitchen was a mess and she usually tidied it, and Magda was coming, as well.

Mel had two more cups of tea. She heard Magda arrive so she went out the back door. She wished she hadn't said she'd stay home, she couldn't think what to do with herself. She heard the car come down the drive, the whine of the garage door as it opened and shut; Stuart back from taking the children to school. Was this when Emmanuelle ... and what did Lance ... Spying when you looked at it up close wasn't something you'd want to go in for. There was frost on the ground, the grass was blue with it; it was cold, a raggedy damp morning, the air smoky smelling and sharp in the nostrils. There were flat frail flowers on the camellia bushes, which she looked at with irritation; what had they to do with her? Nothing, not the frost or the air or the bare trees or these pale flowers, nothing belonged to her. Some people, because they see these things, because they breathe them in, believe that they own them, and maybe then it's as if they do, Stuart for instance, mister macho man, he'd walk around and own the morning, but not Mel.

She heard her name called and looking up saw him leaning out of the window of his flat above the garage. He beckoned her.

He was making his breakfast milkshake of honey and eggs, yoghurt and fruit, and offered her a glass. You know Mel, he said, I been thinking. You and me, we could get married. There's this apartment, not bad you'd have to say, we could live here. Whaddya reckon? We'd make a good little team, ay?

She stared at him. These words between them rippled and glimmered. As though they were fish, and the air in the room was a substance like water. And not very good for breathing. She could be

Alice gone through the mirror, and everything looks the same but it's just that little bit twisted so in fact it's wildly different from what you've learned to expect in your own place, but you don't know where the twisting's happened or how it is that the rules have got bent. But people are still expecting you to play their games.

You been into the bundy and coke already? Ten o'clock in the morning and you're away?

Stuart was beaming at her, with his downy hair and his grin like a big innocent milk-swigging baby. Whaddya reckon, ay?

You trying to tell me you're serious?

He just went on sitting on the edge of the table, nodding his head, beaming, his big body quaking with delight.

What about ... what about ... this, this ... *affair* that you've got going on? What happens to that?

Stuart continued to smile. Aw, you know me. Sex is a kind of a hobby with me. It don't mean nothing but.

What if it meant something to me? Would you stop if we got married?

Aw well ... I reckon its days are maybe numbered, anyway. I tell you what, you wait and see. See if we don't make a good little team. His chest heaved with chuckles under his sweat shirt. He hardly ever wore his uniform now. You wait and see, he said again, and Mel looked at his eyes crinkling and his chest heaving with a kind of wonder: what will he do next?

Stuart's excitement was because he'd worked out his blackmail scheme. It wasn't original, he'd seen it in a movie. He meant that he and Mel were a good team because he'd never have thought of turning it to his own use if she hadn't brought the idea up. In the movie one bloke puts the hard word on the other, the rich one, he says to him Of course it's not really blackmail buddy, and buddy says Godammit not really blackmail, and slaps his leg and laughs and gives him what he wants. Which is a decent packet of shares in buddy's company and, this is the important part, teaching him how to use them so he can make money for himself. Very decent and clean and the real beauty of it is it's one-off. When it's done it's done, none of that nasty business of having to keep on paying that would wear out the friendliest of relationships.

When Stuart says to Lance, It's not really blackmail, Lance says back, just like in the movie, Not really blackmail, but he doesn't laugh, his voice is cold. No, says Stuart, of course not, and Lance nods, his old courteous self. Blackmail over what?

Well, you wouldn' want madam to know, would you.

Know what?

Well, about you and me, ay?

How would she find out? You wouldn't tell her, would you?

Stuart looks at him.

Are you planning to tell her?

Well, no, that's the thing, I don' wanna tell her, I don' think she should know.

I see, says Lance. And what exactly do you require?

Well, see, I haven' got much to come and go on, well, you'd know, you pays me, and so I thought, what if you was to give me some shares, because that's how people get rich, right? and you could show me what to do with them and then I, well, I'd be okay too. And that'd be it, kaput, finito.

I see, says Lance. And if I don't, you'll tell my wife about you and me.

Like I said, I don' wanna do that. We're good friends, aren' we? We've had good times.

I wonder what you'd say. Would you tell her that you and I were in love?

Stuart squirms. The movie doesn't happen like this. The man laughs and slaps his leg and calls him buddy, he says great idea buddy, admiring, pleased even, you could say. Of course it's a different blackmail in the movie, it's telling the wife too but somcthing about the bloke and a girl only it hasn't really happened, it was really his wife after all, that was it, so it's quite a good joke there too, maybe you need that part of the joke for it to be really funny. Stuart is starting to feel a bit worried. He's sitting on a chair in the guest-room, back to front as usual, Lance is still in bed, the day has turned grey and sleety, too cold for swimming even in a heated pool, he's upright against the pillows and resting against his chest is a book with a black cover and gold squiggles, *Bleak House*, Stuart can see the name, and bleak is a good word for the day this morning, Lance too.

I see, he says, and this is beginning to get on Stuart's nerves. I see. A parcel of shares plus expertise. He stops and gazes, his eyes very wide, gazes out the window, but you can tell he's not seeing any-thing there, it's all inside his head. Well, he says, I don't see why not.

Stuart's pleased baby smile shines out. Great, he says. Great. He jumps up, stretching, so the perfectly cut muscles outline them-selves under his shirt. We can still do the massages, and things, he says. I didn' mean we should stop anything.

I see. Well, perhaps not today. Today I don't feel quite up to it. And besides, we have to think about your first lesson on how to play the stock exchange.

Oh yeah, says Stuart. Play, that's a good one. You teaching me, yeah. Will it be hard? his voice is doleful, then he smiles. Ya reckon I'll be a good student?

Why not? You're pretty good at body-building, and massage, and ... other arts. Why not finance? On the other hand, perhaps concentration on certain skills would be wiser, cobblers and lasts and such like.

Stuart gives an uneasy grin. He hasn't a clue what Lance is talking about. Yeah, he says.

No Health

When Stuart had gone Lance got out of bed. He stood in the shower for a long time, letting the water run over him. He washed himself three times. He rubbed at the soap so that it frothed on his left arm, he knew it was there. You could probably do massages for yourself, only in part of course. Your own fingers finding the dips and folds of your muscles, dabbling and sliding through the oil. But it wouldn't be the same. No eyes of the other to see what was happening. He turned the tap on hard so the water's force was like needles pricking his skin. Then he dressed carefully and went in search of Emmanuelle.

He found her coming down the stairs with a tray, which seemed odd but he didn't want to have to go into that. He stopped in front of her, and looked at her, his gaze encompassing her and the expression on his face that of a man who finds grace, perhaps unexpected, in looking. Emmanuelle's face showed her astonishment at this.

I wanted to talk to you, she said quickly.

And I to you, he nodded.

About Stuart ...

Ah.

I want to have him for a bit. There's a lot of things — wait till I tell you what's happening with Susie — anyway I was thinking there's Stuart and he's our chauffeur and I'd like him to be of some use to me, for a change. Not all the time, I don't mean, but sometimes.

Ah, said Lance again. I was about to say, maybe we should let him go.

I thought ... you needed him.

Maybe I don't any more. That's what I want to talk to you about. But of course, if you have use for him, we must keep him.

By this time they were in the kitchen. Emmanuelle had put the tray down. They were standing looking at one another, paying attention. Emmanuelle wasn't tidying the tray, or the table with its debris of breakfast, she stood with her head bent slightly so she looked up through her lashes at him, her hair was tucked behind her ears, one hand rested on a chair back. He saw her fingers slightly curled and the luminous unpainted pinkness of her nails. She was wearing her pale blue morning tracksuit and he noticed how the colour became her, how fine her skin was, her face without make-up clear, vulnerable, needing care.

You have a candid face, he said.

Candid, she repeated, as though the word were a small hard piece of toffee in her mouth. Maybe setting her teeth on edge, just a little.

Mmm, he said. He understood that she knew about him and Stuart. I have to talk to you, he repeated.

Maybe you're better, she said. She reached out and touched his shoulder, the left one, cupping it in her palm. Cured. The phases all gone.

He shook his head, quite violently. I doubt cured, he said. *There is no health in us.* They both looked a bit surprised at these words, and Emmanuelle said, I'd better tell you quick. Gavin's dead. Susie's here ...

Gavin ...

An accident, last night.

She'd hardly finished describing the events of the night when there was a loud banging on the front door knocker.

That might be the police, she said.

It sounded like the might of the law, said Lance. Their mouths curled upwards in faint complicit smiles. For this moment they were a husband and wife in their own house with their own language, and intent on keeping its safety around them. I've talked to Donald Slatkin, she said, he's handling it.

Oh good, Donald Slatkin.

The knocker banged again. Somewhere the noise of the vacuum cleaner ceased, and Magda's heavy footsteps made for the front door.

It looks as though it could be all right, said Emmanuelle. Not murder, or anything. I think.

The Days Pass

Emmanuelle has a chauffeur and she makes use of him. She orders him here, there; says wait, come back. Takes Susie home to her house to pack some clothes. The white room no longer has a body in it, but the blood remains; it is as though the furniture, the carpet, the fabrics have begun to rust, as though time has passed in a place neglected and desolate and corruption has set in. The lilies are rotting and there is an old brown smell of life gone bad. The glitter of the little silver boxes is obscenely bright among the debris. Emmanuelle shuts the door and won't let Susie in. We'll get some cleaners, she says. Professionals.

They go to Susie's mother's house to collect Nathan. He can come and stay too, he can have the other bed in William's room. William will be pleased, at least at first. They'll fight a bit and be naughty and not go to sleep soon enough, and Maud will be jealous and superior, but it will be fun. Susie's mother lives in a small wooden house in Bexley full of Afghan rugs crocheted while she watches the television all day. When Susie was born, or Susan as she was then, she started collecting the wishbones every time she roasted a chook, and got her friends to do the same, and by the time Susie got married to Gavin she had enough to paint them all with gold paint and use them to decorate the placecards at the wedding breakfast. You had to wash and dry them carefully at the time, of course. They were tied with apricot ribbon to match the bridesmaids' dresses. She'd got this handy hint out of the *Women's Weekly*, which was full of useful advice to a young bride from another country. Mrs Shubert has been told the official version of Gavin's death, over the phone; she looks sideways at them and says, Stumbled and fell on a whisky glass, ay, and about the corners of her mouth lurk sly phrases like Pissed again, and That's what you get for screwing around, but Mrs Shubert doesn't say any of these things, not this time, just pulls her face into a brief grimace that might be satisfaction, or seemly sorrow, or even a nod at vengeance, the Lord's of course. You never know, she says, and crosses her arms across her chest, you never know. Emmanuelle feels sadder than at any time so far because there is so little grief for Gavin, but then she thinks of his parents and Nicole and the devastation they will be undergoing, and of Nathan who hasn't been told yet, they haven't worked out what to say to him yet, and considers that grief there will be, in sufficient measure. Grief, and fury too: the rage of Nicole. Nicole who will have longed, and despaired, and hoped, and won, and then lost the lovely man out of the embrace of victory. She thinks of Brian. He was a lovely man once. But never embraced in victory. She remembers all the trains she never stepped under.

Stuart carries suitcases in and out of houses, drops her at the entrance to the supermarket, comes back and picks her up, heaves the bags from trolley to boot. He fetches the children from school. He takes Susie to the lawyers. He hasn't had time to tell Mel about Lance and the blackmail. What will he tell her? That Lance said yes. That was the message, and of course there's the lesson, but not seeing the joke is a bit of a worry. Though maybe a sense of humour isn't Lance's strong point. And then he remembers: rich, this is it, rich, and a tide of joy rises in a wave from his feet swirling up through his bowels his chest his brain and beats there so he can't think and certainly doesn't wonder why there are all these precise errands and Emmanuelle in charge.

Emmanuelle says to Susie, I'll fix up a room for you, if you like, and Susie replies, Oh, okay, thanks, in such a disappointed voice that Em says Unless you'd rather stay with me, and they both smile with pleasure and of course this is what they want to do. They go to bed with mugs of hot cocoa like girls in a dorm which neither of them ever was but they've read all the books. They lie in bed in the dark and say things they wouldn't if they were sitting up looking at one another in lit spaces. Emmanuelle thinks this is what it would have been like to have a sister. She never had one but if she had would she have been like Susie, born of her parents into that neat household? Snow White and Rose Red. Rose Red the lively one, dark haired and playful. Snow White good and industrious. Not the better part if you had the choice. But loving one another dearly. Each a mirror for the other, a mirror of might-have-beens. As well as eerily exact reflections. The bodies to clothe, the bras and knickers and shirts of silk, the sleeping smells of flesh, the bleeding and blow-drying, the anxious applying of creams. Not girls in a fairy story but grown women stepping smartly towards the grave. That is the message of the body's decay, for decay it does, even in women in their prime, like Snow and Red here. Snow and Red: you could laugh, if you had the courage; two women in a big bed in the dark of night, while their husbands are elsewhere.

In her sedated sleep Susie moans, and sighs, and turns sharply as though to shake something off. Sometimes her breath stops, and Emmanuelle waits for it to start again. This is the kind of bed on which a steam-roller is supposed to be able to drive down one side without disturbing the person sleeping on the other. If so Emmanuelle must be a pea-sensitive princess; maybe she could sleep through a steam-roller but not through Susie. Susie wakes chastened and groggy after the long chemical nights, and ponders him, her husband, the dead man of whom it is understood no ill will be spoken. She dabs ti-tree oil on her cuts. That they should sting still, and Gavin be dead. She doesn't need to go to classes to learn how to grieve, she's good at it already. She celebrates him, her tears flow, she is sad, she is mournful. And, Emmanuelle has to wonder, secretly, secretly pleased?

The days pass, and the incredible accident takes on the shape first of fact, then of inevitability.

The days pass, there are meals. Lance opens bottles of wine. Susie is fond of wine, he brings out champagne before dinner, he watches her sniff its bubbles with a shadowy glint in his pewter eyes. He looks at Emmanuelle too, she remembers how she thought he does not love me because he does not look at me; she returns his gaze with a look that says you dare not speak to me as you promised and he passes her a glass of champagne with a shrug that replies we are never alone any more, even in bed you are not alone any more. She doesn't care, there will be time. The murder of Gavin, as sometimes she says it to herself, the death of Gavin has marked the changing of everything, and for now there is the pleasure of considering what will come of it. There is a moment of poise, before the next way must be taken, before it needs to be chosen; there is a sense of excitement because this time she sees it, and means to choose clear-eyed. There must have been moments like this in the past; she looks back on herself, starry eyed, cloudy eyed, blind, never noticing them. This time she is noticing.

The days pass. The law follows its processes, so do the newspapers. They frolic with catchy headlines on the third page, the fifth: Death by whisky glass. Drinking is a health hazard. Whisky proves fatal. Whisky the unkindest cut of all. Their facetiousness enrages Emmanuelle. Lance points out that the jokiness must mean no foul play is suspected. The reports don't bother Susie because nobody lets her see them.

Lance says to Emmanuelle, You have a Greek view of death.

Proper respect must be paid. You'd have broken the law to bury your brother. All serious societies have their ways of respecting death, she replies. In some they put the bodies out for the vultures. It's a matter of thinking. I hope people will think about me when I'm dead. Not grieve, just think.

Lance spends a lot of time on the phone. He gets up for breakfast and then goes into the study. He telephones Donald Slatkin. Business is on his mind again. Several times he passes Stuart and says, Ah, the lesson, tapping with his finger the cleft in his chin, but it is never the moment. Stuart is kept busy these days. No time for massages. Errands all the day. Lance does his exercises on his own. He watches his left hand press the buttons that dial the telephone with firm little clicks.

Lance's birthday is in four days' time. Percy and Lou will be back from Alaska by then. A quiet family lunch will be held. Now she's decided not to give him the Wandjina painting Emmanuelle has to find something else for a present. Try Frankie's again. That morning at breakfast Lance says, Why don't we take a trip? Why don't we go to ... well, what about New York? We could call it a birthday present.

Emmanuelle looks at him, astonished.

William says, New York! Will we go in a aeroplane that flies?

Lance says, I thought just Mummy and I would go, not children, this time. What about school?

Emmanuelle says, We haven't had our talk.

Where better than New York?

New York is a very dangerous city, says Maud. It's got muggers.

How do you know, Emmanuelle asks.

Charlotte's daddy got mugged in New York. They took all his money and his plastic as well.

Plastic what, asks William.

We'd be very careful, says Lance.

After that conversation Emmanuelle sat in the back of the car while Stuart drove steadily through the traffic and wondered whether she and Lance will actually go to New York. They've never been. To Europe, several times, last year with the children, but to New York, never. She thought of planning to do something, of thinking ahead about it. This time next week I'll be on the plane, flying to New York. You know this, you believe it, here are the tickets, the passport, the visa stuck and stamped, but somehow it's not real. You know the days will pass and you'll be there in that place doing that thing and yet somehow this present moment is all there is, that later moment has no power, and then when it does happen you look back on the unbelieving time and say to yourself, see, here we are. Didn't we know it all the time? And she thought, death will be like that; is; has been. You think, one day, soon, later, and it's not real. And then one day you'll be finding yourself in that moment, like the plane going to New York, and you'll be dying, and you'll be living through the moments of death, and maybe it will be expected and logical, like the plane journey, and with interest and pleasure at the end of it. Your body staring eyed and lolling mouthed, but the little manikin of the soul buckling its seat belt and looking forward to the free drinks and the next stop.

Lance wouldn't think so. Lance took no comfort in souls, not little manikins or pure spirits.

At Frankie's in Mosman she found a faience plate with two figures, in a landscape proclaimed by one tree, one flower and three blades of grass. The figures were painted with lively little dashes of blue; you could see the energy of the hand that made them. More than two hundred years ago. The plate was quite large, and oval, not cracked or chipped, but worn. The figures were a man and a woman, and the energy of their depiction made them look happy. It cost a lot of money, and Lance will like it.

The days pass. Nathan had been told that daddy isn't coming back any more. Has Nicole got him, he asks. Lying in their sisterly bed that night Susie relates this story to Em. Who gasps. Little pitchers, says Susie, contrition in her voice. Then she gives a hiccup, and suddenly they are both laughing, violent hooting sobbing laughter that curls them up and flings them flat with legs crossed to stop them pissing themselves and leaves them worn out and shocked and is much more terrible than the grief they've been plodding their way through these last days. Laughter lays you bare and shows you what you think.

Maud, when she hears that Nathan's daddy is dead, dead is the word that Emmanuelle uses, none of this passing on going away nonsense, says to him, So, he ought to be on the right hand of God; there. She jabs the table with her hand, the left one. It would be good if you could ask him what it's like. But you never seem to be able to. She sighs, in her bossy way, and gives him a chocolate biscuit. Nathan is beginning to perceive the importance of losing a father, but isn't aware of grief yet; that's for the rest of his life.

Maud remembers the video she saw at Sunday School about Lazarus rising from the dead, and asks her mother what he said, what did he tell people about what it was like. When Emmanuelle says that nobody knows, nobody seems to have written it down, Maud can't believe it; how could they be so stupid, she says, her voice full of scorn; she will talk to Miss Manifold about it, next Sunday, somebody must know.

The days pass, though Mel feels their slowness like an iron band round her head. The clamour of the household does nothing to lighten or lessen its weight. She's back pretending to go to hotel school. Sometimes Bianca can get away and sit in coffee shops with her, or wander the streets window-shopping, though she would like to give that up, so depressing it's become, all these clothes she can't afford and wouldn't look any good in, but Bianca is supposed to take her free time in the afternoons so she's not often available. She's back to long telephone calls and the salty sting of peanuts on her lips, however much she rubs them with Vaseline her lips are always cracked, these days.

She's had no words with Stuart. He beams as he passes her, and waves his hand, with his finger and thumb forming a circle, an O that makes his face go daft with grinning. Fancy being married to that oaf. She's trudging back from the station through a thin sleety rain, whatever has happened to the smiling sun of winter, when she hears a tootling tune played on a car horn and stops and he picks her up. What's a good-looking girl like you doing in a place like this, he cackles, and it doesn't occur to her that he means it, about the good-looking. Well, he says, our little scheme, and taps the side of his nose, our little scheme, she looks like a beauty.

What, she says. She's had such a boring morning she could scream.

Y'know, to make some money. Make us rich. He looks at her as though he's squizzing a dumbcluck. Blackmail? he says, with a leering drawl.

Shit. Did you do it? As she says these words she has no idea whether she really thought he would. Whether she was just throwing the idea around, playing at tough games. People say a lot of things and never do them. She feels a bit queasy at the fact suddenly shaping itself, solid, in front of her.

Yeah. Didn' you think I would. I went up to him and I said, Lance ...

Lance? she shrieks. Lance?

Yeah. I says Lance ...

You fool. You moron. You total bloody fuckwit. It's her. It's her. She's the one to blackmail. I can't believe this. Can't you get anything right? Don't you even know where you're putting it? It's fucking Emmanuelle is the one to blackmail. Emmanuelle.

Her too? says Stuart.

Black Puddings Forever

Emmanuelle, on one of these passing days, got a telephone call. Susie actually answered, and passed the phone to her. A man about an antique, she said. Emmanuelle felt a little clutch of fright, but hadn't time to work out why. A voice said: It was a very fine piece, but it was passed in for lack of bidders.

It was Knight, of course. She remembered, the telephone call on the evening of Gavin's death, the cryptic message about the antique auction, when was it for, a day already passed, she'd completely forgotten in all the excitement. Oh, she said, oh, I forgot. Mmm, I noticed, said Knight. Well, since the piece is still available, would you like to make a time for a private view?

Why not, she replied. This afternoon?

Whoa. Okay, why not. Same time, same place.

She put the phone down, giggling. It suits you, Susie said, buying antiques. Brings out the colour in your cheeks and the sparkle in your eyes. Can I come too?

No. But I might tell you about it.

She called Stuart and booked him for the afternoon. You needn't wait, she told him, when he dropped her off at the hotel, come back in three hours. She'd learned not to explain to him where she was going.

It's a kind of game, meeting a lover in a hotel and when you play it you join everyone else who's ever done so. The elaborate nonchalance, the purposeful-casual anonymous walk, the quick scanning for possible recognisers. The alibis should they be needed. The strategies planned ahead. Knight always arrives first, she rings him from the lobby so he can give her the room number. Standing with the phone, lounging, eyes alert. So far she's not met anybody she knows. She likes this part, the tension of it, which gives a quick nervous edge to meeting. So you can arrive in the room, slightly breathless, and fall into the arms of your lover, waiting impatiently.

Today he's leaning against the window looking at the piled buildings of the city beneath. He looks up quizzically, but is not impatient. She goes to him and kisses him. What I've to tell you, she says. But not yet.

She's wearing jeans and a jumper and loafers and begins to take them off. Not a lady in town today I see, he says. A lady, do you think I'm a lady? She's offended. Candid face, and a lady. I'm beginning to think I've got an image problem.

By this time she's naked, and so is he; he says Oh no, not an image problem, and they are making love in their tender friendly way. It's when they're lying together afterwards that it occurs to her that the sense of ease, of speech unlocked, she has had with Susie is a kind of betrayal of Knight. On top of forgetting their meeting. Which she still hasn't explained.

You know Gavin Prothero, she said.

The Computer King?

Well, that's the name of the business.

The pleasures of good narrative are not wasted on Emmanuelle. She tells her story with gusto, with glee, and is surprised to find she's turned Susie into a heroine whose bully of a husband destroyed himself by his own misprizing of a good woman.

Knight says: Are you envious?

She goes still. And cold, it's cold in this stuffy pastel room. She pulls the bedclothes up. Envious, she says, a small flat statement of a word. Why would I be? But she knows what he means, her question is a shield put up against him, and he recognises that. He turns on his back and slides her head on to his chest.

I've got some news too. Not so dramatic as yours; probably just as well. He's silent for a moment. Fiona's pregnant. Well, I suppose I should say, we're pregnant.

Oh. That's good. That's very good. Isn't it? She tips her head back to see his face, but it's a craggy and unreadable view from this angle.

Yes, he says. It's what we intended. And she's chosen her moment, not to wait any longer. Apparently she's not been using any contraception for a while, without saying anything to me; so I shouldn't have the ups and downs of trying, just the success. And now, here it is.

Are you happy?

Yes, I am. It's what we planned. Hoped for. There's always a certain pleasure in plans working out.

She listens in vain for any joy in his voice. She props herself on one elbow and examines his face, with her eyes, with her fingers. He lies with his eyes closed. His face is calm as an effigy. On the other hand, he says, I wouldn't have minded if it hadn't happened. At my age. You get set in your ways. I like my life the way it is. His arm tightens across her back.

Having babies changes your life, says Emmanuelle. I think now how carelessly people go in for it. Without taking any thought. And then a child is born and you're faced with the fact that your life will never be the same again. You will never be the same again. You know what hostages to fortune means. You thought it was a cliche, and so it is, it's just entirely true as well.

Emmanuelle's body has gone taut while she says this. He can feel the seriousness of her words in the tightness of her muscles. He looks curiously at her bent head.

Do you mind that?

It's my life. How can I say I mind it? And in some ways it's very good for you. Turns you into a more thoughtful person. More aware of fate. Do you see what I mean? Less ... less full of hubris, more humble, I suppose. But all the same I do think you should know what you're letting yourself in for.

It might be good for Fiona and me to be more humble.

Oh, I'm sure.

I can't say I've noticed having children makes people more content, though. They still want things. They're not any happier with their lot.

Still wishing for black puddings and sticking them on noses.

Ooh, black puddings, says Knight. My father made wonderful black puddings. Fiona can't stand them. Do you like black puddings, Emmie?

Mmm. Especially French ones, all juicy, I don't like the dry and doughy kind. And cooked with onions and apples.

Aah. Wouldn't it be good if we were eating a black pudding now, this very minute.

I know a shop that makes quite decent ones. Not far from here.

With some good bread and a bottle of red.

And thou.

Beside me in the wilderness.

Black pudding would make the wilderness civilised.

And you'd make it paradise.

Paradise enough, remember?

Paradise enough will suit me.

It's a pretty structure they're building, the lovers and the black pudding. They wish it would happen, but will do nothing to make it. And yet for a while the words are it, they don't need the smell of frying or the grease on their lips.

Black puddings in the air, says Knight.

There is more silence, in which Emmanuelle thinks of saying: I've got some news about Lance, too. I have discovered that he is gay. She lies held tight beside him, her fingers exploring his chest, the shape of its muscles, the way the hair grows, the little bulge of flesh beneath his ribs that will one day turn him into a portly man. I have discovered my husband is gay. She has also discovered that she has no intention of saying these words to Knight. This is a fact between herself and Lance; loyalty is owed here still.

She says, Your wife will have to have tests. Scans and things. They'll find out the sex of the baby. Will you want to know?

God. I've never thought of it.

Don't, she says, for your sake and everybody else's. Some things should not be known until the suitable moment.

You know, she says, something like this, Gavin's death I mean, it's marking a change. I don't think it's doing the changing, but it's marking it. Like a buoy in rough seas.

Emmie. Knight turns to face her. I don't want things to change. I want this to stay the same.

It's not, already. You're a father-to-be. She knows she's being disingenuous here, because it's Lance as well, but of course he doesn't, and then she goes on to offer him a pure if hypothetical honesty. You know, she says, I've sometimes imagined another life in which we were together, we left our spouses and went off and were just us. Black puddings forever. I knew it wouldn't happen, but it was a nice thing to think of. A kind of alternative scenario for the story of my life, that I could live in sometimes.

I did too. The same thing. I didn't think you would. I thought it would be only me that would think that.

What if you asked me?

Would you say yes?

The room fills with sadness like a glass with wine. Wine to sip, and taste, and discuss the vintage, remember the valley where the grapes grew, the view of the mountains beyond, the conversation of the winemaker proud of his skill. To hold up to the light, to admire its colour, its texture in the glass, the bouquet, to sip and sip and taste every mouthful and when it is drunk sigh and put the glass down and regret that it is finished and go on to the next thing. A sadness of rare and excellent vintage.

Though this is not necessarily the last bottle. The cellar is not empty yet.

They put on their clothes and step out into a violet dusk and go their separate ways.

A Little Goldmine

The day was set for the inquest. It's really quite routine, said the lawyer. Susie thought she heard doubt in his voice. She took Emmanuelle with her to help buy a black dress, something sober but fetching. She looked at herself in the fitting room mirror and thought is this the image of a grieving wife? She felt sad and tired, hardly able even to remember the passionate desire to possess aroused by Gavin's leaving. She kept thinking Poor Gavin, as a kind of reproach to herself, and then remembered there was Nicole to mourn him. Poor Gavin, his life not lived, his hopes unflowered. She concentrated on thinking these thoughts because she didn't want to consider that she might be going to have feelings of relief, the house all hers, the business ... Poor Gavin. Her eyes filled with tears as she turned to look at the fit of the dress round her hips. It was black wool crepe, high-necked and demure, not dowdy but not too smart either, sexy if you wanted to find it so but not blatant about it. For all these reasons it cost a lot of money.

A good investment, said the saleswoman. Yes, thought Susie, if it saves me from a manslaughter charge. Or murder. She shivered, and the tears welled. A classic like this, the woman went on, you can wear it for years. Years, said Susie, and at this the saleswoman noticed her distress. Oh dear, she said. A mourning ... ?

Emmanuelle nodded. A loved one, said the woman. Oh dear, I'm sorry.

Murder, said Susie, when they were alone in the lift. Murder. Or manslaughter. And all I've got to save me is a little black dress.

You've got a good lawyer, said Emmanuelle. And an innocent heart.

I don't know, said Susie. I don't like to look at my heart. It worries me.

It's innocent, said Emmanuelle. I've looked at it, I know.

To cheer Susie up she told her Miss Forbes' maxim, about the sense of being well-dressed producing a feeling of inner tranquillity that religion is powerless to bestow, but she was too preoccupied to be much amused. Emmanuelle was uneasy about her own behaviour. She wondered if she should have lied, said she was there when it happened, that Gavin turned and tripped and fell on the glass, all without any intent or action on Susie's part. But she hadn't thought of it soon enough, and then she was afraid if she said such a thing she would be caught out, the ambulance men would know that she hadn't been there, or the police would work it out, or some busybody would tell them. No point in lying if you get found out.

There was already one lie going on. Sam Cropp the lawyer had told Susie not to say that Gavin had left her. That could be damaging. He told her to admit to an argument, that should be all right, an argument about selling the house, Gavin wanting to and Susie disagreeing, that way there was a bit of anger flying round but not of a murderous kind. You don't kill your husband because you don't want to sell a house. And of course you're telling the truth, said Sam Cropp, you were arguing about selling the house. We're just not mentioning the context.

What about Nicole, said Susie. She won't keep quiet about that. Why should she?

Aah, said Sam Cropp. I take your point there. Mmm. Yes. A sticky one.

What about offering her a bribe, said Lance.

What of? Susie said.

Dangerous, said Emmanuelle. Might put the idea in her head.

Money, said Lance. Money makes a good bribe.

But I don't know whether I have any. If the verdict is ... isn't in my favour, well, what happens to the money?

Nathan, I expect.

Sam Cropp said the idea didn't seem to be in Nicole's head. At least there was no evidence of it so far. Maybe Susie should lie low. Keep mum.

Lie low, said Susie. Lilos I have known.

Emmanuelle and Susie smiled in one another's eyes. Sam Cropp said Pardon? Lance said, Have you tried thinking from Nicole's point of view?

She must be pretty distraught, said Susie. Seeing everything within her grasp then losing it.

Gavin, don't you mean? Losing him? said Lance.

Gavin, and life with Gavin. Being his wife, all that, said Susie. It's not just a person.

So, she will be prostrate. Desolate. Her heart broken, said Lance.

Yeah, said Susie. Something like that.

Susie seemed to go out quite often, messages, shopping, visiting her mother, organising Nathan's life, but Emmanuelle didn't have the solitude she'd had before when she sat in her yellow chair and read in a slow thoughtful way and pondered what the words said. She no longer went to the bookroom, there always seemed to be some activity crackling through the house that needed her attention. And she and Lance had still not talked. Sometimes they looked at one another across the hubbub around them, caught one another's eyes in the conscious gaze of lovers which says, later there will be time for the real conversation, at the moment we are here and it is quite amusing, the serious will wait, there is no hurry. Luxurious in their patience. Emmanuelle often thought of the irony of this patience, now; now that they weren't lovers and their marriage only a form, but still its peacefulness soothed her; how ironic, she said to herself, and accepted it.

The evenings were like dinner parties. Susie sat over meals and there was a lot of talk, sometimes not cheerful but always energetic. Occasionally laughter, though Susie's didn't trumpet in the old way. Lance opened more bottles of wine, Emmanuelle made coffee, Susie brought chocolates. I should go back to my own house, said Susie, but she didn't, except to get more clothes. The inquest seemed a distant event.

One morning when Susie was putting the breakfast dishes in the dishwasher and Emmanuelle was making more coffee there was a knock at the front door. Emmanuelle opened it to a young woman with long brown hair and round smoky glasses. I'd like to see Mrs Prothero, she said, in a quiet firm voice. Emmanuelle asked, Who shall I say, though she thought she knew. My name's Karabalis, said the woman.

Karabalis turned out to be Nicole's surname. Susie recognised her, not so much because she remembered her face from the livid Polaroid photograph but because Nicole was who she had to be.

Emmanuelle said, I'm making some coffee, why don't we go into the kitchen and have it? Thinking that blackmail might be more difficult in a kitchen. That threats would not fit with a homely place of women's work. Though of course there is nothing queasy about kitchens, sites of knives and blood and the dailiness of dirty dishes. Inexorable the work of kitchens and entirely unsentimental.

Nicole sat at the table. She had a very pretty round chin that she stuck out at them, while she kept her eyes lowered, fixed on her hands with fingers plaited and clasped tight so they looked like pinkish sun-starved plants. Emmanuelle poured the coffee and Susie leant against the sink, waiting. Her head was tipped to one side and she examined the young woman's face, her thin cheeks and narrow mouth, the round chin and clean brown hair. Susie's expression said: So this is she ... No wonder Nicole kept her eyes downcast.

I know you'll think I'm cheeky coming here, she said. I thought you might not want to talk to me, so I didn't phone. She paused, but nobody else spoke, so she went on. Gavin, Gavin was in love with me. He wanted to marry me. He's dead now and he can't. I wanted to marry him too.

Nicole kept stopping, as though she wanted her words to stay in the air, not be chased away by the next sentence.

I was fond of him, she said, but I wasn't in love with him. It was what we did. I mean the business ... that business was as much me as him. In recent years. More. It wouldn't have happened the way it was without me. People thought I was the secretary but I wasn't. I made it work. Gavin knew the computers, but otherwise ... That's why I wanted to marry him.

Nicole's plaited fingers were twisted so tight and pinkish pale they looked like water lily roots.

Well, I can't now. I have no rights. But there's one thing ... if I were to say that Gavin had left you, was living with me, well, they might not think his death was an accident. They might think you were mad with him for leaving you and so you decided to kill him.

Might they, said Susie.

Yes, said Nicole. At last she looked up. I'm good at that business, she said. It needs somebody who is. I could keep on being. If I was a partner, well, I'd run it, I'd do the work. It'd be a little goldmine for us to share.

I was thinking of selling it, said Susie. Buying a dress shop.

Oh no. No. Nicole's lilyroot fingers untwisted and clutched the tabletop. No. That would be a crime. A terrible thing. You'd be mad.

Would I, said Susie.

Yes. A dress shop is more business than dresses. You might know dresses but do you know business? It would be a risk. I know. Whereas Computer King ... I know what's happened in the four years I've been there, it's going from strength to strength even with the recession, and that's mostly in fact I could say entirely my doing.

Dresses are more interesting than computers, said Susie.

Not when you go bankrupt. Or you're in gaol. Nicole stuck her chin out, her shapely round and rosy chin, the prettiest part of her face it was, and looked with her neat hazel eyes at Susie. I think I should tell people about Gavin not living with you any more, about Gavin divorcing you and marrying me. It's better to tell the truth in the long run.

Blackmail, said Susie. Hmm. I was wondering how to blackmail you, and now I see it's you blackmailing me.

Blackmail me? said Nicole. Ah, so I wouldn't tell people about me and Gavin. So you saw the danger in that, too.

She is sharp, thought Emmanuelle.

Nicole was smiling. Not a triumphant smile, or one that made judgments of irony or anger, a smile that was pleased to understand. It didn't make her any prettier, but it made you interested in her. So, she said, and here I am offering it to you on a plate. Isn't that kind of me.

And somehow it seemed that it was. Susie said, I don't suppose I want a dress shop. Though I had thought of it. I suppose this might be a better idea. Mutual blackmail. Maybe we deserve each other.

Emmanuelle had been wondering what it was about Nicole that had made Gavin leave his wife for her. Now she understood the passion for something outside themselves, the business they were constructing which had its own life and theirs was part of it and there was no place for Susie. It was love on common ground. Otherwise, Nicole was young, her flesh was new, and taut across her bones, her skin had a bloom like a newly picked fruit, she was sexy in the way that babies are, good at making adults want to kiss their necks and cheeks and hair, greedy for their innocence. But women know and so do men that this bloom fades, and that would leave

Nicole a slight pleasant woman and nondescript. But then when she shouted No and was passionate and smiled it was easy to see how her spirit would charm people, they'd think they were cleverer than this ordinary young woman but the charm would be coils of iron and that could turn out to be pleasurable too, you'd be caught and not want to escape. And cool Nicole would have her way.

Like now with Susie. And Emmanuelle too. Though she did think to ask should they believe Nicole was good at the business just because she told them so. How could they be certain?

You can't really, said Nicole. You just have to take the risk. Though you could check that it's done super well in the past three years or so.

That's true, said Susie. That's how we could buy the house. I remember Gavin saying he was quite pleased.

He took me on, said Nicole, he called me his secretary but really I was there to organise the place, keep things in order, you know, and he didn't have to pay me much because I came straight from school. And that's the thing, I still don't have any qualifications, not on paper. He gave me raises because he knew I did good work but still it wasn't like being a real partner, though really I was, I learned the business and the computers too, I've got a knack for them, I'm a good trouble-shooter, and when he wanted us to go together I thought why not, we should be partners, I really wanted us to be partners. You'll see that I'll do a good job, we'll prosper, see if we don't.

Partners, said Susie. Prothero and Karabalis.

Prothero Wife and Mistress, muttered Emmanuelle, or do I mean Widow and Mistress. But so softly they didn't have to take any notice.

What about alphabetical order? said Nicole.

No, said Susie. Partnership, okay. Equal shares. But Prothero was there first.

All right, said Nicole.

We'd better get Sam Cropp and do it all legally. Could be good fun. Maybe I'll make a brilliant businessperson.

I thought you'd be a sleeping partner, said Emmanuelle.

Susie giggled. Maybe the odd nap. But otherwise, I intend to rise and shine.

I think we'll make a good team. Nicole smiled, and for a moment the brightness of her smiling teeth dazzled the older women.

You'll have to watch her, said Emmanuelle, when she'd gone.

I know, said Susie. But I'm sure she's sincere.

Sincere, oh yes. But single-minded. And selfish.

No harm in that. So am I, from now on.

Susie began to smile in a broad and uncontrollable way. What's funny, asked Emmanuelle.

Not funny, said Susie. But still her lips curved, though she tried to look solemn. Poor Gavin, she said. He thought Nicole was in love with him. Life plays terrible jokes on people.

I think you're enjoying this one.

I'm trying not to.

Emmanuelle examined her. The smile was bright, but it wobbled. Her eyes shone with tears.

Gloating is a word that comes to mind.

She was in love with him, in her way.

Oh, in her way.

You sound like Maud when you say gloating. I'm trying not to. Part of me feels very sad.

For the vanity of human hopes.

Mmm. Tell me, Em, how does it feel, to have such neat words for everything? Always the right phrase.

Other people's. Not mine. So they're a comfort, I suppose. Shows somebody's BTDT.

What's that mean?

Been there, done that. So Maud says. It's the thing at school.

Later in the day Emmanuelle took the train into town, since Stuart had the day off. For a change she walked up to the station. The suburb was very still, the stillness made denser by the sound of birds singing through the leafless air. The houses were folded in behind their cosseting gardens. There were no people at all. She walked past the police station at the top of the avenue and through the subway under the highway and over the footbridge to the railway station. Its shiny new paint and clean polished appearance made it look like part of a model train set, in contrast to the melancholy of the closed shops on the highway, the now derelict and always gimcrack buildings with zigzag awnings, empty and broken-windowed, waiting for demolition. There were a couple of arty shops, gamely, grimly hanging on through shrunken opening hours; they seemed likely to give up soon. Whenever Lou came to visit she mourned the pretty useful shops of her day. Things change, said Emmanuelle. People drive these days, to Chatswood or Turramurra. They change, yes, says Lou, but they don't improve.

Emmanuelle stood under the fretted awning of the railway station. The wooden hands on the clock said that the next train was due five minutes ago. She likes change. There's a kind of excitement in it, even if it's bad. It might make you feel a bit breathless and sick, but it also makes you sharp and edgy and conscious of life happening.

She sat on the top storey of the train and looked at the familiar scenes along the line. The swags of greenery against the patterned sandstone of the cuttings. The muscular eucalypts that were taller than the carriages even when the line was elevated. Coral trees with scarlet vigorous fingers clutching handfuls of sky. The blue glass secretive towers of Chatswood. As the train pulled into Artarmon she caught sight of a man running for the train and knew she wouldn't see if he caught it, a man with his arm in a yellow sling and running with immense leaping strides, so as to make you feel nervous for his injury. You saw things from trains, a bedroom window a long arm's reach away, with tumbled sheets and peacock feathers in a vase, two people on a staircase arguing, a couple of old women walking stiffly and talking to one another with animated schoolgirl faces, a child slyly picking up a stone, and they were all fragments of a narrative that for you would never have a beginning or an end, no matter how you longed to know what happened, that were moments spun from a turning planet into the void, but of immense importance to the people whose outcomes would follow.

Often the line ran close to the highway, and in one place there were buildings with fancy brick fronts facing on to the road and behind corrugated iron sheds with rounded roofs, Nissen huts they probably were. In the next seat was a man in a wide-brimmed hat of stiffened tweed sitting beside a schoolboy with fair hair flopping fashionably over one eye. The man tapped on the window with a knobbled stick. There, he said, you can see the truth behind the facades, and pointed at the Nissen huts.

Is it a good truth, or a bad, asked Emmanuelle, but the man took no notice. Fancy brick where it shows, he said, and look at the back. Look at it.

The curved corrugated iron of the huts seemed to grow out of the lush hillside of long bright grasses and ivy and tumbled paling fences in the grip of morning glory. They were shabby, Emmanuelle could see that, and they were beautiful too. More beautiful than the stepped and figured gingery brick fronts on the highway. After Wolstonecraft the city appeared from time to time ahead, beyond the bays and inlets of the harbour, still distant enough to be an entity, an intricately modelled work of art in which high rise buildings and smog and narrow streets did not have to be suffered but could be understood as a marvellous creation.

The train was a shiny new red and blue one, befitting the prettily painted, flower-bedded stations it passed through, but there were already graffiti on its gleaming white enamelled walls. Emmanuelle took a fine felt-tipped pen out of her bag and wrote in neat large letters: The truth is many. The fair-haired schoolboy watched her with astonished eyes. With a grave flourish of her hand, she offered him the words.

Small Gifts

What was going on between Lance and Emmanuelle was a courtship of separation. Those long looks across crowded rooms, knowing, promising, melancholy, postponing the moment when the sharpness of yes or no, of acceptance of refusal, would change everything, would bring energy and excitement, or desolation and emptiness: they knew they were temporary, that they couldn't stay in this luxury forever.

Why not? Lance asked himself. He discerned that what counts is to live in important moments, whether they are happy or sad. That is why a funeral is a good thing, before the long empty days that will follow the death. These were important moments, and he savoured them, though they were threaded with pain. There was a hard grace in them. The pleasure of making love to Stuart now seemed over-ripe and pulpy, like tropical fruits whose deliciousness is the decay they verge on. Now was like walking along a beach on a grey day, the sky and sea drained of colour and a salty sting in the breeze; a more temperate and yet harsher beauty. He walked there, in his lean frame so much stronger now thanks to Stuart, walked strict and solitary, and Stuart went with him in the fleshy scented shape of a romantic memory, Lance almost grateful that he needn't be a presence; safer to wish he was and know he wouldn't be.

He brought Emmanuelle gifts, things that said to her, see, I know what you like; and he was right. An orchid in a blue and white pot, with spikes of creamy thick-petalled flowers. A book about water gardens. A compact disc of Kathleen Ferrier singing the songs Lou sang. A yellow lacquer box patterned with lilies. Things he came across, picked up, happened to notice. Whose message was, I think about you a lot. She took them with only the faintest eyebrow raise of irony; she knew her role was to smile and accept with pretty distant manners.

Mel bent close to the orchid and sniffed it before she remembered it would have no smell, just a slight vegetable odour. She pressed her lips to one of the waxy blooms and imagined it was someone's flesh she was kissing. She knocked it off and when she picked it up she wanted to squeeze it, crush it, tear it.

She had finally believed Stuart when he told her he wasn't having an affair with Emmanuelle, that it was Lance who was the person to blackmail: Believe me, I know, he said, over and over, with a kind of laugh she hated hearing. She hated everything, the stupid phone calls with Bianca, the meaningless train trips, the pretence of hotel school, the embarrassment of being wrong about her employers' sex lives, she was so full of hatred for these things she couldn't hold it in any more. She decided to tell Emmanuelle the truth.

They were in the kitchen. The children were in the playroom watching television. Emmanuelle was slicing garlic cloves and sticking them in a leg of lamb. Mel stood in the middle of the room and blurted it out. She said It's a lie that I've been doing any courses. I was only pretending. I've been deceiving you. Emmanuelle stood astonished and watched her for a moment, dragging out all these punishing words. Oh my poor Mel, she said. She wanted to go over and hug her, but there was something in the bleak way the girl stood, straight and with her legs braced, with her head at a stiff angle, that stopped her. It also reminded her of something.

Emmanuelle went over to her and took her hand and led her

to the table. Sit down, she said. Let's have a cup of tea. Tea. What can tea do for us? Oh dear. Oh Mel, I wish you'd told me at the beginning.

They wouldn't have me, said Mel. There were all these pretty girls, slim, with really nice manners, what chance did I have.

Mel was sitting down now, but she still held her head up. Her eyes were full of tears but she wasn't letting them fall.

I should have known, said Emmanuelle. I should have realised that you couldn't have been going ... that hospitality courses don't work like that ... I haven't been good to you, have I. You've been so good to us, and how have we repaid you.

You think I've been good?

Of course you have. You've been terrific with the children, they behave well with you. They love you. She paused. Is hotel work what you really want to do?

It seemed a good idea. There aren't a lot of things you can get into, with my qualifications.

What are they, exactly?

I didn't even finish high school.

Mel, what do you really want to do? What would be your dearest wish for yourself in the future?

My excellent wish-list, you mean? That's what Bianca's boss is always talking about. The electorate's excellent wish-list. She turned her face away from Emmanuelle, and stared at the orchids with dull eyes. I don't know, she said. I can't think of a single thing to wish for.

Emmanuelle looked at her pale brown face, her dark wiry hair, the fierce line of her brows. She saw the fine blue lines of a tattoo across her cheek. Not in fact, she was remembering from a painting she'd seen at the Gallery, of a Maori princess, so it said, a young warrior-like woman with a spear and her face tattooed in bands across her cheeks and chin, defiant and fierce-browed; this was what Mel reminded her of.

She said, We have to mend that. We have to find you something to wish for.

Mel frowned.

I know, said Emmanuelle. What about driving? What if we get you some driving lessons? That'll be a start. I reckon you'll make a good driver.

That's not a career, said Mel, but she looked pleased. Then she said, You mean like Stuart?

Emmanuelle shook her head. A career might take a little more thought. But driving could be something to wish for, in the meantime.

How can I? I didn't finish school.

Were you good at school?

A smile slid across her face. Sometimes.

Sometimes?

If I wanted to be.

Do you think you might want to be now?

It's too late.

You like reading, don't you?

Yeah. But just for fun.

You're a bright girl. What about going to college? Or university?

Mel flounced her shoulders. That's not for people like me.

Why not, if you're clever enough? All sorts of people much thicker than you go on to study these days. You could have a go at getting university entrance. I'm pretty sure there are courses you can do, if you missed out on the first round. It'd give you a breathing space, to work out what you really want. Instead of pretending to go to hotel school, you could do that.

I thought you'd give me the boot.

Why? When you do a good job.

I lied to you.

Well. You only have to think about your own lies, and you can understand other people's. The truth is many, she said, with a small smile remembering the train.

Would it be as easy as that? Mel's voice was full of wonder. Stay here and go to courses, and then get into university?

Not easy. Bloody hard work. But it could be done. If you want to.

Mel leaned her elbows on the table and let her body sag. Emmanuelle got up and put her arms around her. I'm sorry you've had such a hard time, she said. Mel began to cry. Not all her anger washed away with her tears, but a bit of it did.

Emmanuelle went up to her bookroom and found the book on colonial art with the painting of the Maori princess. She looked more like a chief, a kind of Boadicea. The resemblance was striking. She wondered how to go about showing it to Mel.

In the end she took the book downstairs and sat at the kitchen table reading it. When Maud came in after 'Playschool' she leant on her mother and looked over her shoulder. Who's that, she asked. She's a Maori princess, said Emmanuelle. Isn't she beautiful? She looks like Mel, said Maud. Except for the patterns on her face. She went up to Mel and stroked her cheeks. That would be nice, she said. Blue patterns on your skin. Like face painting.

William came and looked too. She's got legs like Mel, he said.

Do I really look like her, asked Mel.

Yes, said Emmanuelle.

Maybe you're a Maori princess, said Maud.

Mel screwed up her face. A princess? Yeah, for sure.

I don't know about the princess bit, said Emmanuelle. That's a colonial thing, anyway, if you read this book. This woman's probably a warrior or something. But what about being ... Maori?

I wouldn't know, would I. Never had any relations ... Maybe, Mel said. Maybe that's what I am. How would you find out?

When Lance came in they were all in the study looking up encyclopaedias. He was in a sardonic mood because he'd been giving

Stuart his first lesson in how to play the stockmarket. He'd put together a small portfolio of shares for him to trade with. Don't do anything for a while, he told him, just watch them, read, learn. Check the financial pages regularly. At the moment they're nice and solid.

Will it be difficult, asked Stuart, squinting at the flimsy paper, the computer printouts, the rows of small black figures shimmering out of line.

Not when you get the knack, said Lance. And as I say, you can just leave them and they'll prosper, in their own way.

I was hoping to get really rich.

Well, when you understand it, and can sell high, buy low, said Lance. You've got to get the expertise though. No point in buying low if they drop lower.

Stuart looked wan. Lance said, Tell me something. Do you regard this as blackmail?

Blackmail? Did I ever say blackmail?

Possibly not. I think it's better to see it as the gesture of a grateful employer. Regard me as your benefactor. In a one-off sense. Of course, you should feel free to ask my advice at any time. See how you go.

What about the massages? said Stuart.

Yes. There doesn't seem to have been a lot of opportunity lately. And I reckon it's time I got back to work. Suddenly Lance gave him a sly smile. They were good massages, he said. I won't forget them.

Stuart looked pleased. Yeah? he said. Well, any time. He fanned through the papers Lance had given him. Thing is, he said, I'm thinking of getting married.

Oh? Anybody I know?

Mel. I think we'd make a good little team. We could both move into my flat ... any obs?

Pardon? Oh, objections. Well ... I suppose I did think you might be moving on soon. I mean, when I'm pronounced fit to drive, and now Emmanuelle's got her licence again.

Aw, said Stuart. Out of a job then.

Well, we'll have to see. There's the firm. No hurry though. Anyway, you might have made your fortune by then.

Stuart looked wan again. Lance's expression was suddenly contrite. But I'm not congratulating you. You and Mel. Wonderful news. I hope you'll be very happy.

Yeah. She hasn't said yes yet. I reckon she will, but.

When Lance found Mel pink-faced and bright-eyed in the study with the rest of his family he took her hand and kissed her formally on each of her rosy cheeks. I believe felicitations are in order, he said. Mel looked bemused, and Emmanuelle asked why?

The marriage ... I've just heard you're getting married, to Stuart.

What! I wouldn't marry him if ... if he was the richest man in the world.

He has plans, said Lance gravely.

I wouldn't marry him if he was the last man on earth.

I see, said Lance.

Has he asked you? said Emmanuelle.

I could be bridesmaid, said Maud, twirling her skirt.

What about me, said William.

They don't have boy bridesmaids, said Maud.

Well, I suppose he did, growled Mel. But I didn't say yes.

Did you say no?

I wasn't sure he meant it. I don't want to get married. I'm not ready for it. And not to Stuart. Ever.

Good idea, said Lance.

I'm planning a quite different life, said Mel.

At that moment Susie and Nathan came home. She'd brought a tray of chocolate eclairs for dinner, proper ones with yellow pastry cream inside. It was easy to have doubts about Susie continuing to fit into her new svelte clothes. Maybe even the inquest dress could be in danger of becoming too tight.

Birthday

I keep having this dream, said Emmanuelle. Of not being able to see. It's not my sight that's gone wrong, it's my eyelids that are all gummed up. Stuck together. Sometimes I manage to prise open just a slit, and it's all sticky and gluey and I still can't see, it's a tremendous effort, in fact I think it's one of those effort dreams, when you can't make something work, you try and try and it doesn't work.

I should be the one with the bad eye dreams, said Susie. I'm the one who's practically blind.

And then, when I do wake up, said Emmanuelle, I still think it's so, I'm too worried to open my eyes, I think they'll be stuck up with glue, all milky and opaque, and then when I finally manage it I'm surprised, I can see after all.

The lunch party for Lance's birthday was to be elaborate. Emmanuelle supposed that food in Alaska would be blubbery and bland, so she wanted to welcome back Lou and Percy with food full of colour and spicy flavours. It was like old times, making lists, starting days ahead, shopping. There was a boned fowl stuffed with pistachio nuts and ham and chicken mince, grilled peppers loaded with garlic, quail split and marinating in thyme and juniper berries, a bowl of tiny potatoes to eat hot with aioli and celery and radishes, slices of raw cured tuna with sweet onion and dill and horseradish, frangipani tarts with sliced pears in precise glazed patterns, smelly Milawa cheeses and walnut bread, miniature tomatoes with hot-house basil and heavy green olive oil, asparagus on an oval platter with shaved Parmesan cheese, strawberries sprinkled with balsamic vinegar. And of course a birthday cake with at Maud's insistence enough candles. It was a feast, it was far too much, five adults and three children would never eat it. It was a gesture of lavishness and hospitality, grand, excessive, and an offering of love of an intimate kind. She'd chosen the favourite dishes of everybody involved, even the children, who'd been asked what they liked best in the world. Nathan had said McDonald's. Emmanuelle regarded all this bounty with ancient housewifely satisfaction. The tiled shelves of the larder, a chilly room out of reach of the sun, with windows open to the cold winter air, were laden with bowls and platters and baskets of food, to be assembled at the last minute. The mistress of such an array of goodness must be a happy woman, prosperity and comfort were in her grasp, the world could hold no wicked surprises. And indeed Emmanuelle has sometimes felt like her old self in these days like the old days, the self who saw with clarity a fruitful present and expected the future to emulate it, a self whose discontents, even, were innocent. But she isn't her old self, the context in which that person flourished has gone forever. It's merely pleasant to recapture it, briefly, and try to forget how irrelevant it all is, now. If there is a valedictory quality about it that may be because all feasts are poten-tially the last; tomorrow we die is always on the cards.

She went to bed with everything done that could be, her back aching and her calves sore, and dreamed of eyes too gummed up to open, and woke with pleased surprise that she could see, and put on a yellow silk kimono that Lance had given her years ago and took his present to him in bed.

He likes it, she knew he would. He brushes delicate fingertips across the sketchy couple. Amazing, he says. So few strokes, and how alive they are. He turns it over. Ah, Moustiers. Faience de Moustiers. Do you remember, the little village in Provence? Moustiers Sainte Marie, it was called. We ate chicken with lavender honey. Poulet fermier au lavande de miel. Remember how strange it sounded and how good it tasted? And in the afternoon we went to the museum and looked at stuff like this? Oh, and there was a gorge with a huge chain across, put there by some chap coming back from the crusades, after years in captivity ... some sort of vow. Remember?

Remember. Remembering's no help when it's now you're trying to make sense of, she mutters.

Now, says Lance. Now's our talk. Isn't it.

His fingers trace the scalloped edge of the plate. His eyes watch, the lids downcast. These are what break your heart, the curled hand, the thick black lashes, break your heart and you sit and weep for the loss of them. Your body sits on the end of a bed, pensive and dry-eyed, the weeping is inside and the pieces of your broken heart slosh around in its salty tides.

Ingrown weeping. Like ingrown toenails. Hard to take seriously, unless you're the sufferer. You sit cross-legged on the end of a bed, the yellow silk rests like a sigh against your knee, somebody unravelled the cocoons of how many grubs to spin threads and weave this fabric, somebody drew patterns of white curly-headed peonies to print on it, and maybe their hearts cracked and sloshed around in tears and the sharp edges pierced the delicate inner flesh of their bodies, but still the silk was made and it remains, it is beautiful however unhappy the humans who wove and sewed and bought and wore it. As the man and woman are sharp and full of life on the faience plate though the person who painted them has been dead these two hundred years and doubtless knew misery in life. Rest your hand on yellow silk, lay your fingers on the scalloped edge of a painted plate; you know what they are and they will remain so. And for a moment you may believe this is enough. For several moments, if it is the round eyes and poignant stony breastbones of the

Wandjina that you contemplate. That you've kept for yourself instead of giving to your husband for his birthday.

Lance said, I am not any good at talking. I've looked at you and known that I should say ... But I don't. It's cowardice. Self-indulgence. Postponement. He paused, listening to all these words, offering himself performing them. And of course you know, that Stuart and I ...

Emmanuelle was generous. Yes, she said. I saw you, one day, by the pool. The day I ran over the dog. And the old man wailed.

A purplish smudge mottled Lance's neck and the soft skin of his jaw, his cheeks. But he said, Ran over a dog?

I didn't get around to telling you. Because of what I saw. It was only a glimpse, I didn't watch.

That, what you saw, I think it's true, about me. I wondered if it was a kind of adventure, part of coming out of the stroke, trying different things, and soon I'd be myself again, and that would be behind, part of the illness, like, like, well, you know ... that terrible lunch in the garden. But I don't think it is ... part of the stroke, somehow. I mean I think I have to say that I'm starting to be myself again, but, well, your self changes, I'm not that old self any more, not exactly. I don't mean I'm in love with Stuart. Though for a while I thought I was. But Stuart isn't the point. It's me. I think I am ... His words seemed to come out of an old worn-out machine that could hardly turn them out any more, however much effort the operator makes. I have to get used to the names, he said.

Emmanuelle didn't say anything. It seemed a kind of punishment that Lance who had so long avoided talking about feelings should now have such difficult ones to articulate. She didn't want to help him. But after a pause she spoke.

What are you going to do?

He gazed at her. He pinched his bottom lip between his teeth. What if I said, nothing?

Nothing ...

The plate lay on the bed beside them, the sketchy man and woman. The happy couple, Lance said. We're a happy couple, in our way. We like one another. Don't we? We could go on like this.

Emmanuelle unfolded her legs. She had been sitting on the opposite side of the bed from Lance. She got off and began to walk across the room, back and forth.

It's hardly a marriage.

It could be one version.

What about sex?

Sex, sighed Lance. I don't feel much interested. Friendship seems more important, the way I feel now.

And what about me?

I thought you might value friendship too.

If you never make love to someone it's hard to stop being angry with them. Sex dissolves anger.

Friends cope.

Emmanuelle's pacing was turning into stamping, she was walking faster and harder, swinging sharply at each end. Homosexual men are notoriously promiscuous, she said. I suppose you'll expect to take lovers whenever you feel like it.

That's not what I'm saying, not now anyway. I am saying ... celibate. Do you mean you think that's what you'll want? Taking a lover?

Emmanuelle stopped pacing and looked out the window, so her back was turned to Lance. Lucky she'd decided not to have lunch outside, it was raining, in great slanting lines that smashed as they hit the terrace. She considered saying I already have one, but then thought that maybe cunning was more important than honesty.

Men go to gay bars and pick people up, she said, still with her back to him. Rough trade, isn't that what it's called? Is Stuart rough trade?

I don't know.

They were both looking out at the rain, at the grey sky and the grey slanting rain, at the cold puddles and the sodden lawns.

I don't know about the future, said Lance. I can't foresee it and I reckon promises are dangerous. I don't know about my health, except that I can't trust it. I just think that this now is good, and we should let it go on and see what happens, not smash it up in any drastic way.

What if I want a divorce?

Then you must have one, of course.

The irony was a gift. She took it with a small smile, turning back into the room. Her gown was brightly yellow against the grey rain outside.

Would we have conversations?

We always have.

No. That's the point. There was a time when you were too busy to talk.

Not now. We talk now.

I don't know, she said. It's all too hard for me. We're having people for lunch.

The family, he said. Families are not to be sneezed at. Children. A fruitful life.

Lou and Percy are in love with one another. They have been for fifty years.

I know. I don't think I can give you that kind of passion. But I do love you dearly.

And if I want to be in love?

I don't know what you can do about that. Do you?

You're hard, she said.

We all have to get on as best we can. I'm offering company and affection and faith and a good life together.

Bleak but honest.

I like the truth, said Lance.

I'd better go and get on with lunch, she said. It was a temporary comfort that she hadn't offered him her own truth. Knight was a secret she wasn't yet ready to tell. She took his hand and kissed it. Happy birthday.

The fire burned once in the fireplace and a second time in reflection in the windows, sketching its yellow flames against the grey rain. It was necessary to have the lamps lit, so it seemed like night; the dining room was a place of gleaming surfaces designed to keep the dark at bay, to encircle in their own space of light and warmth the circle of people who sat in an intertwining of backs and elbows and turned their smiling faces upon one another, as though they were knitted together against whatever lay outside. This was the first time they'd used this room since Lance's stroke, it had sat, Magda-polished and deserted, through all those months. Soon the season would be spring again, and a year passed, and maybe by that anniversary it would be possible to say, Lance is cured. But not, Lance is his old self again.

Emmanuelle watched him, watched Lou and her regarding of him, saw doubt turn to relief. Ooh, you look so well, she said. The shock was Percy, so lean, his hands and neck all sinew; even under his clothes his arms and legs seemed made of cords and blades of bone, without flesh. His eyes were so sunken into his head it was like looking into a cave for the distant silty shine of a pool or patch of water in its depths. He seemed well, and said he was, Lou was cheerful and didn't fuss, but her attention was like a small ghostly manikin of herself hovering at his shoulder. When they were in the kitchen together before lunch Emmanuelle asked her if Percy was still the man she'd married. Lou said in a suspicious way, What do you mean? Emmanuelle wanted to know had he changed in any drastic inner way, or was he still basically the same person.

Well, he's got older of course, who hasn't, but underneath he's the same lovely old Percy. Why do you ask?

Emmanuelle had meant this to be a way of talking about Lance, but Lou fixed it on Percy. I suppose people do change, she said, but you change along with them so it doesn't really register. Fifty-three years this year, she said, you grow together. She smiled as she said this, but there was a faint bluish shadow of anxiety in the planes of her face, in the tones of her voice. When Lance asked her about Alaska she said Oh, it was marvellous, we've got a lot of photographs, but had to be questioned closely on what they'd done. They'd bought Lance an Inuit sculpture of a seal, that was sturdy and solid to hold.

Emmanuelle asked what the food was like. Not a patch on this, said Percy. But he ate very little of it. Lou wanted to try a bit of everything. The galantine is a triumph, she said.

What's galantine? asked William.

It's a boned fowl, boned and stuffed, said Lou.

What's that mean?

You get a chicken, and you take the bones out and you fill it up with nice things, chicken mince, and ham, and pistachio nuts, see the green pistachio nuts? Emmanuelle put a slice on his plate.

It looks like faded salami, said Maud.

William was suspicious. Where's its arms and legs?

They're there. But they've had the bones taken out, see? So you can slice it in nice round slices.

How does a chicken walk without any bones? asked William, but nobody else felt like getting involved in one of his circular question and answer conversations. He crammed a big piece of galantine into his mouth, chewed with three exaggerated bites and swallowed it. Suddenly his eyes bulged with panic and he began to choke. Emmanuelle stood him on his chair with his back to her and clutched him violently round the middle several times until a wad of food was dislodged and flung on to the front of Lance's jumper. William heaved several breaths that turned into sobs when he was sure he could manage them. Maud looked severe, and curious, and worried. Lance said in a fierce voice, There's a lesson for you! Maybe next time you'll chew food properly. William sobbed more loudly. Nathan joined in. Susie scraped the wad of food off Lance's jumper with a tissue. There's a bit of bone in it, she announced, a little thin sharp shard. The butcher didn't do a very good job.

Lance picked William up and hugged him. Emmanuelle said I think we should all sit down and go on with our lunch. Look, empty plates, empty glasses. She began pouring more wine.

At that moment there was a loud knock on the door. People exchanged nervous glances. Lance said I'll go, as though he expected burglars. There was a man in a red dinner suit and a black top hat, with a bunch of large silver balloons. Where's the birthday boy? he cried. Where's the party? He capered, his feet made clicking noises on the marble floor.

Come on, said Susie to Maud, and took her hand. Come on, she beckoned Lou and Percy, so they all followed her out to the hall, where the man stopped trying to do Fred Astaire taps, took off his hat, bowed from the waist and sang Happy Birthday in a serious tenor voice. Then he bowed again, and held out his hand with the balloons. But before Lance could take them he let go, so they all floated up to the ceiling and bobbed there, strings dangling. One trailed a long silver banner, saying Happy Birthday from Balloonaloon in gold letters. They all had smiling faces of different character.

This was Susie's present to Lance. He was pleased, in a dry way, but Maud and William and Nathan were thrilled. They counted them out, a third each, and moved them about all over the house. At first the balloons rested against the ceiling, then they dipped and swayed and batted; gradually they dropped lower and lower till you walked among them at knee and waist level as though you were being mobbed by heart-shaped grinning aliens, until finally they cowered on the floor, wizened and wrinkled and smelly, and even the children thought it time for them to go.

Miasma

When you lie in bed at night and your life seems full of intractable things you can sometimes will yourself to make them have happy outcomes. This is not difficult when there is something evident and important that you desire. So Susie can make the coroner bring in a report of accidental death. She inherits the money and the business without any problem and Nicole of the round dotted *is* runs it for her. This is easily sorted out. She can go on from there to consider selling the house, it's not a suitable house anymore and anyway the vibes are bad, and of course she gets an enormous price because it's just what somebody wants, she doesn't have to explain this yet, just specify a large sum, so she can buy a cottage in Darlinghurst, perhaps, with a secret tropical garden like the one she saw recently in *Vogue Living*, with whitewashed spaces and a tiled floor, or maybe an apartment of a spacious kind in a block overlooking Hyde Park with balconies and a doorman, or what about a terrace in Paddington, not the latest fashion but always desirable, and she could have enough left over from her enormous sum (no need to remember the chunk of this the current mortgage will take) to buy some neat designer shack at Pearl Beach, or possibly on the Hawkesbury, with access only by boat, and the svelte and slender

Susie will give marvellous parties and flash long brown legs in the disporting water and there will be beautiful men. This is wishful grazing; once you've butted your way through that first intractable, the inquest, the coroner's report, then whole fields of possibilities are yours to browse on, and their sweetness will distract you utterly.

For others it is not so easy. Lou organises Percy's health. The results of the tests are ... but this is already difficult. They can't be negative, there has to be something wrong, to account for Percy's thinness and tiredness, but it has to be easily remediable, so he can be completely cured, and Lou doesn't know what that will be, she tries to see Percy fattening and his energy coming back, she takes them to Venice and sits them in a gondola, to Paris and a pavement cafe, to Stratford upon Avon and Shakespeare, all the comfortable old classical tourist tricks they haven't done for years, but she can't stop Percy beside her getting thinner and frailer, she can't keep him in good flesh though she takes him to Vienna and they eat Sachertorte and coffee with extra cream. She tosses and groans but can't toss off the recalcitrant imagination, she tries to bring it back to the doctor, beaming, the results are fine most pleasing you'll be very happy, but what are they exactly says the recalcitrant imagination, I need to know what they are.

Lance in his small hours turns away from the future and tries to dwell on the past. The good things that have happened and why shouldn't they come again. He thinks of his children and how the world changed when they were born and what will become of them — see, that's the future, you meant to stay in the past. He thinks of the first time he saw Emmanuelle and the gravity of her beauty and how he desired it. At that time when he didn't know he was gay or queer or whatever word he must now use for himself, like Gary Shield he went to university with, seeing him in town the other day in jeans shrunk to his skin and a purple shirt open to the waist with a thick gold chain and a ring in his ear and pointed hand gestures, his hair shorn to a grey stubble over his bumpy skull; how did he recognise him? You could hope you wouldn't turn out like Gary Shield but was hoping for something not to happen the best outcome you could dream up for yourself? What about bodies and love and the wash of desire in the gut, should you dream of sex and not do it, or do it and not dream of it?

And what about your wife, can you expect her to stay when you offer so little, possessing her in your own way but what's in it for her?

And Emmanuelle. Emmanuelle lies and wonders how given absolute choice she would order her life. Choice she has: Lance has made his offer, she can take his or make her own. She thinks: if Lance were his old self, if Lance were not gay. But this is a cheat, you can't construct happy outcomes on wishing facts undone. This is bringing in magic, it's real flounder-fish wishing, remember what did for the old woman in the end was wanting to be God, if you get hold of the right translation that is, whereas what's needed is simply supposing that the way things will turn out is well, and then picturing what that well might be. Constructing scenarios. Best case scenarios, as Bianca's boss probably wouldn't say. If Fiona were not pregnant ... another cheat? Not necessarily. What if you were to organise a miscarriage for Fiona, which puts her off children and indeed marriage, so then Knight is free and you can make all sorts of pleasant opportunities out of that. But do you want to go off with Knight? A man whose first name you don't even know. Knight is a lover, in bed on afternoons in dull hotels, with sadness like wine to be sipped and savoured. Why not savour sadness with your husband? Why assume husbands are for being happy with? A melancholy celibacy could have its pleasures; what you need to do is perceive them. Or, why don't you try to understand the happiness, the cool grave kind like you, Emmanuelle, the happiness he is offering you. A thoughtful companion and two children whom both of you love, don't lose the force of it, love, a fine house and a fruitful life. A very house-and-garden view of the good life, tidied up to have its picture taken.

And what's wrong with that. Passion? Passion on a shoe-string?
Passion doesn't last and shoe-strings snap especially when you're
pulling yourself up by them. Shoe-strings, boot straps, laces. In a
fine pair of polished Beltrami brogues, you're fond of fine objects.
Why not passion as well in the picture-magazine house and garden
... ah, maybe you're grown up when you learn you can't have everything. You have to choose, the lot is not available. Except on ham-
burgers. You could be single again and live in a little house with a
garden that's all yours, a house like your bookroom plus kitchen
and bath, but how many bedrooms? who's in them? who's paying
for them? Maybe you should get a job make a career good enough
for Mel good enough for you. Back to publishing and the slush pile
and a salary so petite it was hard to take seriously ...

Choice you have: the world is all before you, where to choose. But Eve had
Adam, they were a couple, he wasn't a possibility of refusal. As
Knight isn't a possibility of choice, and neither is Lance if it's a real
husband you want. And all the choices that have been made since
Adam and Eve's day limit the number available to you now. Like the
choices your parents made, to bring you up dutiful for one, and it
worked, you are. You have a name that means God with us, and you
haven't given up on him yet, whatever you think of the church. You
believe in behaving well, out of pride maybe, self-regarding; should
you have wished for the gift of behaving badly? But you don't
suppose things can turn out well if you don't behave well, so you
have no faith in the usefulness of behaving badly. Though alas not
the reverse; you can't believe that behaving well will ensure things
turning out well.

> *So lulla lulla lulla lulla bye bye*
> *Dost thou want the moon to play with?*
> *Or the stars to run away with?*
> *They'll come if you don't cry*

So her father sang, and in his voice the moon and the stars were available for a good little girl, for a while. One day. Until she learned that some days don't ever come, and some offers are worth the love they are made with, nothing more. And if you are lucky, nothing less.

If you sing loving lullabies to your children, you can hope they'll remember them, and you.

In a city the size of Sydney where however many of you are lying sleepless in the small hours what miasma sighs and seeps into the already dirty air? That's not smog you see next day, it's exhalations of fear and desire and the sweat of wrestling with intractables. The day comes and you go tidily on your way doing one thing after another making an orderly life mostly but the miasma's there, you're breathing in it. They should put it on the television in a graph, miasma level: medium, high, extreme. Is it ever other than extreme? Maybe in the country where there's less of us like cars full of lead polluting the air.

Sometimes you lie awake until the sky whitens. Singing birds sound like a schoolyard of children before the bell goes. Maybe then you sleep, just as the early risers are springing up. When the alarm sounds you might have been asleep no more than a minute.

The alarm wakes Susie and Emmanuelle, still sleeping in the one big bed. Snow White and Rose Red, one in a white cotton nightie the other in black lace. This is why there are stereotypes, so people can fit into them. Their dead-of-night watchings overlapped, though neither let on. Emmanuelle could have wandered happily through Susie's outcomes, helping choose white muslin curtains for the cottage, or mushroom-coloured carpet for the flat, and gilt-finished wall sconces. Though Susie wouldn't have had much fun keeping Em company. Emmanuelle wonders why she doesn't tell her friend about her predicaments; sharing confidences is what bedmates do. She's had an idea of talking to Lou about Lance being gay, a wise and discreet woman and closely involved you could say, but now with this business of Percy's health she doesn't like to worry her more.

Susie stretches and yawns to rev herself up for getting out of bed. Emmanuelle says, You could say your wish came true, couldn't you.

You mean about getting thin? Hopefully it's not temporary.

No, not that. Remember when you told me about Gavin going off with Nicole, you said ... you said you'd sometimes wished that you were a widow, because then you could mourn his death ...

A silence grows between them, large, heavy, pressing against them.

Until Susie says, So you think I wished Gavin dead?

Well, you wished it, it happened.

But I didn't make it happen.

No, I'm not saying that.

And what about this limbo I'm living in now? Widow indeed, but maybe a murderer.

Susie! You know that's not going to happen.

Do I.

Yes.

Another silence hunkers down between them.

Susie says, What about your wishes? What have you wished for?

I once wished for the power to make dangerous choices.

Did you get it?

I don't know. I don't think I know where danger lies. Except ... well, I suppose you could say I did get it, because all choices are dangerous. Thing is, you don't find out just how much until after you've made them.

Have you ever wished Lance dead?

I've wished him different.

And did that come true?

Not in ways that I'd have chosen.

Maybe Lance would've. Oh shit. I didn't mean the stroke.

Mmm. Some of them I think he might've.

Emmanuelle got out of bed and went into the shower. She had a habit of taking long showers because once in there she started to think and forgot to come out. This morning she was pondering why she wanted to talk about Lance being gay to Lou and not to Susie. Because Lou was family, because Lou would have more sense of responsibility, she wasn't so frivolous as Susie ... Because she wouldn't want to break up the family. Aah. Does this mean that Emmanuelle wants her mother-in-law to tell her to stay where she is, is this what she wants to hear?

Just as likely to be the other way round, Susie saying stay put, Lou fearful of the absence of passion. It's Lou's idea that sex dissolves anger, that a marriage without sex is a marriage full of anger.

Have you drowned, shouts Susie. There are three starving children out here.

Emmanuelle thinks that being alive is like reading a book. You might think you've got a fair idea of the plot but you don't actually know what's going to happen next, you're as much a mystery to yourself as a character in a novel. Perhaps the secret is just to keep turning the pages.

In the kitchen Lance is making coffee. He looks at her with a faint hopeful smile. She likes being looked at by Lance. She looks back at him, repressing her smile into a little rueful twist. They have a great deal to say to one another still.

Do you think we'll ever sleep together again? she asks.

Lance looks dismayed, and blushes.

People can be bisexual, Emmanuelle goes on. I believe it's quite common. It's like being an urban person who's fond of bush walking.

Lance finds this very funny, which means he gives a little hoot of a laugh. Would you mind if we ... he's saying, when the children come in. Their faces fill with light when they observe their parents smiling. A bookroom solitude in a little house wouldn't be much fun for Maud and William. Not like Nathan disporting with his mother in the waters of the Hawkesbury.

During the afternoon the rain stopped and a tremulous sun shone out of the grey sky. Suddenly it was a quivery spring day; the bare tree branches swelled with glistening drops like new buds and the leaves of the eucalypts shed tiny cascades. The sky was nacreous as a pearl shell promising something precious out of irritation. Lance walked down the garden to the bush at the bottom of it and went a little way in, but the trees would shiver in the wind and shower water over his head and down his neck; he went as far as a stand of sapling pepper trees and came out again. He'd picked a sprig from one of them and snuffed in its cool spice smell, he breathed deeply and felt it fume up into his head and down into his lungs and enter his bloodstream, cleansing and quickening, so you could suppose. He remembered, but as a fact, not a sensation, the odours of rose and jasmine in Stuart's massage oils. How he had surrendered to the languor of them. Maybe he would again. You could look forward to things, and back on things, and the senses of them were much the same, they weren't happening now, but in an imagined other time. Now was the sharp exciting smell of the pepper tree in his nostrils, the rainy scent of a washed clean earth, and air so luminous he felt himself gently dazzled by it. There was a rainbow in every trembling water drop. He looked up and saw Emmanuelle picking lemons, tipping her face up and closing her eyes and laughing to herself as she plucked showers of raindrops along with the fruit. She was wearing leggings and a tunic of the blue colour in a china plate, and she held the picked lemons in the crook of her arm. Their yellow against the blue of her dress was a painting that has been made over and over, lemons in a blue bowl, lemons on a blue cloth, madonna and child with lemons against a blue robe, a laughing blue-gowned girl with lemon-coloured hair, and Lance's dazzled eyes saw it. People often live in paintings, but they do not often recognise it.

She walked down the slope and he walked up. Both their faces were pearled with rain drops. Smell, he said, and held out the sprig of pepper tree. Ah, she sighed, closing her eyes and sniffing, isn't it good. We should get into the habit of calling the house by its name. Peppertrees is a nice name for a house. He took some of her lemons and smelt their different pungency.

They didn't walk straight up to the house but made a circuit of the garden, as they used to when they first came to live there, carrying Maud in a babysling. Emmanuelle, who liked things orderly in her head as well as in her surroundings, asked a question she'd wanted to know the answer of for months. It was also as though she were testing Lance, to see if he could cope with her desire to talk about things. Do you remember, she said, telling me you weren't a nincompoop? A while ago now. Why did you say that?

In that other time. Well may you ask. I'd seen it in a *Playboy* magazine. An article on words. You know, people reading *Playboy* for the articles. It said a nincompoop originally meant a man who hadn't seen his wife's private parts. That's why he's a fool and a blockhead.

I see. But it wasn't true. Then. Whatever happens in the future.

They were passing the end of the garage, above which was Stuart's flat. He was leaning out of his window calling out to Mel, who'd been putting the children's bikes away. He spoke in a whisper that could be heard all over the garden.

Hey Mel ... I've got the shares, I've got all the paperwork, it's all there, now we can go ahead.

We? said Mel.

Yeah. I'm not sure what it all means, m'self, it was your idea remember, you're the brains of the outfit, Mel.

Outfit?

We're getting married, aren't we.

You may be, I'm not.

But Mel, I thought ...

No.

What about the shares? When we work out how to do 'em, and get rich?

I don't know about any shares.

The blackmail, hissed Stuart. I can't do them on me own. I need you.

No. 'Fraid not. I'm not staying here. I'm going back to New Zealand. I've got reason to think I've got Maori blood and that's really something in New Zealand these days and I'm going to go home and find out all about it. Then I might go to university. Do law, I think I'd be a good lawyer. Might get to be a judge one day.

Mel turned away and ran up the lawn, through the wisteria walk where it reached the house by the guest room windows, across the terrace and into the kitchen. Emmanuelle remembered the flitting figure she'd seen from the bedroom window.

Lance, did you ever sleep with Mel?

Jeesus. No.

Oh. I think I'd better go and tell her ...

I think she knows.

Tell her I made a mistake ...

Emmanuelle ran away up the lawn past the guest room, under the brawny bare branches of the wisteria, across the terrace, to the kitchen and its lights shining yellow through the quietly falling dusk. Where Susie was making tea and feeding the three children with bread and hazelnut paste which Emmanuelle never would have bought, herself.

Again

Maud came home from school. Charlotte's got a new baby, she said. I wish we had a new baby. Hers is a baby sister. She's allowed to give it its bottle. Can we get a baby sister?

Maud, sweetheart, it's not always easy. It's one thing to wish for a baby sister ... wishes don't always come true, you know ... or not in good ways.

I know a story about wishes, said William. He began to tell the tale of the man and his wife and the three wishes, the husband wasting the first one on a black pudding, the wife wasting the second one on sticking it on the husband's nose, and the third one — wouldn't you leave it there and use the last wish for something really important? too bad if you had a husband with a sausage on his nose — wasted on taking it off again.

I've heard that story before, a lot of times, said Maud.

We can hear it again, said Emmanuelle. A good story's always worth telling again.

So William told it all over again, and at the end he said, Do you know what I wish? I wish ... I wish we could have some black pudding, for dinner, tonight, could we?

Black pudding forever, said Emmanuelle.

Marion Halligan

Winner of the 1992 *Age* Book of the Year Award for her collection of short stories *The Worry Box*.

Lovers' Knots

If your house was burning down, what would you save? The money, the silver, the compact disc collection? The original Dali print? The last plate from your great-grandmother's dinner set? Standing like a spectator on the lawn, hearing the greedy eating of the flames at your possessions, smelling the noisome smoke of your belongings, suddenly you disobey. You bunch up your skirt or your shirt in a mask against the heat and run inside like a footballer ducking detaining hands, to save your precious ... what?

The boxes of photographs ...

From Ada the matriarch to Eva the waif, from gentle Alice to sharp-eyed Sebastian ... a family saga reduced to the shapely form of its best stories. A novel about ways of seeing and means of living ...

The much acclaimed writer Marion Halligan has written a brilliant evocation of life in Australia. The stories swapped between generations fill this large novel with passion and sorrow.

Marion Halligan's writing is as shining with life as the rivers that flow through these pages. The style is as polished as the amber its women wear and the story as full of pictures as the files of the photographer Mikelis who needs his camera to see the world.

Lovers' Knots is one of the year's finest novels.

'... crackling with life and mortality ... Halligan's magical word pictures have that serene intensity that is now her hallmark.'

Robert Dessaix

Minerva rrp $14.95
ISBN 1 86330 158 3

Marion Halligan

Winner of the *Age* Book of the Year Award

The Worry Box

Stories of unease, of youth and death and age, of violence and deceit ...

In this collection from the winner of the Steele Rudd Award, Marion Halligan shows us our flawed world in all its tawdry splendour. She holds up a mirror to its follies and phobias and takes us on a journey through the mirror's surface into a cracked and glittering other life that reflects and illuminates our own.

'The tears of love melted the evil magician's mirror' ... but outside fairy stories may not be so lucky.

Yet, however out of joint, this time is all we have, and Halligan celebrates it with wit, compassion and a black delight in its humour.

'Marion Halligan is a dangerously seductive writer.'

Diana Simmonds, *Bulletin*

'Like all the best writing, so simply done and graceful, it looks easy and is hellish to achieve ... [Marion Halligan] threads the meaning of a sentence like a needle through silk.'

Kate Llewellyn

Minerva rrp $14.95 pb
ISBN 1 86330 238 7